Th   nity,
he to   ness
that

Er   ding
heart, Leslie looked angry and bemused.

"Why did you do that?" she asked.

Marcus laughed. "Only you, Leslie, would ask such a question. I kissed you because I wanted to and I admit I found it most enjoyable. Did you?"

"I don't know. I have never been kissed before," she answered ingenuously, and then ashamed that she had been so forthright, continued. "But you must not do it again."

"I don't think I can promise that," Marcus teased. Before Leslie could make any response he had run lightly down the steps, jumped into his carriage and was away. Standing in the darkened hall, she felt abandoned.

WATCH FOR THESE ZEBRA REGENCIES

LADY STEPHANIE   (0-8217-5341-X, $4.50)
by Jeanne Savery
Lady Stephanie Morris has only one true love: the family estate she has managed ever since her mother died. But then Lord Anthony Rider arrives on her estate, claiming he has plans for both the land and the woman. Stephanie soon realizes she's fallen in love with a man whose sensual caresses will plunge her into a world of peril and intrigue . . . a man as dangerous as he is irresistible.

BRIGHTON BEAUTY   (0-8217-5340-1, $4.50)
by Marilyn Clay
Chelsea Grant, pretty and poor, naively takes school friend Alayna Marchmont's place and spends a month in the country. The devastating man had sailed from Honduras to claim his promised bride, Miss Marchmont. An affair of the heart may lead to disaster . . . unless a resourceful Brighton beauty finds a way to stop a masquerade and keep a lord's love.

LORD DIABLO'S DEMISE   (0-8217-5338-X, $4.50)
by Meg-Lynn Roberts
The sinfully handsome Lord Harry Glendower was a gambler and the black sheep of his family. About to be forced into a marriage of convenience, the devilish fellow engineered his own demise, never having dreamed that faking his death would lead him to the heavenly refuge of spirited heiress Gwyn Morgan, the daughter of a physician.

A PERILOUS ATTRACTION   (0-8217-5339-8, $4.50)
by Dawn Aldridge Poore
Alissa Morgan is stunned when a frantic passenger thrusts her baby into Alissa's arms and flees, having heard rumors that a notorious highwayman posed a threat to their coach. Handsome stranger Hugh Sebastian secretly possesses the treasured necklace the highwayman seeks and volunteers to pose as Alissa's husband to save her reputation. With a lost baby and missing necklace in their care, the couple embarks on a journey into peril—and passion.

Available wherever paperbacks are sold, or order direct from the Publisher. Send cover price plus 50¢ per copy for mailing and handling to Penguin USA, P.O. Box 999, c/o Dept. 17109, Bergenfield, NJ 07621. Residents of New York and Tennessee must include sales tax. DO NOT SEND CASH.

Violet Hamilton

Love's Masquerade

ZEBRA BOOKS
KENSINGTON PUBLISHING CORP.

ZEBRA BOOKS are published by

Kensington Publishing Corp.
850 Third Avenue
New York, NY 10022

Copyright © 1996 by Violet Hamilton

Zebra and the Z logo Reg. U.S. Pat. & TM Off

First Printing: September, 1996
10 9 8 7 6 5 4 3 2 1

Printed in the United States of America

Chapter One

"Haven't you finished yet?" Sir Alan Dansforth asked his daughter, his tone querulous and demanding.

"Almost, Father," Leslie answered patiently, not looking up from her work. She was making a fair copy of a lengthy dispatch her father had dictated earlier, before he succumbed to his current bout of illness, a malady he attributed to vague digestive disturbances, but Leslie acknowledged was the result of over-indulgence in food and wine.

Sir Alan, driven from England by gambling debts and scandal involving the wife of a notable peer, had been forced to wander from one European watering hole to another, his resources dwindling because of his inability to stay away from the gambling tables and taverns. Finally, he had agreed to take on the role of foreign correspondent for *The Times* and Leslie was now copying his fortnightly letter to London from Vienna.

Despite his reputation and failing health brought on by dissipation, Sir Alan still retained vestiges of the handsome features and winning personality that had conquered both tavern wenches and the town's most elegant matrons. Al-

though only in his late forties, he looked much older with
rapidly graying hair and the ravages of his wasted life apparent in the deep lines scoring his face. But his brilliant
blue eyes could still sparkle with excitement and his smile
charm all who met him.

His daughter, Leslie, his companion and nurse for the
past three years since leaving her seminary in Bath, paid
for by the last of her mother's marriage portion, had inherited her father's handsome looks, but her character
lacked his instability. Perhaps because of her experience
in dealing with her wastrel father, she found most society
distasteful, preferring books to people, and disdaining fashion. Her father complained that she was in danger of
becoming a blue stocking and a dowd, unable to attract a
suitable husband, but she just laughed and kept to her path.
She might have reproached him with the knowledge that
his own way of life prevented her from meeting the kind
of gentleman who would make a suitable husband, but she
felt reproaches were useless. For all her definite charm of
face and figure, no matter how she disregarded her appearance, she attracted many men, much to her disgust, for
she doubted the sincerity of their intentions and found
them selfish, vain and arrogant.

Although Sir Alan felt demeaned by his journalist chores
for *The Times,* Leslie found his work fascinating. The political intrigues at the court of Joseph II in Vienna, the
ploys of Prince Metternich, the autocratic but impotent at-
titudes in the fading Holy Roman Empire, Austria's weak-
ened position in the aftermath of Napoleon's defeat offered
her a rare opportunity to observe the changing face of Europe and the balance of power struggle among the victors
after the Congress of Vienna. Her insight and assessment
of events was far more incisive than that of her father who

believed what he saw and was told, reporting the obvious rather than investigating the motives of his sources. England had emerged from the struggle with Napoleon under the redoubtable Wellington as the commanding presence in the councils of Europe. Sir Alan with all the arrogance of his class and background, however much he had fallen from grace, accepted his country's dominance as right and proper, never questioning the ambitions or tactics of England's rulers. Leslie was more astute.

"If you hurry to the consul's office with that dispatch he can send it off in the next bag," her father urged, eager to have his responsibility discharged. "Why is it taking you so long?"

Leslie, well used to dealing with her father's petulance, merely went on with her work, forbearing from reminding him that his own pleasures had taken precedence over his assignment so that the dispatch was already late. Neither did she mention that she had amended several of his comments and edited the article to strengthen its impact. She knew he rarely asked to see the final copy.

At last looking up from her work, she said casually, "All done, now. I will be off to Mr. Lester's with this immediately. And it's such a lovely day I might walk in the colonnade afterwards. With Metternich and the court here to take the waters there might be some news you could use."

"You shouldn't be strolling about without a chaperone. You will give an impression of laxity," Sir Alan complained. Only occasionally did he remember his paternal duties and the strictures of the society in which he was reared. He conveniently forgot that Leslie had seen him disgracefully drunk and rescued him from situations that might have appalled a less resilient and resourceful girl.

"Nonsense, Father. What could happen to me in broad daylight among patients taking the waters? Not a very debauched scene, I think," she answered paying little heed to her parent, pinning a plain straw bonnet on her short dark curls, and carefully placing the copied dispatch in a large reticule.

"Is there anything you need, Father," she asked, looking at her father a bit anxiously. Sitting in a large armchair with a rug over his knees, and the sun striking his greying hair from the long windows of the apartment he looked his age and more, tired and pale. Although she knew his current indisposition was brought about by a marathon drinking bout in a low tavern in the seedier section of Carlsbad, she could not repress an affectionate sympathy for his unhappy state. She knew, full well, that as soon as he had recovered he would return to his dissolute habits despite his remorse and promises of reform.

Looking up at his daughter, so fresh and expectant, so healthy, Sir Alan felt one of those rare pangs of remorse and said ruefully, "You are a darling girl to put up with your old reprobate of a father. You should be making your come out in London not nursing this old wreck in a seedy spa."

"Carlsbad is not a seedy spa but a charming historic town where the nobility of Europe come to cure their ailments. And you are not a reprobate, just unable to resist temptation. Now, have a nice rest and I will be back within an hour or two."

"Thank you, Leslie," Sir Alan nodded and closed his eyes, having made what he considered a suitable recompense for causing Leslie any trouble.

Quite used to her father's fits of conscience, Leslie sensibly paid him no more heed and hurried out of the apartment, eager to enjoy some of the fine spring weather along the banks of the Tepla River that bisected this medieval town with its melange of Renaissance and Gothic architecture and the light-hearted gaiety of its Bohemian citizens.

Quickly accomplishing her errand at the British consul's office, where she was received grudgingly, for the proper and precise Mr. Lester frowned on *The Times'* correspondents using the diplomatic bag for their dispatches. This was fairly recent practice, introduced during the French blockade of the ports before Waterloo, preventing the mail from the continent to be delivered. *The Times'* proprietor had introduced the use of foreign correspondents at that time, and Sir Alan was only one among a half a dozen men reporting from the capitals of Europe.

Leslie gave Mr. Lester one of her most charming smiles and thanked him effusively for his trouble so that he was somewhat chastened by his previous ill humor, which had been her intention.

"Sir Alan may not know that his new employer has just arrived in town," he confided smugly. Lester was a square-faced, dull young man, with thinning brown hair who had obtained his post through a nebulous connection with Lord Sidmouth, and by his mother's badgering of the Home Secretary. He was a collector of gossip and a good news source so Leslie cultivated him, although she found him a tedious bore.

"You mean Mr. Walter," Leslie said, referring to the proprietor of *The Times*.

"No, the new editor, and I understand he is a great one for the ladies," Lester smirked.

"Really. How up to the mark you are, Mr. Lester. Well, I must be on my way. Good day," Leslie slipped away before Lester could properly interpret her remark, but on the whole he believed he had scored.

Really, Lester was a poor representative of His Majesty's government, Leslie concluded as she walked briskly down the boulevard adjacent to the river, enjoying the sun on her face and watching the carriages making a stately progress toward the waters whose health-giving properties were the reason for the prosperity of this old town. Leslie herself found the waters noxious and doubted that anything so foul tasting could restore damaged livers and cure gout, but that was an opinion she kept to herself.

Thirteen different fountains ejected the waters from springs some six thousand feet below the ground, and each tap claimed to offer a different combination of minerals destined to heal a variety of ailments. The spa had been discovered by Charles IV, Czech king and Holy Roman Emperor in the early fourteenth century, while on a hunting trip. Since then Carlsbad had grown in popularity and was favored resort of the Austrian court.

As she strolled along the avenue that followed the winding path of the river Leslie enjoyed the soft April breeze that ruffled the budding trees lining the esplanade and put all thoughts of Vienna from her mind. Spring was coming early to Carlsbad and memories of the difficult winter in the hidebound Austrian capital were temporarily forgotten. As she neared the colonnades, an impressive classical facade open to the weather that housed the various waters, she paused to observe the various patients indulging in the cure. There were few native Bohemians but a score of fashionably dressed Europeans with the money and the leisure to spend weeks at the spa recovering from the dissipations of the winter. Lingering to observe the scene, her gaze was drawn to an attractive couple strolling arm in arm ahead of her. The woman wore a fetching walking dress of azure merino faced in cream with a matching spencer and her companion wore the de rigeur dress of the man about town, cream kersey britches and a dark well cut coat with sparkling white linen. They appeared completely absorbed in one another, obviously enjoying the day and each other, grimacing as they drank from the odd spouted mugs sold to the patrons of the waters. Leslie smiled at the picture, so intent on the couple she did not at first heed the voice calling her name.

"Ah, Fraulein Dansforth. What a fortunate meeting." A gentleman had caught up with her and touched her on the arm.

Leslie turned, barely repressing a recoil of repugnance. Yes, it was the odious Count Felix von Ronberg, a notorious Austrian libertine, who had tried to press his attentions upon her in Vienna. She had welcomed the move to Carlsbad, not the least because it removed her from any chance meetings with the man, and now to her dismay he had turned up here, too, no doubt following members of the court. At first glance Leslie's repugnance might be difficult to fathom. The count was a well-set-up man in his late thirties with hot dark eyes and a sensuous mouth which betrayed his appetites, but he had a certain rakish appeal accented by the dueling scar that scarred his left cheek. He had a fearsome reputation with women and well-brought up respectable girls were warned not to encourage him, although he was considered a formidable catch, being both well connected and extremely wealthy. He had great influence at court, despite the rumors about his past, including the mysterious death of a young wife at one of his isolated Bohemian castles. He had seen Leslie in Vienna, shopping in the Kartnerstrasse and scraped an acquaintance with her at an embassy gathering. From the beginning she had no illusions about what he wanted from her and had done her best to depress his intentions.

"Good afternoon, count. I suppose you have come to take the waters after a hectic season," she said, implying that his life of debauchery might finally be exacting its toll.

If he found her greeting far from enthusiastic he ignored it and bowed formally over the hand she reluctantly extended. "How charming you look, strolling among the poor sufferers. It is obvious you have no need of the healing proprieties of these dubious waters."

Leslie remained obstinately silent, hoping he would realize she did not welcome his presence and take himself off, but her aloofness did not appear to affect him.

"My carriage is just down the avenue. Why not join me in a delightful ramble into the countryside. Surely you wish to take advantage of this glorious day," he urged smoothly, ignoring the cold look she cast on him.

"I'm afraid I must decline, count. My father is not well and I must return to him immediately."

"Surely he could spare you for an hour or two. I promise to return you safely to his side. I am always delighted to renew my acquaintance with him, such a charming fellow," he insisted, his condescending reference to Sir Alan grating on Leslie. She knew her father had found the count obliging. She suspected he had borrowed money from von Ronberg who encouraged Sir Alan to chance his luck at the gaming tables and was quite prepared to frank him if the Englishman ran out of funds. In answer to Leslie's complaints about the count, Sir Alan had protested that he cultivated him because he was a good source of gossip about the court. And von Ronberg was also a friend of the powerful Prince Metternich who masterminded every decision of the Austrian king, Joseph II. Leslie hesitated to tell her father that she feared the count had designs on her virtue. In his cups Sir Alan could become belligerent and might easily provoke an incident that would result in his banishment from the Vienna, the loss of his job, and even worse.

"I must refuse, count," she said determined not to be lured into a tête à tête with the man.

But he was not so easily dismissed. An ugly light darkened his eyes for a moment before he quickly masked his feelings with a smile.

"I think it would be to your advantage to accept my courteous offer," he countered taking her arm in a firm grasp and pushing her toward the street, away from the eyes of the promenaders and patients, always eager for distraction and the hint of scandal. Soft as his voice was it held a threat that angered Leslie and stiffened her resolve to defy him.

Leslie did not want to create a scene, but she had no wish to spend another minute in the count's company, and had no aversion to letting him know it.

"Count von Ronberg. I think I have made it quite plain that I do not find your company enjoyable, and I dislike being forced into a situation that makes me appear careless of my reputation. To be frank you are a man no respectable girl can afford to be seen with. I must decline your invitation, and insist you release me." Leslie spoke softly but with some urgency, conscious that several patrons of the spa were watching her with cynical amusement. A pair of gentlemen moved toward her.

They came to Leslie's side even as the count, now in an ugly mood, seemed considering abducting her by force.

"Good afternoon. May we be of some assistance? I rather think you are English as we are, and we must introduce ourselves." The fair-haired gentleman bowed and looked admiringly at Leslie, ignoring the count.

Von Ronberg, furious at the interruption, flushed and losing control was about to strike the interloper, when he was halted by a fierce grip on his hand. "I think not, sir," the dark haired man insisted quietly, but not releasing his grasp. Turning to Leslie he, too, bowed, "Marcus Kingsley, at your service, madam, and this is my graceless friend, Jonathan Stirling," he drawled in the cool tones that identified the well-bred Englishman.

"How kind, sir. I am Leslie Dansforth," she answered both relieved and amused by her compatriots adept handling of the count, who was mastering his rage with difficulty, but not to be outdone in courtesy by these brash foreigners.

"I believe you misunderstood the situation, my dear sirs. Miss Dansforth was just about to accompany me on a drive. We are old friends." His tone was light but his expression ugly.

"I think the lady was a bit reluctant. If she would prefer to be escorted home we are just the fellows to oblige," Marcus continued still affable, but with a determination that did not escape the count. Glancing around he saw that their small drama was becoming the focus of intense interest, and he suspected he did not appear to the best advantage. Marcus and Jonathan waited, prepared to challenge the count further if that was necessary, but von Ronberg, not liking the odds and ever conscious of his dignity, admitted defeat.

"If I have caused you any embarrassment, Miss Dansforth, I apologize. I will make my amends at a more suitable time and place," he warned, and bowing curtly, ignoring the two Englishmen marched away, anger in every lineament.

"An ugly customer, that one," Jonathan remarked watching the arrogant stride.

"Thank you so much. He can be obtuse and fails to understand why every female he meets does not find him engaging," Leslie admitted with a slight smile. She liked the look of Jonathan, whose open face, warm brown eyes and sleepy smile bespoke a gentle engaging personality. She was not so sure about his companion. Marcus Kinsley, some inches taller, with dark hair falling over a high forehead, hooded grey eyes and a square cut chin hinting of obstinancy was not so much handsome as commanding in appearance.

Marcus eyed Leslie in a considering fashion she could not quite interpret. "It is a bit unusual to see a female of your obvious respectability walking alone, even in the informal ambiance of this backwater spa," he said, hoping to fluster her into some kind of explanation.

"Really, sir. And can you tell just what kind of a female I am?" Leslie answered tartly. She was beginning to think she had only exchanged one licentious male for another whose only mitigating asset was that he had rescued her from the count. Turning her back slightly on Kingsley she smiled at Jonathan Stirling as the easier of her two cavaliers.

"I believe you should be the chief recipient of my gratitude, Mr. Stirling," she said, hoping to depress Kingsley, who she thought typical of the arrogant Englishman marching through Europe as though he owned it, disdaining the natives and refusing to learn any language but his own.

Jonathan blushed, aware that Marcus was regarding him with amusement, understanding exactly what Miss Dansforth intended to convey, a rebuke to him. "Not at all, not at all. And may we have your direction, unless you want to spend some time taking the waters," he suggested kindly.

"Alas, I have dallied here long enough and have obligations at home. But you must want to sample the famous potions. Do not let me detain you," Leslie suggested.

Marcus interrupted. "We have already tasted the waters, nasty stuff, and since our way fortuitously lies with yours we will accompany you. Who knows, that rather sinister Austrian might be lurking outside ready to spirit you away," Marcus mocked.

Not liking his suggestion, nor him much, Leslie's only response was an indifferent shrug, ignoring his hint that he knew her direction. Jonathan, rather worried by the antipathy between his companions, hastened to explain.

"I don't believe you know that Kingsley here is the new editor of *The Times*. He is making a tour of the European capitals to meet with his correspondents, and after a brief stay in Vienna, we hurried on here to meet Sir Alan. Your father, I think."

"Thank you, Jonathan, for so adeptly offering my bona fides," Marcus said sarcastically.

"And what is your role, Mr. Stirling?" Leslie asked as they strolled from the colonnades, refusing to express awe or dismay at Jonathan's news.

"I am just a scribbler, that poor fellow who must earn his bread criticizing the efforts of others because he can produce nothing but drivel himself," Jonathan joked.

Liking his modesty, a refreshing change from most men she met, Leslie gave him an approving smile. "I suppose that means you are the paper's literary critic. I must look for your work."

If Marcus disliked the decisive Miss Dansforth's preference for his friend he showed no evidence of it, only observing her with a discerning eye as they walked on, listening to the exchange between the two. Jonathan, always susceptible, was charmed, he realized. He, himself, found Miss Dansforth, although well worth another look, entirely too independent for his taste. Marcus Kingsley considered females necessary to his well being, but not worthy of much respect unless they were over sixty and been tempered by a life time of experience. He wondered just how much influence Miss Dansforth had upon her father, of whom Marcus had some cause to think might be a reprobate. Miss Dansforth might do well to remember that he was her father's employer and use a few womanly wiles to impress him.

If Leslie had a great deal to learn about the new editor of *The Times,* he, in his turn, might himself be surprised by the daughter of his Vienna correspondent.

Chapter Two

As Leslie and her escorts walked across the Gogol Bridge and up the rather steep rise of Zamecky Vrch where the Dansforth apartment was situated, she began to have second thoughts about allowing Marcus Kingsley to meet her father today. Sir Alan was not at his best and the astute Mr. Kingsley would no doubt grasp the reason why. She believed Jonathan Stirling would be more compassionate, not so harsh on her father's delinquencies, but she expected no such tolerance from Mr. Kingsley. Although he behaved with perfect courtesy toward her, Leslie sensed a certain cynical assessment in his attitude. He probably thought she had deliberately enticed the odious Count von Ronberg and then, playing the teasing flirt, had retreated in a false show of maidenly reticence. Leslie had decided she did not much care for Marcus Kingsley, but she could hardly treat the man scornfully if her father was to retain his job. Well, she could only hope Sir Alan had recovered enough from his indulgences of the last evening to exhibit some of that famous charm when he met his new chief. Leslie herself had no illusions about her parent. Not that she did not feel great affection toward him but she also had to admit that he was irresponsible, profligate and a practiced liar. These were not characteristics liable to win him favor in the eyes of Mr. Kingsley, she decided.

"How long have you been in Carlsbad, Miss Dansforth," Marcus asked idly as if to break the rather uncomfortable silence of the walk.

"About three weeks. Father thought he must follow Prince Metternich and the court, most of whom take the cure here after the season. King Joseph himself is expected within the week. Also it is sometimes easier to discover news in the informal atmosphere of the spa than in the more restricted atmosphere of the Hofburg," Leslie said stiffly. She despised herself for making any effort to placate the man, but she had a nasty feeling that he meant trouble.

"And what have you, or should I say Sir Alan, discovered?" Marcus asked.

Leslie, by now thoroughly irritated by Marcus Kingsley's patronizing airs, replied coldly, "Only that Princess Caroline is expected here with her Italian lover, Bartolomeo Bargami, and that a Bonapartist ex-officer approached a former servant of the Duke of Wellington and offered him money to assassinate the Duke. It is all in father's latest letter that I have just dispatched," she ended curtly, knowing that she had been rattling on, but determined to impress Sir Alan's new editor.

As they mounted the steps to the Dansforth apartment, Marcus allowed himself a small smile, which he hid behind his hand. Obviously Miss Dansforth had not taken to him, and hoped by her exciting budget of news to show how diligent and clever her father had been. Marcus, even before meeting Sir Alan, had an idea that Miss Dansforth herself was the author of much of the Vienna letter that ran every fortnight in *The Times*. Marcus disliked managing females, who pretended to a grasp of affairs he felt few of them understood. He had always regarded women as relaxation in leisure hours, but for hard discussion and analysis only men were competent. It was a view that Leslie had sensed and one which she despised.

However, she was prepared to swallow her ire and check her tongue in order to insure that Sir Alan would treat his unexpected guests with a measure of civility.

Opening the door and ushering in her guests, Leslie called out quickly to her father, hoping to give him enough warning of what was to come. "I have brought you some unexpected guests from London, Father."

Jonathan, who had some idea of what Leslie hoped to accomplish, felt embarrassed and a bit annoyed with Marcus. He had not been slow to perceive that Miss Dansforth and Marcus had not exactly taken to one another. From a selfish point of view that suited him, as he found her quite delightful, but he did not want her animosity toward Marcus to include him. Despite his loyalty and friendship with Marcus there were lengths he was not prepared to go in condoning his friend's behavior. Maneuvering to place himself ahead of Marcus and just behind his hostess he was the first to be introduced.

"Father, this is Mr. Jonathan Stirling, a colleague from *The Times,* and Mr. Marcus Kingsley, the newly appointed editor," she introduced the two men knowing Kingsley might take umbrage at coming second to his friend. Sir Alan made no effort to rise, but waved his guests to a chair in a lordly manner, and then suggested Leslie might find some refreshments.

"Tea would be most appreciated," Jonathan suggested tactfully, feeling that Sir Alan might be wise to delay any further intake of wine. He had enough experience to realize that Leslie's father was suffering from the effects of overindulgence rather than real invalidism.

"Well, Mr. Kingsley, this is a surprise. I had not been informed in the change of management," Sir Alan informed the visitors as if he were in the complete confidence of the proprietor of *The Times,* which was far from the truth.

"John decided he was bored with the journalist trade and his co-editor Stoddart likewise wanted to seek other opportunities, so I inherited the position of editor-in-chief. Jonathan here is *The Times* literary critic and an old friend. Now we are making a tour of Europe to check in with our correspondents in the various capitals. We learned in Vienna that you had come here." Marcus was careful to temper his assumption of power. He believed he knew the type of man with whom he was dealing. Sir Alan, well connected and proud, no matter his altered circumstances, would take offense easily, and Marcus was willing to treat him carefully until he had decided his worth to the newspaper.

"Going to vet us all and then decide whether we are worth keeping," Sir Alan said shrewdly, surprising Marcus who had not expected such astuteness. Before he could either confirm or deny Sir Alan's assessment, Leslie returned with a laden tray, that Jonathan hurried to relieve her of, placing it on a nearby table.

Realizing that he must make an effort to throw off his malaise and impress this young jackanapes (for that is how Sir Alan privately looked upon Marcus) with his credentials, Sir Alan assumed an air of fellowship. Unfortunately before he could exert the charm for which he was noted, Marcus had begun a story about Crabb Robinson, *The Times* first and most famous correspondent who had covered the Peninsula War. Sir Alan did not take kindly to memories of this fabled correspondent, whom he had met years ago and disliked as a common journeyman.

Leslie cast a wary glance at her father as she poured the tea and passed the cakes. He must behave himself, and she tried to convey a warning, but she doubted he caught it. Sir Alan was perfectly capable of whistling away his job in a fit of haughty pique and that would be disastrous, for the Dansforths desperately needed the money. Although Leslie decried the necessity, it might be sensible to try to placate Mr. Kingsley.

"Certainly you are very young to have been appointed to such a responsible post." She flattered as Marcus' tale of Crabb Robinson came to a close.

"Well, I was on hand, writing literary criticism for the paper when Johnny Walter decided to retreat to Berkshire and become a country gentleman. I will really miss the critic's chair but Jonathan will fill my seat ably, I know."

Leslie thought there was probably a great deal more to the story than that but she reluctantly applauded Marcus Kingsley's modesty in not crowing about his appointment. She gave him the benefit of the doubt, having a firm sense of justice, but it did not make her like him the better. But by now Sir Alan had gathered his wits and realizing what was at stake set out to satisfy his new employer that he was without a peer in this business of reporting on the news and rumors from the Austrian court.

When the pair signified after an hour that they must take their leave, Sir Alan believed he had completely settled the affair, that Mr. Kingsley was convinced of the wisdom of leaving him in his post. He felt he might venture a request.

"I would rather like to return to London for a spell, renew old contacts, always helpful in this business.

Haven't been home more than two years now," Sir Alan reminisced. He wondered if Marcus knew the reason for his hurried exit and subsequent exile. If Kingsley was aware of the scandal surrounding Sir Alan he kept his own counsel.

Deciding that this young man could be easily manipulated, Sir Alan could not resist playing his chief care. "It would be nice to see my cousin again, Rothfield, you know. He's getting on a bit, the old earl, and might pop off at any times," Sir Alan spoke wistfully, even a bit diffidently about his noble relative, with whom he shared no intimacy as far as Leslie knew. And somehow she did not think this last ploy would impress Marcus either.

"Actually, he looked quite well when I saw him at White's last month just before we sailed." Marcus may have settled Sir Alan's pretensions but did nothing to endear himself to Leslie who scorned such snobberies.

Marcus made no promises about an extended leave and soon after this last exchange he and Jonathan left. Both the Dansforths felt uneasy about the interview, for that was essentially what it was, and reluctant to discuss it. Still, Leslie thought her father ought to understand this new change of command at *The Times* could endanger his own position.

"And what did you think of Mr. Kingsley, Father?" she asked tentatively.

"Has a very good opinion of himself, that young fellow. He might be wise to take some advice from those who have had more experience in these matters," Sir Alan insisted pompously. Not for the world would he admit to his daughter he found the situation ominous and feared for his own future. He accepted that Leslie had proved an invaluable ally but he held the old fashioned idea that women must be protected. He might admit in his more honest moments that most of the protection in their case had been wielded by his daughter, but he clung to the notions of chivalry in which he had been raised. He really felt ashamed that Leslie was exiled here pandering to his needs when she should be enjoying a debutante's life in London. Perhaps if he could get back to England he might make some effort at rapprochement with the old earl. After all the man must have some family feeling, although he had shown few signs of it when Sir Alan had asked him for help during his past troubles. Most of the time Sir Alan could ignore his own transgressions, unwilling to blame himself for the reduced circumstances in which they lived. But he was not a stupid man, only a selfish one, and he knew in his heart that he had failed Leslie as a father. It was not a pleasant thought to live with so he rarely entertained it.

Leslie, who did not want to discuss Marcus, refused to give her opinion of the new editor but did offer, "I liked Mr. Stirling. He appeared a modest affable man, although in the shadow of his more dominate friend."

Since Leslie rarely confessed to finding a man agreeable, Sir Alan was encouraged. Tardily remembering his duties as a parent, asked, "And how did you happen to meet that pair?"

Leslie hesitated, unwilling to report on the distasteful encounter with Count von Ronberg. She knew her father would be both rueful and embarrassed, not wanting to admit his indebtedness to the count.

"Oh, they were taking the waters and we just began to chat," she said weakly, expecting recriminations.

"Such rag-tailed manners the young have. You should not speak to strange gentlemen on the street. In this case they seem to be unexceptional, and you would have met them in any case, but you cannot be too careful," Sir Alan reproved huffily.

"Of course, Father. It was very ill considered of me," Leslie agreed meekly. No need for her father to learn of the real incident. And she only prayed that the count would take his congé and leave them alone. His influence on her father was unfortunate and she had to step warily when discussing the count with her susceptible parent who did not wholly understand the count's intentions toward her, or if he did wanted to ignore them. So typical Leslie thought, her father upbraiding her for speaking to the two Englishmen before they were properly introduced yet refusing to see the real threat implicit in the count's attentions. To forestall any more questions or reproaches she gathered up the tea things and left the room, leaving her father prey to some rather vague apprehensions.

Marcus and Jonathan strolled along the Louka, the boulevard leading to the Grand Pupp, where they were lodging. The two hundred year old hostelry had played host to most of Europe's royalty and aristocrats during its long career and currently welcomed Metternich himself. Marcus, who did not believe in economizing on his tours, had justified the hotel's high prices by reminding Jonathan that they needed to be at the center of news. And Jonathan admitted that wherever Metternich was intrigue and power politics followed. Both young men were followers of Henry Brougham, the radical member of Parliament who pressed for reform, but Marcus did not feel that his political persuasions should deny him a certain standard of comfort, if not luxury.

Accustomed to allowing Marcus to take the lead in their discussions Jonathan waited to hear his opinion of Sir Alan and the lovely Leslie. Marcus did not hurry to oblige, but it was obvious he was giving some thought to the problem of Sir Alan. At last he ventured to share his thoughts.

"I'm not sure that Dansforth is up to the job. Vienna is a hotbed of political intrigue just now for Metternich has his itchy hands in every European affair, on one hand cozing up to us and behind our backs cultivating the Tsar, who has this Holy Alliance nonsense threatening the balance of power. And then there is a great deal of unrest in the Austrian provinces. Can Sir Alan handle all this? I doubt it."

Ignoring any reference to Dansforth's abilities, Jonathan, with a reformist fervor, leapt on the last point made by Marcus. "Yes, it's dreadful, the autocratic control of Austria. Look at these Bohemians, at one time kings and rulers. Now the poor people are not even allowed to speak their own language, and must learn German if they want to get on."

"All too true, Jon, but we cannot expect enlightened ideas about government from foreigners," Marcus explained with the Englishman's conviction that Europeans, and indeed all not born in his tight little island, would never attain the freedoms and liberties of his countrymen.

"Well, certainly not from Metternich and Tsar Alexander," Jonathan agreed, hoping to distract Marcus from his concerns about Sir Alan. He suspected, judging from the shabby apartment and the lack of servants, that the Dansforths were existing on the edge of genteel poverty, and if so, the salary paid by *The Times* to Sir Alan was vital to their subsistence. His compassionate nature was moved by their plight, but perhaps more moved by the thought of Miss Dansforth.

But Marcus was not to be distracted. "I think we will have to replace Sir Alan. Let him come back to London and

ease him out gradually. I have a promising candidate to replace him, Robinson's nephew," he confided.

"I believe the Dansforths depend on his salary from the
paper," Jonathan said, rather unhappy over the thought of
the charming Miss Dansforth coping with further
economies in her living style.

"Probably," Marcus agreed with a frown. He was not
callous, only determined to make a success of his new position and to push *The Times* toward preeminence. And Sir
Alan did not appear to fit into the future he planned. He
wanted young, ambitious and industrious men covering
Europe's capitals for his newspaper. Sir Alan did not possess any of these qualities, and his health appeared dubious.

Jonathan, about to appeal to Marcus, bit back his words
as they turned into the courtyard of the hotel. The lobby
was crowded with fashionable guests, greeting friends,
gossiping and eyeing each newcomer with avid interest.
These wealthy patrons of the spa were easily bored with
the tame amusements of Carlsbad and found a healthy
regime of waters, walks and a reduced diet quickly lost its
charms. Carlsbad might advertise its chief attraction as the
curative powers of its springs but Europe's well-born were
more often lured to the resort by the very society they had
left at home. Of course, there were the usual hangers-on,
and the raffish exiles who wandered fretfully about the continent, victims of their own transgressions. This was the
height of Carlsbad's season and Marcus and Jonathan noticed several distinguished gentlemen with their ladies
among the throng in the lobby and on the terrace of the
Grand Pupp.

"Come up to the room, Jon, and we will thrash out this
question of the Dansforths and the other correspondents. I

can't spend much more time here and some hard decisions must be made," Marcus insisted brusquely, shouldering his way through the crowd and making for the stairway. Jonathan followed but with a small smile. Marcus had already made his decision and he was not usually dissuaded from a course of action once his mind was made up. Still, Jonathan would do his best to urge the claims of the Dansforths, for he had been most impressed with the lovely Leslie and thought she needed a defender, from the odious count, from her father, and even from Marcus.

Chapter Three

The Dansforths arrived in early June to find London enjoying a spell of fine weather and celebrating the opening of John Rennie's fine new arched Waterloo Bridge. On the day of the state dedication the bank on either side of the Thames thronged with the citizenry, rich and poor, determined to enjoy the "Waterloo Fair." On the Thames itself masses of wherries and larger ships jostled each other for the prime positions, their passengers hoping to catch a glimpse of the Waterloo heroes present on the great occasion. Even the Duke of Wellington himself deigned to honor the festivities, riding in the Admiralty barge to view the shining structure festooned with flags. Vendors of oysters, whelks, gingerbread and oranges worked the crowd, distracting customers from the jugglers, the dancing bears, the musicians and dancers who vied for coins. Gypsies, pickpockets, sneak thieves and worse darted through the masses relieving the unwary of their purses, but most of London's citizenry enjoyed the day, the color, the excitement and the memory of the Iron Duke leading the nation to victory.

Prices had risen since Sir Alan's last visit to London so

that finding clean, reasonable lodgings was not an easy
task. Leslie felt most fortunate to secure rooms off the
Strand near the Haymarket, the haunts of theatrical com-
panies. The district was not too respectable, but Mrs.
Gorey, their landlady was a kindly, garrulous soul, a retired
dresser that Leslie found obliging. Her father, as might be
expected, decried the unfashionable address, but soon settled down, spending much of his time in the various pubs
near the theaters, drinking away what little money remained from their savings. He had received a formal letter from Marcus terminating his employment, with the
suggestion that the paper might consider buying occasional
articles on suitable subjects. Leslie hiding behind her father's name, had already submitted two that were accepted.
Sir Alan, complaining about the shabby treatment he had
received from *The Times,* laid it at the door of that "bumptious young fellow" who had taken over the direction of
the paper. He had attempted to beard Marcus in his office
but had been prevented from reaching his quarry, by a
burly porter. Marcus had made no effort to contact the
Dansforths after Sir Alan's dismissal, but Jonathan, learning of their direction, had been an assiduous caller in their
rooms.

   Of course, he heard Sir Alan's complaints about his
friend, but of an easy going and affable nature, Jonathan
let most of the diatribes pass over his head and con-
centrated on Leslie. He thought she was a female of in-
credible efficiency, talent and resourcefulness, as well as
compassionate and forbearing of her father's feckless
habits. Jonathan would never admit that if these praise-
worthy qualities had been displayed in a less attractive
package he would not have noticed them, for Leslie, for
all her virtues, was an exceedingly lovely girl. She en-

couraged his friendship, although hoping he would not insist on any deeper relationship, for she enjoyed his company and found his amiable dependability a pleasant relief from her father's moods and bouts of dissipation.

Even more appealing was the literary circle to which he introduced her. Jonathan and Marcus, too, were close friends of William Hazlitt, Leigh Hunt and Charles Lamb, all essayists of the first rank, as well as members of an inner circle of radical politicians whose views Leslie thoroughly endorsed. On her first sight of London's back mean streets, away from the stately homes and clean streets of Mayfair, she had been appalled at the filth, disease, the ragged begging children, the drunkenness of idle desperate men and women, who had lost hope. The conquerors of Europe dealt meanly with their own citizens. Leslie had not seen such distressing sights in Vienna and she was both ashamed and indignant that her countrymen were forced into such degradation. Although she had enough humanity to be concerned about these conditions she could do little to ameliorate them even if she had been allowed to join the few women working in the slums to aid the sufferers. The Dansforths were rapidly approaching a desperate level in their own finances, and Leslie had to force her father to face up to their circumstances.

"Our expenses are fast outrunning our income, Father. We must economize more stringently," she explained gently, knowing how reluctant her father was to discuss money.

"I suppose you think I have been spending too much on entertainment, in seeking some companionship to lighten the depths to which I have sunk and dragged you with me," he moaned in the exaggerated manner he often adopted when reproved.

"Oh, come now, Father, it is not that bad. But your quarterly allowance will not be paid for another month and we have few other resources." Leslie tried to soften the situation but she must impress her father with their dilemma.

"I should be scurrying about like these common ink-stained wretches trying to wrest some coppers from our Fleet Street masters," he sneered, now beginning to feel abused and misunderstood.

Leslie sighed, seeing how hopeless it was to direct her father into any realistic view of their affairs. "Not at all, Father, but quite plainly we cannot eat until the end of the month if you insist on frittering our small funds at the grog shops," she spoke impatiently with rather more bitterness than she usually displayed.

Immediately Sir Alan retreated into the self-accusing, pathetic useless dependent, a role he practiced on the occasions when his daughter's attempts to make him see reason had become urgent. Picking up his hat and cane, he moaned, "You are driving me out, quite rightly, to find some source of income, no matter how demeaning, that will allow us to live. I will do my best, my dear," he promised oozing sincerity, and departed, scurrying away from the nasty truths Leslie had forced upon him.

He probably believes he can make some sort of token effort toward finding employment, but then he will stop off at some tavern to slake his thirst after such arduous seeking, and forget all his troubles as well as spending coins we can ill afford Leslie thought. She had hoped, on their first arrival in London, that he might approach his relative, the Earl of Rothfield, with whom he claimed some intimacy, but that idea seemed to have been forgotten along with so many other uncomfortable reminders of his negligence. Leslie, not one to give into despair, felt quite close to that condition on this grey and unseasonable morning. But she knew she must not allow her depressed spirits to take control. Somehow she must think up a clever idea for a new article, that, signed with her father's name, would add to their purse. Perhaps a heart-rendering tale about one of the veterans of the Peninsula War so callously set adrift by an indifferent government.

Aside from insulating himself from any appeals from Sir Alan, Marcus had given no further thought for the Dansforths although Jonathan had pled their cause most movingly. He was completely absorbed in remaking the newspaper along the lines he had outlined, incisive and influential, but profitable as well, for under the terms of his employment he had been given a small share in the paper. He found that his former radical ideals were fast fading under the exigencies of business. Three years ago John Walter had introduced the steam press and now the printers were agitating for more pay to handle the new type. Although circulation had risen to almost five thousand, the seven penny price put *The Times* out of reach for all but the well-to-do literati. There were a host of one and two penny sheets pandering to a cruder readership.

In answer to rising costs and the stamp tax of four pence, Marcus introduced advertising supplements and reduced the page size. As literary critic he had only been concerned with turning the telling phrase. Now he must be equally concerned in turning a profit. It left him little time or interest in personal affairs.

Jonathan had teased him that he was neglecting the mistress he had in keeping for the past year, a languid and luscious lady of dubious background but obvious talent in pleasing gentlemen who had been only too happy to abandon her casual career as a dancer at Covent Garden to please Marcus. He had set her up in rooms across the Thames in Nelson Square but since returning from his European tour had spent little time with her. Marcus was fortunate in not relying on his salary for his livelihood. His father, a prudent and successful solicitor, had left his only child with a comfortable income. Still, he was determined to make his mark as a journalist, to guide *The Times* to success and to make it an organ of influence in the affairs of the nation. Noble sentiments, he sometimes thought cynically, but of no use if he could not insure the financial stability of the newspaper.

If Marcus appeared indifferent to the fate of the Dansforths he could plead that other, more vital concerns occupied him. But Jonathan was a worthy champion of their cause and it was at his urging that Marcus encouraged his staff editor to approve the occasional articles Sir Alan submitted. He had been particularly impressed by a fierce attack on the Prince Regent, whose profligate spending in depressed times, had caused an outcry. Earlier in the year Prinny's coach had been attacked by a mob incensed because of the repressive measures passed by Parliament and for which the populace blamed the Prince Regent. While men, women and children were hungry, Prinny was spending thousands of pounds on his Pavilion at Brighton.

Marcus had never forgiven the Prince Regent for the imprisonment of Leigh Hunt and his brother John, editor of *The Examiner*. The Hunts had called the Prince Regent "a violator of his word, a libertine over head and heels in debt and disgrace, a despiser of domestic ties, the companion of gambler and demireps, a man who has just closed half a century without one single claim of the gratitude of his country . . ." The Hunts were arrested and charged "with intent to traduce and vilify His Royal Highness". Despite a brilliant defense by Henry Brougham they were fined five hundred pounds apiece and sentenced to two years at Horsemonger Lane Gaol. Marcus, along with Percy Shelley, Charles Lamb and John Keats had all visited Leigh Hunt there and raised a subscription for "the brave and enlightened man."

The Dansforth article echoed all of Marcus' heart-felt beliefs about his ruler and the state of the country. He was surprised by the author's perception and humanity as well as the skilled turn of phrase in which he expressed his views. He doubted that Sir Alan entertained such radical opinions and he wondered if Miss Dansforth could have been the source. The idea piqued his interest. Of course there was the rare woman who thought incisively, embraced the rights of the people and wrote well, but certainly if Leslie Dansforth combined all these qualities she was an exception. Marcus had a very jaundiced opinion of the intellectual abilities of women. Still, Leslie Dansforth could not be completely banished and she lingered on the edge of his awareness, soon to take a dominant role in circumstances he could never have imagined.

Sir Alan, all unsuspecting that his daughter was submitting articles, whose precepts he would have scorned, under his name to *The Times,* set out from their lodgings in an aggrieved mood. Really, Leslie was becoming a most managing female and not the dutiful daughter who would cherish him, a role he had designed for her. That there was some justice in her insistence of economy and reform of his life, he might admit grudgingly to quiet her complaints, but Sir Alan really felt that he had been singled out by a cruel fate. It was not of his doing that his affairs had degenerated in such a fashion. Perhaps if his poor wife had lived, he mused, knowing all too well that gentle lady had never opposed him no matter how outrageously he had behaved, things would be better. Leslie probably inherited her stiff-necked manners and moralizing from the Rothfields, a prosy, mean-spirited, bigoted family, he thought. Well, he would not take criticism from his daughter. The more his mind dwelt on his troubles, the more miserable his situation appeared, the more he sought relief from his troubles. He decided he would just make a brief visit to the Dog and Bottle, a rather low tavern beyond Covent Garden before deciding his next move.

Sir Alan always felt more comfortable in the company of men less well born than himself. He could restore his conceit by bragging of past glories and association with the high and mighty. To strengthen his image he often indulged in generous if foolish gestures such as buying drinks for the whole tavern, especially after he had taken the odd glass. And this afternoon was no different except that among the customers in the Dog and Bottle was a scurvy fellow well known for his mean and argumentative disposition and feared for his great strength. Jim "Bruiser" Parkes was a former Guardsman with a grudge against the world. A good soldier who had fought doggedly in the Peninsula and at Waterloo, he had been released from the army after Napoleon's defeat, as had so many other veterans now swelling the unemployment ranks.

Bitter and violent, he cadged a living of sorts by robbing the unwary and begging from his former officers, a nasty customer indeed, and Sir Alan would have stepped more warily if ale had not relaxed his normal caution. Before he quite understood how it happened he had become embroiled in a slanging match with the Bruiser who had the temerity to criticize Wellington. If Sir Alan had not been overflown by his own rhetoric and bottled courage he would have heeded the warnings of his fellow drinkers. With some experience of the Bruiser's temper they tried to quiet Sir Alan, but he would take no advice from these inferiors. The tavern keeper, too, expressed the wish that both Sir Alan and the Bruiser would take their custom elsewhere but by that time it was too late. In a fit of rage because Sir Alan had called him a traitor, the Bruiser hit out at the toff who annoyed him and Sir Alan fell back, hitting his head on the stone fireplace. Efforts to revive him were useless. He had died in a drunken brawl. Aghast and sobered by his handiwork, the Bruiser, uttering threats against any who informed the constables on him, made a rapid exit, leaving the tavern keeper to tidy up the mess.

"Dump the gent in the river, Burt. Don't want any busybodies nosing around here, do we?" suggested one of his regulars, a rough dock worker. "These gaffers who come down here slumming get what they deserve," he suggested.

"It was an accident, and all," Burt pleaded.

"Yah, and who'll believe that one. You want the Bruiser back here rubbing your face on the bar?"

Possibly, that would have been Sir Alan's fate, to be dropped carelessly in the Thames, jettisoned as useless cargo, had it not been for one rather more humane patron, Pride, who slipped out while the argument continued and fetched a constable. His motive was not wholly charitable for he thought there might be some reward for the information from grateful relatives. And he suspected that if Burt and some of the rest started dividing up the contents of Sir Alan's pockets and stripping him of his clothes, watch and chain, he would not be among those who shared in the loot.

The constable, a grizzled veteran, who was no stranger to tavern fights, arrived before the Dog and Bottle's ghouls could do more than wrangle over the body. The more wary patrons had slipped away in the wake of the Bruiser, not wanting to become involved. Not that the Charlies, as the constables were called, had much power to apprehend a criminal. But they were entitled to a reward, as was any citizen, if they could bring the perpetrator to justice in the magistrate's court. Tom Higgens, always eager to augment his salary of twenty pounds a year, hurried to the Dog and Bottle with his informant, who kept nattering away about the reward. Neither Higgens nor Pride, who had fetched him, were shocked by the death. London was the most lawless city in Europe, the only one without a professional police force, and death, rape and robbery were commonplace along the docks. It was not unusual for the nobs from Mayfair to sample the low life in the Thames side taverns, and often they came to grief.

Higgens examined the dead man and rifled through his pocketbook, reluctantly surrendered by Burt, the barman. He had not needed to learn Sir Alan's name and direction before realizing that the dead man was a toff.

"Good thing you summoned me, Burt. This gent has a title to his name and who knows what else. Ever been here afore?" he asked Burt.

"Can't say as he has, but he might of. We get some toffs in here some nights, throwing their blunt around and sniffing at the likes of decent men," Burt whined.

"And how did he come to end up on the floor with a great bloody bruise on his noggin?" Higgens asked, having a good idea what had happened. "Who hit him?"

The half dozen or so men standing around looked at each other, their eyes shifting downwards. They would not be foolish enough to accuse the Bruiser.

"Come on, Burt. The man didn't just fall down on his own," Higgens urged, suspecting he would never learn the real tale. Even Bob Pride eager for a reward had enough regard for his own health to keep mum about the Bruiser.

"Well, the magistrate and coroner will settle the matter. I'll just take his valuables along to give to his relations. Bad enough the toff stuck his spoon in the wall without being robbed," Higgens said, knowing full well what the Dog and Bottle crew had in mind. He gathered up Sir Alan's watch and chain, his pocketbook, and tugged the signet ring off his stiffening finger.

"I'm leaving you in charge, Burt. See that no one disturbs the body whilst I report this, understand. It'll be the worse for you if you don't," he threatened. "As for you, Bob Pride, if there is a reward I'll remember you did your duty."

Having settled the matter to his satisfaction he left after a raking glance around the bar, as if to remember who had witnessed Sir Alan's death and could be held responsible.

" 'Twas an accident," one of the men whined.

"Was it? We'll see," countered Higgens and took his leave.

Dusk was darkening the room where Leslie was struggling to put her turbulent thoughts on paper. Hearing the knock on the door, she looked up, puzzled as to who should come calling at this hour. She hadn't realize the time, nor the length of her father's absence. Could he have forgotten his key again? She lit a candle on the sideboard and hurried to answer the summons.

The man standing on the threshold raised his hat, "Miss Dansforth?" he queried, rather surprised to see the young woman, and hating his task for he was a compassionate man despite his experience of death.

"Yes, I am Miss Dansforth," Leslie agreed, a sudden premonition of the stranger's errand sobering her voice.

"May I come in?" he asked in a soothing quiet tone. It was unfortunate the young lady appeared to be alone, with no one to offer comfort when he had revealed the shocking news he had to give her.

"Of course," Leslie stepped aside and waved him into the room. "Who are you?" she said, realizing she might have been unwary to allow him in so easily.

"I'm from the coroner's office, ma'am, and I am the bearer of sad news. Your father is dead, killed in a nasty tavern brawl, I fear." He looked apprehensive, expecting hysterics, a fainting, screaming female, for few received the news he brought in silence. But Leslie only gasped, her face paling, and subsided into a chair. Somehow she was not surprised that her father had met such a sordid end.

"Are you all right?" the man muttered, not sure of what to do. "Is there anyone I can call for you?" He continued kindly, admiring her stoic reception of the appalling tragedy.

"No, no thank you. But please, tell me what happened?" she asked with what he thought an unmaidenly avid interest.

"In the Dog and Bottle, a low dive near the docks. What a man like him was doin' there, I can't imagine, but it was the death of him," the coroner's officer reported baldly.

Getting no reaction from the silent female he plodded

on, "I'm afraid you will have to come and identify the body." Then realizing the enormity of his request, "Surely there is some relative, a man, who might assist you."

"No, no. There is no one," Leslie replied bleakly. Never had she felt so alone, so frightened, her normal resilience completely shattered by her father's wretched end.

"Tomorrow will be time enough, if you could come to where he is," he stammered, not knowing what comfort to offer. "At Newgate, that is."

"Yes, yes, I will be there," Leslie agreed, hardly knowing what she said, eager for this seedy little man to take his leave. "Is that all?"

"I guess so, ma'am. Will you be all right?"

"Yes, thank you for coming."

Seeing there was no more to be said, and feeling ill at ease, the coroner's officer sidled out. Rarely did he have to bring the dreadful news of a death to such a one, he thought, shaking his head, and wondering a bit what would happen to the girl. She seemed so alone.

And Leslie, still huddled in her chair, uncomprehending, realized that Sir Alan's death had left her not only alone but without friends or resources. What was she to do?

At noon the next day Marcus, reading a leader about the increase in immigration to Canada of England's unhappy citizens, was annoyed to be disturbed by Jonathan Stirling, who entered his office wearing a grave face and an unusual frown. Rarely was Jon's equanimity disturbed and Marcus put aside his papers and gestured to his friend to take a seat.

"You are looking most grave and unlike yourself, Jon old boy. What's the trouble?" Marcus asked jovially.

"Sir Alan Dansforth is dead," Jonathan announced bluntly.

"Heart, I suppose. The man was a heavy drinker," Marcus said, not too surprised.

"He was killed in some kind of tavern brawl down by the docks, leaving Leslie without a penny," Jonathan stated brutally. For some reason he blamed Marcus, almost disliking his friend for his calm acceptance of the shattering news.

"Unfortunate. I am sorry to hear it, but what can I do?"

"I want you to give her some work," Jonathan insisted as though the suggestion that Marcus employ the bereaved girl was not the most shocking departure from accepted standards. Women were not hired as journalists, no matter how talented they might be.

"Well, I don't think—" Marcus began, only to be interrupted by Jonathan before he could frame a conciliatory sentence.

"She has no relatives, no source of support. Do you want her turned out into the streets," Jonathan cried, his voice implacable.

"No, of course not. But it's not my responsibility." Marcus hesitated, realizing how his friend was affected, and not knowing quite how to frame his suggestion then plunged into his ill considered words. "Since you appear to care deeply for Miss Dansforth, this should be your chance. Marriage would solve all her difficulties." Marcus hoped he did not sound as cynical as he felt, but he knew Jon's attraction to Miss Dansforth, and he thought this was his chance to win his heart's desire. Marcus himself believed marriage to be the ultimate bondage, but he doubted Jon shared his views, and his friend was surely in the toils of Miss Dansforth.

"She turned me down," Jon said bleakly.

Marcus, realizing his friend's disappointment, was at a loss. He wanted to help him, but was afraid any words of his would only exacerbate Jon's disappointment and frustration.

"I feel so helpless. She won't accept me, nor would she let me lend her any money. Sir Alan's affairs are in a muddle, although there should be some relief when his quarterly allowance from his father's estate arrives. But that's a fortnight away, and Leslie is not sure that the funds will be forthcoming when the man of business learns of Sir Alan's death. It's criminal that men make no provision for their dependents," Jonathan fumed.

"Have you spoken to the fellow who handles these matters?" Marcus asked trying to be practical.

"Yes, the fool just shakes his head and says he will look into the matter, but that is of no use to Leslie now."

"I see. Well, I have the germ of an idea. I will have to think about it. Try not to worry, Jon. I'm sure Miss Dansforth, a managing female, will cope."

"You're a heartless beast, Marcus," Jonathan cried and stormed out of the office, leaving Marcus a bit ashamed. But he quickly recovered, deciding that he would have to give his idea more thought, but daring as it was, it might solve both Miss Dansforth's difficulties and his own.

Chapter Four

The days following her father's death had taxed Leslie's courage and endurance to the uttermost. First there had been the grim duty of identifying Sir Alan's body in the cold bleak precincts of the morgue. Then she had to answer the coroner's endless questions to satisfy the authorities, drab men, callous and uncaring of her personal tragedy having seen too many deaths. Jonathan Stirling had tried to comfort and support her, and she was grateful for his presence as she coped with all the meaningless details and during the brief funeral that had followed.

His proposal of marriage had been the final token of his concern, but she could not accept this comfortable solution to her loneliness and sorrow. She did not love him and he deserved more, although he asked for little but her consent, insisting he would not demand more than she could give. Leslie was accustomed to shouldering her problems alone and Jonathan's kind and caring protection had offered her a safe harbor, but she could not treat him as a convenience.

Exasperating and demanding as Sir Alan had been she had always been sure of his love for her. She had feared he might eventually end as he had done, but when it happened, so suddenly, so sordidly, she had not been prepared. Now she was faced with an uncertain, even frightening, future. She had considered contacting the old Earl of Rothfield as he was her only known relative but had abandoned the idea almost at once. She doubted that he would welcome her advances. He had spurned her father during his life and now that Sir Alan was gone he would feel little but relief to be rid of an embarrassing and unwanted connection. And it would be a betrayal of her father. She could not accept the charity of a man who had treated her father so hardly.

Sitting alone in her shadowed sitting room, she realized that whatever security remained to her might not outlast the month. The rent on these shabby quarters was paid until then, but no matter how stringent her economies she could see no way of staying on after that date. Her father's solicitor, a weedy man with an unpleasant sniff and soiled linen, had proved to be of no help. She suspected he was dishonest and although Jonathan had championed her interests strongly, it did not appear to have spurred Mr. Pickens to offer her any advance on her father's allowance due at the end of June if indeed, he intended to pay it all. Jonathan had threatened him with dire proceedings if he did not produce the funds, but Leslie feared the man would do little.

Her options were few. Since marriage was not the answer her only recourse was to offer herself as a governess or companion to whomever might be foolish enough to desire her services. Neither position appealed to her, but she supposed she would have to contact some suitable agency and hope for a post. Teaching children in a household where she would be regarded as little better than a servant, or being at the beck and call of some querulous old dowager, even if she were fortunate enough to be employed in either of these unattractive posts, had little appeal. Yet, again she added up the few pounds available. Perhaps if she could write enough articles—but that alternative, too, was closed to her. No longer could she shelter under her father's name and pursue his journalistic calling. Perhaps one of her former schoolmates might offer a suggestion, but the thought of writing a begging letter was repugnant to her. Pride was a luxury Leslie could not afford, but she found it difficult to abandon.

Sighing she rose to light a few candles and dispel the gloom of the room, wishing she could banish her own unhappiness as easily. She walked to the window, gazing out on the street where the clerks and tradesman, having put up their shutters were hurrying home to their evening meal. As she stared out, envying those with home and families to welcome them, she noticed a tall well-dressed man walking up the steps to the entrance of her boarding house. She had a casual acquaintance with the other members of Mrs. Gorey's establishment and could not recall that they numbered among them any such respectable and well turned out person. Idly she wondered at his business, then turned away thinking she must make herself some supper. To her surprise she heard a knock on her door followed by Mrs. Gorey's gentle voice, "Are you in Miss Dansforth?"

"Yes, Mrs. Gorey. Do come in?" Leslie realized she had not seen or spoken to a soul all day. Even her landlady would be a relief from her thoughts. Mrs. Gorey was a kindly, but doleful soul, a widow always moaning the death of her husband, now departed these ten years, not the most cheerful companion for she had an avid interest in death and had tried Leslie's patience with her efforts at consolation. Still, the poor woman had good intentions so Leslie tried to summon up some enthusiasm for her arrival.

"Sorry to disturb you, dear. I know you must want to grieve in privacy but a very handsome, well behaved gentleman has called to see you. Not the usual one, your friend, Mr. Stirling," Mrs. Gorey announced, curiosity rampant, but respect for Leslie's bereavement restraining her from further questions. "Mr. Kingsley, he says."

Leslie greeted the news with little interest, but supposed she had little reason to refuse him. Perhaps he might be the bearer of money owed to Sir Alan, although she doubted any was due. A cursory condolence call was more probable.

"Show him up, Mrs. Gorey," Leslie agreed, then taking pity on Mrs. Gorey's obvious interest she said, "He was my father's employer, the editor of *The Times,* a thoroughly respectable gentleman, as you observed."

Satisfied, Mrs. Gorey nodded in agreement, as if she had known all along and hurried out to usher him in.

"Good evening, Miss Dansforth. I hope this is not an inconvenient time to call," Marcus said, entering the room removing his hat and giving a slight bow. If he felt any awkwardness at this meeting he was too experienced to show it.

He saw a tall girl with a wealth of waving brown hair, carelessly arranged, painfully thin with a thin nose and high cheekbones, her most striking feature a pair of deep violet eyes fringed with heavy lashes. She was dressed in a shabby black gown fashioned of cheap material and a white shawl, neat but indifferent to style. Marcus preferred lush blonds with enticing smiles and beguiling manners. Miss Dansforth had none of the attributes he looked for in the women he usually pursued, but he was prepared to put aside his prejudices for he needed her.

"Not at all, Mr. Kingsley, very kind of you. I saw you at father's funeral, but you hurried away before I could speak to you," Leslie said with no hint of bitterness although at the time she had felt he was just fulfilling an onerous duty by appearing at the brief rites.

"Yes, well, please accept my condolences on your loss," Marcus said formally, feeling rather uncomfortable. As he remembered from their brief exchange in Carlsbad, Miss Dansforth was adept at producing this atmosphere.

"Certainly. Won't you sit down."

Leslie wondered a bit at his call. Certainly she had not taken to the man in Carlsbad, and he had not appeared to approve of her either, so what was the reason for this unexpected visit. He did not seem the type to be overly burdened with a conscience. Nor had he respected Sir Alan. Remembering how he had terminated her father's connection with *The Times* Leslie frowned, glaring at the man she felt somewhat responsible for Sir Alan's death.

Marcus, who had a good idea of what she was thinking, and of her dislike of him, wondered why he had thought for a moment that his wild plan might work. Still, he had made the effort and all she could do was refuse, throw him out, and that would be the end of it. For a moment he hoped that would be the situation, but then he recalled his own dilemma.

"Actually this is a matter of business, Miss Dansforth. I understand you are in need of employment and I think I might be able to provide it, to both our benefits," he hurriedly added. He suspected that Miss Dansforth would reject any offer that she believed might smack of charity.

She waited uneasily. What on earth was the man sug-

gesting. It said a great deal for Leslie's good sense as well
as her innocence that she never dreamt he might offer her
carte blanche, a suspicion a more worldly female might
have instantly assumed. Females less respectable than
Leslie, and less self reliant, would expect such overtures
to be made in her circumstances.

"As Jonathan may have told you I have been making
some sweeping changes in the staff of *The Times*. It is necessary if the paper is to achieve the first rank, and I am
determined that it shall. For some time I have been dissatisfied with the gentleman who edits the page one personals, what we call waggishly, the agony column, a great
reader attraction. Fortunately he has just come into a small
competence and bored with the job, has left. We have been
all turning our hand to it, but it requires a full time person,
for the supplicants are increasing at a rapid rate. Good for
circulation although I could wish our news columns and
leaders were the chief reason." Marcus wondered if he
sounded pedantic, explaining matters beyond Leslie's
understanding.

Leslie understood his requirements but doubted she
could fulfill them. Much as she needed employment she
doubted that she had the skills or experience to edit a personal column. Yet she would be foolish to refuse him out
of hand.

"What makes you think I could undertake this job" she
asked shortly. The idea of being beholden to Marcus
Kingsley for her daily bread had little appeal, but she reminded herself she was in no position to be choosy.

"You write fairly well. Yes, before you interrupt, let me
assure you I am convinced you edited, if did not actually
write, some of your father's dispatches. You appear sensible and well organized. I need someone dependable and

conscientious. No one need know your identity. I thought we could call you Pythius, the oracle at Apollo, I believe, or some such Greek pseudonym. A little mystery would add spice to your advice."

Not liking his description of her qualities, conscientious, dependable and sensible, Leslie frowned and deliberated.

"It's really just common sense, but the poor fools have to unburden themselves, and we benefit," Marcus coaxed, displaying all the persuasive charm which had usually stood him in good stead. He wondered idly why he was so determined to win Leslie's approval for the appointment. She should be falling all over herself to agree, but her very stubbornness intrigued him. What a prickly female she was.

"I suppose I could give it a try," Leslie conceded reluctantly. "How would we arrange matters?"

"I would bring you the letters, inconvenient, but the fewer people who know your identity the better, I think. I brought a few along today and you could see how you do."

Still, she hesitated, but then turned away, and looked at the accounts on her desk. Beggars could not make demands, but her pride rebelled at being beholden to this condescending man. Perhaps, she was being unfair. Obviously he needed an editor for his personal column, and she was convinced the task would not be beyond her abilities. Certainly not as challenging as reporting on continental affairs, but then she needed work of some sort and this was far more stimulating than teaching or going as a companion.

"We haven't discussed money?" Marcus persisted, seeing that she wavered, and wondering at his own determination to secure her services. Certainly he could hire a more eager and obliging editor for the wretched business.

Marcus found the agony column a dead bore, only wondering at the desperation and gullibility of the applicants who sought advice. But he was practical enough to realize the value of the feature to *The Times*. She would consent. He would make it worth her while.

"Yes, that is a decisive factor," Leslie agreed, not liking to admit how desperate she was, but sensing that this self confident man understood her situation.

"I can let you have five pounds in advance and then shall we say two pounds weekly," Marcus offered, believing that was quite generous.

"Fifty shillings," Leslie bargained, feeling she might as well chance her luck.

"Done," Marcus agreed, knowing he would have paid that to a man and probably more. The transaction completed he was anxious to be on his way. There was some quality about Miss Dansforth that disturbed him and he wanted to be on his way before the affair became more complicated.

He handed her the sheaf of letters he had brought, and prepared to leave.

"How often does the column run?" Leslie asked, practical and brisk, now that the agreement had been sealed.

"Four times a week. And here is the promised five pounds," Marcus placed the money casually on the desk. He was not accustomed to dealing in this fashion with his staff, but, of course, the circumstances were unique.

"Thank you. I should be able to turn in the first column in two days. I will settle to it right away." Leslie felt slightly embarrassed, but grateful, and resentful at the same time. A welter of emotion Marcus would find unbusinesslike she knew. Then, as she walked toward the door.

"May I tell Jonathan?" Leslie asked.

"If you must, but swear him to secrecy. We must keep your identity hidden. Good-bye, Miss Dansforth." And he was gone before she could ask any further awkward questions.

Leslie picked up the five pound note and gazed at it in amazement. What had she agreed to do? Well, at least it would give her a respite from her pressing economic problems, and if it didn't work out to that arrogant Mr. Kingsley's satisfaction she was no worse off than before and had gained some time to seek other employment. She smiled a bit grimly. He might have charm as well as ability but she found him difficult and smug, too armored in self-conceit, having won his laurels too early and so easily. He had not the gentle affable airs of his friend from whom he might learn a good deal, she decided angrily. He made her feel like a pensioner, and that was not a position she welcomed.

Before she could wonder further at this startling change in her affairs, the ubiquitous Mrs. Gorey knocked and then appeared in her doorway like a messenger of gloom.

She was carrying a huge bundle of white roses.

"A foreign gentleman came by while your other visitor was here and asked me to give you these. Very well spoken he was and came in a bang-up carriage, he did. I told him you were occupied and he said he would return," Mrs. Gorey informed her cosily, and handed over the bouquet, waiting to see if any information was forthcoming.

But Leslie was experienced at dealing with her landlady's curiosity, and only thanked her briefly, unwilling to divulge any clues to the identity of her caller. She could not imagine who the caller could be but she was not prepared to quiz Mrs. Gorey.

Seeing that further questions would avail little, Mrs.

Gorey surrendered. "I have a nice veal chop for your supper, dear, when you are ready."

"That will be fine, Mrs. Gorey. Thank you for all your trouble," Leslie signified that the audience was concluded and Mrs. Gorey bustled away.

Leslie jammed the roses in the water pitcher, and looked at the note accompanying them with a nervous presentiment.

Count Felix von Ronberg, ensconced in his carriage some yards down the street from Leslie's rooms, frowned. He had not liked being refused admittance and sensed that Leslie was entertaining a man, who might possibly be a rival. Marcus, striding briskly down the steps and turning in the opposite direction, relieved to have the uncomfortable interview behind him, did not notice the spanking equipage some yards away. If he had he might have wondered seeing such a smart carriage in these shabby streets and suspected their passenger might be calling on Miss Dansforth. And he would have recognized the count. The count, for his part, had no difficulty in recognizing Marcus as the bumptious young fellow who had interrupted his conversation with Leslie in Carlsbad and swore softly to himself. He would not countenance that young man's interference just when it looked like he might be able to lure Leslie into his bed. She had become an obsession with him, not only because of her beauty, but because of her indifference to his attentions. He would not allow her to defeat him again. Now she was alone, and for the moment unprotected. It was a fortunate chance that he had read Sir Alan's obituary some days past. He believed her father's death and his arrival in London promised an interesting and rewarding turn of events, and this time he would be the conqueror. Giving a sharp rap on the door of the coach to signal his coachman to proceed, he sat back, a curious malignant smile on his face.

Marcus was not enjoying himself. He felt irritable and restless, an uncommon state. Upon leaving Leslie, thinking he had handled the interview well and achieved his goal, he had called on his mistress, Dinah Darcy, in Nelson Square where he had set her up in a snug little flat expecting some enjoyable hours of relaxation. After a rollicking evening at Astley's Circus, an entertainment much patronized by Dinah, although Marcus thought it a bit vulgar, the pair had returned to Nelson Square to eat a rich supper of lobster, champagne and syllabub. Marcus, usually quite abstemious, decided he had eaten and drunk too much. That must account for his unease. Normally after such an evening he would tumble happily into bed with Dinah, a curvaceous and pleasing blond with an easy going disposition and skilled expertise in the amatory arts. Marcus had discovered her dancing in the chorus at Covent Garden, and since she was of an indolent nature, not interested in pursuing her career, had no trouble on persuading her to come under his protection. Obliging, not rapacious, and of equable temper, she usually soothed him, but tonight he found her rather overblown beauty common and her conversation tedious.

"I think I will take myself off, Dinah," he announced pushing aside his glass of wine and standing up to make his farewells.

"Oh, Marcus, surely not. More pleasures await us," she urged, pouting a bit.

"Not this evening, my sweet. I'm not in the mood. I'll see you soon," he promised and gathering up his hat and cane made a rather abrupt departure.

Dinah, left alone, sensed that Marcus, usually so eager for their romps, had more on his mind than the pressures of business. Could he be tiring, have met another woman? Dinah looked around her cozy sitting room. She would hate to give all this up, return to a precarious life on the stage. And although she had faith in her ability to attract another protector, she doubted she would find one as handsome and generous as Marcus. He made few demands, was a skilled lover, and treated her with every courtesy. She would be hard put to it to find a man who would equal him, remembering with a shudder some of her earlier experiments along this line. But what had she done to displease him? She was faithful, always available and not grasping. That her bounteous charms could prove cloying to a man who was thinking, despite his best efforts, of another woman was beginning to occur to her. Was he considering marriage, of setting up his nursery with some well-born, virtuous girl?

Of course, that was always a possibility, but his legal ties need not bother their relationship. She had never expected marriage, and in fact, would have been surprised if Marcus had offered it. She knew he was a man of education, breeding, and intellectual interest beyond her scope. Sometimes she did not understand his conversation, nor was she much interested in his elevation to the editor's post at *The Times*. She never read the journals, only rifled through the fashion papers and occasionally enjoyed a penny sheet of the more lurid type. She suspected that she bored him with her prattle but after all, that was not what he required of her. A puzzled frown marred her bland face as she prepared to retire to her lonely bed. Could he have found a female who was her equal in bed and could chat about all the high flown ideas that interested Marcus? If so, Dinah realized she was in trouble. She decided she must seek some advice. And where better than the pages of *The Times* itself?

Chapter Five

To Leslie's surprise when she examined the letters handed to her so casually by Marcus she discovered that most of them were quite mundane, offering rewards for the return of lost articles or pets, advertising special rates for certain goods and services and pleas for employment. But there were also cryptic, tragic, joyful and eccentric messages as well. These would lead the column followed by the more typical messages and then there were the letters begging for advice that she must answer. Organizing all this proved to be far more challenging than she had supposed. And some of the pleas engaged her sympathies despite her best intentions.

"Eustace—please come home—Your desperate Mother."

"WA. refuses to wed L.M.—threats are of no avail."

"Sergeant Major Bothwick. Please contact your wife. Children hungry."

And desperate mothers, beset lovers and abandoned wives also wrote for advice on how to remedy their situations. These would tax Leslie to the utmost although she managed to offer reasonable solutions and tempered advice to the most pressing of her correspondents. Of course, it was not just a bundle of unhappy contributions. There were the frivolous and amusing advertisements, too.

A man proposed himself as an excellent husband although he admitted to an "incurable weakness of the knees." Another wanted to sell fourteen embroidered waistcoats because of a sudden financial emergency. A distressed dog owner requested a remedy for his setter who, for no apparent reason, had become gun-wind-and noise-shy.

Marcus had not spelled out to Leslie exactly how she should handle these two quite separate duties—organizing the personals and composing the letters of advice. Obviously she must carefully select those letters she wished to answer to both satisfy the correspondents and interest the readers. At first she felt her replies were dull, prosy and patronizing but she soon evolved a technique, and became absorbed in the problems of these troubled souls whom she would never meet.

How peculiar that someone would turn to a newspaper, a strange anonymous editor, for advice that could decide his whole life. Leslie, who had initially thought the task frivolous, soon changed her mind. She held out hope to unhappy people and probably that was far more useful than writing screeds of analysis of continental politics. Every day her enthusiasm for her work increased and she became thoroughly absorbed in the problems of strangers. Responsibility for their actions as a result of her advice bothered her at first, but Jonathan assured her that she could do little harm and might actually help. Most people just needed to be prodded to use their common sense, he insisted.

Leslie soon realized that Jonathan did not really approve

of her new career. He believed that the only proper future for a female in her circumstances was marriage, preferably to him, but, if not that, to some other available respectable gentleman. He only agreed she had made the right choice when he heard of the alternative.

Count Felix von Ronberg had renewed his attentions, this time under the cloak of providing a solution to Leslie's employment problems. He suggested that she might prove a brilliant social secretary to Princess Esterhazy, the wife of the Austrian Ambassador to London, and a prominent society hostess. Of course, that would involve her moving into the imposing Mayfair embassy. Leslie was not deceived by this altruistic provision for her future. She knew he wanted her under the same roof where it would be far easier for him to seduce her. The idea of moving in the highest circles of London society did not appeal to her and she was well aware of what her position as a dependent of a foreign aristocrat would be. No, she preferred her scribbling, as the count so contemptuously referred to her occupation. Of course, he had no idea of what her scribbling consisted. He assumed she was writing a gothic novel so popular with the ladies, and usually written by one of their number.

"You have wounded me deeply by your refusal to accept this excellent solution for your future," the count informed her during one of the afternoon calls that were becoming more frequent. He brought with him the wife of an underling, whose desire to become Leslie's friend seemed to take second place to a wish to sit by the window and eat bonbons. Unfortunately, because she was with the court, Leslie could not turn him away. He had decided that for the moment the appearance of friendly assistance would serve his real designs toward Leslie, but she was not deceived.

"Let me be frank, sir. The lax moral code of a foreign embassy would do little to enhance my reputation whatever the pretense of my position. I disapprove of the frivolity and extravagance of the ton and would not want to be connected to it in any way, nor would I adapt to a subservient position in an aristocratic household with any ease." Leslie thought she had put her case very well, but she could see by the count's tightened mouth and flush to his cheekbones that he did not take kindly to her references to what she privately called a degenerate life.

"My dear Miss Dansforth you completely misread the situation. And I had no idea, a female of your experience on the continent, would have such puritan standards," he sneered, his temper overcoming his previous efforts to beguile her with soft words.

Leslie, barely able to repress an outbreak of temper, was rescued from intemperate words and behavior by the arrival of Marcus Kingsley. If he were surprised to see the count he did not show it, greeting him with aplomb, as if the acrimonious Carlsbad encounter had never happened.

"Good afternoon," Marcus said nodding briefly but not extending his hand. "I believe we met in Carlsbad," he reminded the count who had not forgotten but refused to be put out of countenance again. Frau Baum nodded when introduced, then returned her attention to her sweets.

"Yes, Mr. Kingsley, I remember," the count acknowledged. Obviously this fellow was on good terms with Miss Dansforth and he must tread warily, hiding his real feelings. Then, sensing that more was expected, "I just called on Miss Dansforth to offer my condolences and offer her some interesting employment."

"Really. And what did Miss Dansforth reply?" Marcus asked.

Leslie, weary of this dueling answered sharply. "I refused." She did not like standing by, a mere observer of the two men's parrying when she was the object of their rivalry.

"But I hope to change her mind. I think on further reflection she will decide it is in her best interests," the count riposted suavely.

A rather uncomfortable silence followed and Leslie was about to suggest they both leave her in peace when Marcus intervened. "I have a matter of business to discuss with Miss Dansforth, Count, so I am sure you will excuse us."

Seeing he had no recourse to this polite dismissal the count bowed over Leslie's hand and retired, Frau Baum in tow. He was bested yet again by this upstart fellow. But he was prepared to wait for his revenge. Driving furiously away from Leslie's lodging he considered his next move, wondering if Leslie had a romantic interest in the crude scribbler.

"Unfortunate that roué turning up again. Has he been giving you problems?" he asked Leslie as he placed his hat and gloves carefully on a nearby table.

"Nothing I can't handle."

"I don't need to warn you that you would be ill-advised to confide in him about the nature of your present employment," Marcus said silkily.

"Certainly not."

"And am I allowed to know what he has offered?" Marcus asked in a tone Leslie found both condescending and arrogant.

"He did not offer me carte blanche if that is what you are thinking."

"It never crossed my mind," Marcus lied. "I am sure you have too much sense to succumb to that mountebank." Somehow the idea of Leslie finding the count appealing was repugnant to him, although he granted it was none of his business. Naturally, the girl would be looking out for her best interests, and becoming the mistress of an Austrian aristocrat might have its attraction.

"He wants me to take a post in the embassy as secretary of Princess Esterhazy," she blurted out.

"Where he will have you under his influence," Marcus observed shrewdly.

"Probably, but it is out of the question. I find the count not to my taste."

Sensing that any further discussion of the matter would only raise Leslie's hackles, Marcus turned briskly to business. "I am very pleased with your first submissions for the personal and advice column. You have a real flair," he complimented her. "I take it you will be willing to continue."

"Yes, but I certainly hope we can keep my identity a secret," Leslie insisted.

Marcus, unlike Jonathan, saw nothing untoward in Leslie's choice of profession. Of a liberal persuasion he entertained no old fashioned ideas on the subject of women's status. After all, there were several respected women novelists, Maria Edgeworth, Jane Austen, and the radical Mary Wollstonecraft, whose daughter, Mary Shelley, was purported to be working on a macabre gothic. Leslie's efforts might be more humble but were equally to be respected.

"If that is your wish. But you are doing nothing of which you need be ashamed," Marcus championed stoutly.

"Perhaps someday we may have female correspondents. I would much prefer to be commenting on political and foreign affairs than dealing with the troubles of the public," Leslie said sadly. But, then thinking she sounded ungrateful, "Not but what I am becoming fascinated by the myriad problems and wants of those who read *The Times.*"

"You will come to enjoy it, and I fancy it will have more reward, not just tangible, than toadying to the Princess Esterhazy." Marcus, although always willing to enjoy the good life, had the political liberal's scorn for the haute monde.

"Have you brought me some more letters?" she asked, feeling it was time to be practical. "I have a new column for you."

"Good. And yes, here they are, and also your fee." Marcus found himself a bit embarrassed at doling out money to Leslie for her services. It put their relationship on a basis he found distasteful, and then wondered why he entertained such foolish feelings.

"Jon does not approve of my working for you," Leslie said as if reading his thoughts.

"He can be an old woman at times. Pay no attention. His nose is a bit out of joint because you refused his proposal," Marcus mocked.

"Jon is a very honorable man."

"And I am not," Marcus conceded. He would not be adverse to embarking on a flirtation with the unusual Miss Dansforth. Then, disgusted at himself, he was reminded that in dalliance he was no better than the count. But who could blame the man, she was an intriguing woman, intelligent, attractive and independent, all qualities challenging to Marcus who could not resist comparing her to Dinah and wondering what she would be like in bed. Beneath that cool facade there must lie passion and commitment, he thought. Well, he would have to deny himself the pleasure of discovering any of Miss Dansforth's depths. A certain disaster to their professional relationship.

Despite his decision to be sensible he found himself issuing an invitation. "I know you are in mourning, but perhaps you might consider a respectable evening at the theater. You must be lonely. Would like to see Edmund Kean as Richard III? I think you would find his performance revolutionary."

Pleased, if surprised, Leslie considered carefully. "Thank you. I would enjoy it. I have heard a great deal about Mr. Kean."

"Well, what about this Friday?" Marcus said more eagerly than he wanted to appear, forgetting he had promised Dinah to take her to Vauxhall Gardens.

"That will be delightful," Leslie agreed. And then, as if ashamed that she had allowed such frivolity to intrude on the business of Marcus' call, settled down to run through the current crop of letters with him.

Sometime later, strolling back to Printing House Square, Marcus wondered what had induced him to invite Miss Dansforth to the theater. He could be embarking on a relationship fraught with problems. Jonathan would be annoyed and he valued Jon's friendship, would not want him to feel he was taking advantage of his position as Leslie's employer. At least it would put paid to the count's pursuit of her if the cad thought another man was in the running. Anyway he wanted to take her to the theater, and Marcus was not in the habit of denying himself what he desired.

Leslie, feeling quite exhilarated, and wondering just why a simple invitation to the theater should inspire such a change in mood, settled down to look through the new batch of personals. One letter in particular touched her. The anonymous writer, a woman, was pleading for advice in holding on to her protector.

> I have had a very happy and generous relationship with a certain gentleman for some time now. But I believe he is tiring, finding me a bore. He is well bred and well educated, and I cannot satisfy all of his interests. In the past this has not mattered too much but lately he appears to be tiring. I do not want him to leave me. Please advise me what to do.
>
> Signed,
> Worried

Poor soul, another demi-rep about to be abandoned by her lover. What happened to these women after their charms had faded? Few of them were provident enough to put money by for their later years. They drifted helplessly from one man to another, as they aged, slipping farther and farther down the social scale until many of them ended on the streets, drunken and diseased. It appalled Leslie to think how near the edge of destitution so many women lived. Even respectable women, governesses, companions, widows of improvident husbands, sank into obscure poverty, friendless, and unless they had caring relatives, destined for tragic old age. She must remember that Marcus had saved her from a like fate and not endanger her professional duties by entertaining a different type of relationship with him. The thought depressed her, but she refused to admit it.

* * *

The count was becoming increasingly frustrated in his plan to make Leslie his mistress. He thought he had been quite clever in securing employment for her in the Austrian Embassy. Princess Esterhazy probably had quite a good idea of why he wanted Leslie to work for her. A cynical intrigante herself she found nothing shocking in her countryman's deliberate intention of luring the girl into his bed. Cloaking her own extra marital affairs in a facade of strict propriety she expected no less from a man with the count's lustful tastes. She was willing to go along with his ploys, believing that she could use them to her own ends. It seemed inconceivable that a girl, thrown on her own resources, would not find the count's offer acceptable. She would be surprised that he had been refused. Confessing his failure to the ambassador's wife would be humiliating. And the count believed that he could lay his disappointment at the door of that upstart journalist, Marcus Kingsley. The man had already thwarted him in his designs for Leslie and he did not accept defeat gracefully.

Could it be that the matter of business the editor confessed to having with Leslie concerned the same offer that the count had in mind? Since the count's relations with women almost always had a sexual motive, he did not accept that another man's actions might be different. He was determined to have Leslie, even if it meant he must abduct her, he decided. She would not escape him and he smiled evilly as he concocted schemes, driving his horses with reckless abandon down Piccadilly.

In his Printing House Square office Marcus faced a disgruntled Jonathan. Marcus had persuaded William Hazlitt, a longtime friend and respected writer, to become his drama critic. He had cajoled Jonathan into taking on the responsibility of political observer, reporting on Parliament, a chore Jonathan viewed with some wariness.

"I understand that luring Hazlitt to write for the paper is a real coup, Marcus, but I wonder if I am the man for this new assignment," Jonathan protested.

"Of course you are. I need someone I trust to cover the lawmakers, scurvy bunch that they are. The country is in turmoil, poor harvests, the Luddites rebelling against the new machinery, unemployment, the Prince Regent's excesses continuing, the Corn Law repeal causing dissension and a rising demand for extended suffrage. I need a good man on Parliament's doings. God knows I have enough on my mind what with labor unrest here, circulation problems and the rivalry of the penny sheets. If *The Times* is ever to become a dominant paper we need to exert Herculean efforts."

"Is Leslie one of your Herculean efforts?" Jonathan asked bitterly. He objected strongly to Marcus' employment of her and felt uneasy as to what the relationship might lead.

"Certainly. She is a talented lady. And a woman's touch is improving the column."

"You find her fascinating, don't you. No wonder, she is unique," Jonathan insisted, worry creasing his brow. He did not like the situation.

"Jonathan, believe me, I would not put a rub in your way. You want to marry her. I understand that, but she has refused you. Do you think she will change her mind?" Marcus waited for the answer with more anxiety than he wanted to admit to himself.

"I don't know. I intend to keep trying to persuade her. I am worried about that Austrian fellow. He is a nasty type and I don't think easily discouraged. Certainly he has no honorable intentions toward her. And how can we protect her?"

"Don't worry. I think Miss Dansforth can protect herself. She would not be foolish enough to have her head turned by the knave's compliments. I wonder what his role is at the embassy? He's a clever rogue. I don't think he came to London just to pursue Miss Dansforth."

"The Prince Regent likes him. They have a lot in common," Jonathan observed shrewdly.

"Poor Prinny. He's so unpopular, and he won't learn. But I think Lady Hertford is keeping him harmlessly occupied for the moment."

Marcus launched into an outline of what he believed *The Times* should advocate in view of the condition of the country and the monarchy, hoping Jonathan would be distracted from further questions about Leslie. Somehow he did not want to confess to his friend that he had invited her to the theater. Of course, it was just a gesture, meant little, really, but Jonathan would not see it that way. He knew all about Dinah and would suspect that Marcus was tiring of her and looking about for a new conquest. He would be both disgusted and angry if he thought for one moment that Marcus had designs on her. Marcus repressed a sigh. Really, a disappointed suitor could be quite tedious and women were death to a friendship. If he were sensible he would leave his relations with Leslie on a professional footing. But he knew he had already gone too far along the path leading to a far deeper and more intimate involvement. It was too late now to retreat.

Chapter Six

The Theater Royal in Drury Lane, designed by Christopher Wren on a commission from Charles II, reigned supreme as the most popular and elegant stage in London. Leslie, whose only experience of English productions, had been one melodrama and a pantomime in Bath, was impressed with the grandeur of the gilded boxes, the heavy velvet draperies, the fashionable audience. From her aisle seat four rows back from the stage she looked about with unabashed curiosity. Three tiers of boxes overlooked the stalls, the center one on the lowest tier obviously the royal box, this evening unoccupied, but every other one filled with extravagantly gowned and jeweled women and their escorts. In the balconies more humble patrons voiced their opinions of the crowd, the coming performance, the actors and engaged in noisy repartee.

Unwilling to admit that this was her initial experience of London's theater, she hesitated to ask Marcus about the occupants of the various boxes, although her curiosity could barely be contained. But he sensed her interest and obliged.

"See there on the right, in the third box, second tier, is

the famous demimondaine, Harriet Wilson, with the crowd of eager gentlemen in attendance."

"I'm surprised. I've heard a great deal about her, and I expected her to be beautiful," Leslie said staring at the notorious brunette, whose chief charm appeared to lie in her saucy manner and bright eyes.

"Her list of protectors is formidable, Craven, Argyll, Devonshire, Hill and Ponsonby. Even Wellington has been rumored to be among her court, but her real love is Ponsonby, so the on dits go."

"Poor girl. Of course, he will not marry her," Leslie said with some asperity.

"No, I fear not. He will become the Earl of Bessborough eventually and wed some well born debutante. It's the way of the world. Harriet, even if she were not a scandal, is the daughter of a shopkeeper, not at all the thing," Marcus reported wryly. Then he went on to point out some of the other stars of the haute monde. Leslie found the spectacle absorbing but she wondered watching the audience how many of the playgoers were really interested in the drama about to be presented. They appeared to be on show, more involved in showing off their gowns and flirting than serious fans of either Kean or Shakespeare. But once the curtains parted and Kean limped onto the stage to declaim, "Now is the winter of our discontent made glorious by this sun of York," she forgot the audience, the theater and even Marcus, so absorbed did she become in the actor's powerful Richard III.

After the first act, still enthralled, at first she did not hear Marcus' suggestion that they stroll through the halls. But emerging from Kean's spell she, at last, consented and they made their way up the aisle into the wide rotunda, thronged with the gossiping patrons.

"Well, what do you think of Kean?" Marcus asked, amused by her distrait air.

"He's brilliant. I wonder what he is like as a man."

"A drunkard, a womanizer, ambitious and jealous of his fame. Not an attractive personality."

"Oh, dear. But as an actor he is superb, so I will think of him only as Richard III," Leslie decided wisely.

The rest of the performance passed in a dream for her, and when they finally left the crowded theater after numerous curtain calls, she thanked Marcus prettily for the evening.

"I thought we might have supper at Grillon's. You must have worked up an appetite," Marcus suggested.

Leslie agreed, reluctant to abandon the magic of the drama. She felt rather like a schoolgirl given a treat by an indulgent brother, but did not want the evening to end. Jonathan and William Hazlitt, the new theater critic for *The Times,* the latter a rather grim gentleman, who had been forced to abandoned spirits because of his past intemperate habits, and drank only strong black tea, made up the party.

"Did you enjoy this evening's performance?" Leslie asked, trying to lighten the atmosphere.

"I saw it some weeks ago, and wrote a critique of it," Hazlitt said in a quelling tone.

Leslie, embarrassed that she had not known of this, refused any other overtures, and despite the lobster patties and champagne, found the meal disappointing. Jonathan kept gazing at her with a hurt but admiring expression she found disturbing. Looking about the hotel, which was crowded with revelers, she felt isolated. Not used to such gaiety, she decided. I am really becoming a recluse, and she felt ashamed of her appearance in her tired black silk gown when she compared her dress to the lavish silks and satins of the other ladies enjoying their supper.

Marcus, realizing her discomfort, brought the meal to an abrupt end, and bidding good-bye to Hazlitt and Jonathan, whisked Leslie away. This was not the way in which he had planned for the evening to end. Not that he expected any romantic climax. It was obvious Leslie did not view him in that light. Just as well he decided ruefully. Although he found her conversation stimulating, her opinions well thought out and intelligent, he wished she could look at him as a friend rather than an employer. If his emotions were confusing he did not recognize them, preferring to delude himself.

On returning her to her lodgings he apologized for Hazlitt.

"I found Mr. Hazlitt intriguing although perhaps a little dour," Leslie confided, "but I am always happy to see Jonathan."

"Perhaps next time we might try a less lugubrious entertainment. You might like a glimpse of Vauxhall Gardens," Marcus returned, not willing to take up the topic of Jonathan.

"I am supposed to be in mourning," Leslie objected, wondering why Marcus was taking so much trouble to amuse her. She was grateful, but puzzled.

Marcus, himself, wondered why he was so insistent on gaining Leslie's approval. After all, though he found her attractive he had no need of another woman in his life. He hesitated, wanting to prolong the evening, hoping for some sign that Leslie returned his regard, then chastising himself for being so foolish. It could only lead to trouble and disappointment for both of them.

"I don't think your father, who enjoyed the good life,

would want you to restrict yourself solely to work," he pleaded.

"No, Father was fond of the fleshpots," Leslie agreed smiling.

"You are a lovely woman, Leslie, quite irresistible, really," Marcus insisted and then as if he could not deny himself the opportunity, took her in his arms and kissed her with a thoroughness that surprised them both.

Emerging from his embrace, flushed and with pounding heart, Leslie looked angry and bemused.

"Why did you do that?" she asked.

Marcus laughed, "Only you, Leslie, would ask such a question. I kissed you because I wanted to and I admit I found it most enjoyable. Did you?"

"I don't know. I have never been kissed before," she answered ingenuously, and then ashamed that she had been so forthright, continued. "But you must not do it again."

"I don't think I can promise that," Marcus teased. "But I am mean to try your patience. I will see you tomorrow," he promised, and then opening her door, pushed her through the entrance, rather as if he could not wait to be rid of her. Before Leslie could make any response he had run lightly down the steps, jumped into his carriage and was away. Standing in the darkened hall, she felt abandoned.

Later, brushing her hair as she prepared for bed, she wondered why he had kissed her. It had meant little to him, just a passing whim, she decided. She would be foolish to read anything more into it but a careless gesture, the result of too much wine, and perhaps his normal climax of an evening with a woman. Beneath that cool ambitious facade, Leslie believed Marcus was a man much experienced in the way of women, and she did not want to end up like Harriet Wilson. What she did want from Marcus she could not fathom, respect certainly, and regard for her abilities with her pen. But did any man think of women as more than the provider of children or as beguiling companions in bed if marriage was not the object. In neither capacity did she think she could accommodate his desires. He must be persuaded that their relationship could not develop along lines she was convinced would only lead to unhappiness for her. Having made this sensible resolution she retired, to lie awake remembering, not Kean's Richard III, but Marcus' compelling embrace.

For Marcus the conclusion of the evening was equally disturbing. Why in the world had he been so stupid to give in to a momentary desire to raise the passions beneath the composed and independent Miss Dansforth? She had enjoyed the play if not the supper and certainly would not repeat the experience if she thought him a cad and a trifler. Somehow her good opinion mattered a great deal. He would have to step warily in the future. Not once during the evening had he given a thought to Dinah Darcy.

Marcus, such an astute and perceptive judge of other men, their talents and foibles, was unable to apply that reasoned judgment to his own turbulent feelings. On the one hand he knew he was foolish to become embroiled with Leslie romantically, on the other she represented an exciting change from his usual amours. Then he laughed a bit bitterly. He was a conceited dolt. She probably would never look upon him in any other way than that of an employer. She had refused Jonathan who had offered her an honorable proposal. Why should she dally with Marcus whose intentions were as reprehensible as those of the salacious Count von Ronberg? Thinking of the Austrian Marcus frowned. At least with him she would not be disgraced nor humiliated. Although, to be honest, if a respectable woman entered into an illegal alliance with a man she immediately earned the scorn and ignominy of her more careful sisters. In London society the sin was not so much in the immoral behavior but in being found out. Marcus, unable to settle down for the night, picked up a tract on the Corn Law and determined to read himself to sleep.

A sleepless night was also passed by Dinah Darcy, smarting over the cancellation of her evening with Marcus, for which he had given no real excuse. She waited with some anxiety for his next appearance. She was sure he would tell her they must part. She was fond of Marcus but fonder of the security he had provided for the past two years. If that was to be denied to her she must be looking about for another protector, not as easy as when she was a member of the chorus in Covent Garden. But perhaps this strange behavior of Marcus was only temporary, a result of his new position, of which she knew little, but supposed it meant added responsibility. Although uneducated, with common tastes and little talents beyond those skills acquired in pleasing a man, Dinah was not stupid. She had a certain shrewdness that enabled her to assess her situation without any illusions. She had been a goose to write to the paper about her suspicion. What if Marcus discovered she was the author demanding advice on how to hold onto him. Did he read the letters himself? As she dressed to go out later that morning she decided she would not buy a paper, although she thought the answer she had requested might be in today's column. Tossing her head, and denying the cold chill she felt at her possible abandonment, she perched a fetching cream bonnet adorned with red cherries

on her blond curls and sallied forth to meet her friend
Gladys for chocolate.

In the morning room of the Austrian Embassy, Princess
Esterhazy was busy with her correspondence, always a
heavy one as she had connections throughout the courts of
Europe. Having dispatched lengthy budgets of news to her
many relations, and friends, she cast an experienced eye
over a list of invitations for a coming dinner honoring the
Duke of Wellington. Then she reluctantly drew another
sheet of the engraved paper on which she wrote her personal letters. She did not want to become involved in this
scheme of Felix von Ronberg's, but she found it impossible to refuse him.

Unfortunately the man knew of a discreditable episode
in her past, and although he was not crude enough to mention this knowledge, he hinted in an odious manner that
compelled her to agree to what he asked. At one time she
had considered a dalliance with the man but some instinct
prevented her from pursuing it. Handsome, rich and well-
born as he was there was an innate cruelty and an incred-
ible self absorption in the man that put her off. She knew
that for some reason he wanted this bourgeois girl, who had
unaccountably refused his advances. And it would be far
more difficult to force her in London than in their own
country, where nobles' exercise of the droit de signeur
was accepted with a resigned shrug. The British were both
more puritanical and hypercritical, the princess decided.
Well, she must get on with it, and if her invitation failed
the count could not blame her. She rather hoped the silly
female would have the good sense not to answer her request for an interview.

Leslie, who had tried to work, and after a fruitless morning had abandoned her pen and strolled around to the British Museum, had decided she would be best away when Marcus called. He could leave his message with Mrs. Gorey. For some reason she did not want to face him after last night, foolish, no doubt, but she was embarrassed. She need not have been. Upon returning to her lodgings Mrs. Gorey informed her that the only visitor she had during her absence was a very uppity footman from the Austrian Embassy who had delivered a letter. Intrigued by this further evidence that Leslie had some mysterious connection with this aristocratic menage Mrs. Gorey's nose twitched with pleasurable anticipation. She would have much to boast about when she next met her crony, Mrs. Appleton from two doors down. Leslie, appreciating Mrs. Gorey's ill concealed curiosity, tore open the letter and obliged her. She read the brief missive quickly, and laughed.

"The Princess Esterhazy requests an interview. Now what do you think of that, Mrs. Gorey?"

"Lawks, a mercy, Miss Dansforth. You would not be going to leave here and take up with those foreigners, would you?"

"Never fear, Mrs. Gorey. I am very happily situated here. Don't you worry."

"Supposed you missed your lunch, Miss Dansforth, so I will bring up some tea in a moment," the lady offered, thinking some recompense must be made for this information. And she really liked Miss Dansforth and would hate to see her leave. None of her other tenants were half so well connected nor so courteous.

Leslie's first reaction was to pen a polite note of refusal to Princess Esterhazy, but she decided she could not behave in such a cavalier manner. Perhaps the lady really needed a social secretary and was unaware of any infamous plan that the count might have hatched. Her curiosity was aroused. She had heard a great deal about the Esterhazys in Vienna, much of it scandalous. She might not have another opportunity to observe the princess whose influence in London society as a patroness of Almacks was so formidable. Before she could change her mind she wrote her polite little note, and only hoped that the count would not be lurking about the embassy ready to pounce on her. But he could hardly seduce her under the eyes of the princess or her raft of servants.

Mrs. Gorey arrived with the promised tea and Leslie realized how hungry she was. She tucked into the meal with a hearty appetite and had barely finished when Mrs. Gorey returned followed closely by Marcus. Leslie gulped down the last swallow of tea and greeted him with what she hoped was a casual air.

"Thank you, Mrs. Gorey," she said to her landlady who, a bit flustered, explained that Mr. Kingsley had not waited to be announced. Then picking up the tray she departed still grumbling.

"Before you say a word of reproach let me explain that I was afraid if I let the good Mrs. Gorey announce me that you would refuse to see me after what you have no doubt decided was my deplorable behavior last evening," Marcus coaxed, thinking to disarm her with penitence.

But Leslie was not deceived. "Do you usually kiss ladies on their doorstep and then come around the next day to apologize. I don't know that I appreciate such conduct. I find it rather hypocritical," Leslie said severely.

"Alas, Leslie, you have exposed me to your critical judgment and found me wanting. You are quite right. I kissed you because I wanted to, and very enjoyable it was for me, if not for you," he mocked, his eyes asking a question. Had she really disliked it?

"You are a rogue, Marcus, and I refuse to take you seriously." Leslie decided that a light bantering tone would suit the situation best. She certainly did not want Marcus to suspect she considered the episode important.

"That is my fate, not to be taken seriously, but I promise to reform, to treat you with the most punctilious courtesy and never encroach in any way. It will be difficult, but I will try." He sighed lugubriously, as if denying himself further treats with the utmost reluctance.

"Enough of this nonsense. Let us get down to business. How are the letters coming?" she demanded, refusing to be drawn into any more analysis of the climax to last evening.

"Very well, and here is a new batch. You seem to have struck a sympathetic chord with the readers. I am hearing a great deal about the popularity of the column." He placed his bundle on her table and noticed the letter addressed to the Princess Esterhazy.

"I don't wish to be accused of prying into your personal affairs, when I am not in your good books at the moment, but I had no idea you were on corresponding terms with Princess Esterhazy."

"You are prying but I don't mind telling you that she has requested I call upon her as she needs a social secretary and believes I might be the proper person. You know all about this from the count's offer the other day."

"But I thought you refused most emphatically," Marcus insisted, frowning. He didn't like this change of mind a bit.

"I did. Oh, dear, you have caught me out in a most reprehensible action. I want to see the embassy and meet the princess. We heard much gossip about the lady in Vienna," Leslie confessed with a smile.

"A good journalist's reply. I can understand that, and you might be able to discover some news for us. The Esterhazys are hand in glove with Metternich and I crave to know more about that wily statesman," Marcus admitted. Then, sensing that he might be trespassing on Leslie's good nature, he added. "But only if you want to, and try to stay out of the clutches of that odious count."

"Not barter my virtue for a good budget of news," Leslie teased, enjoying herself immensely at Marcus' expense.

"Of course not. The man's dreadful, and may even be dangerous. On second thought, I believe you should refuse the princess."

"Nonsense. I am not a child. I will manage brilliantly." Leslie was rather pleased at Marcus' concern for her welfare but had no intention of letting him know that, or of surrendering to his notion that she should obey his dictates.

"Well, when is this interview to take place? I will want a full report and if you do not return at least I will know what steps to take," he growled.

"Tomorrow at eleven o'clock. And what will you do if the Austrians incarcerate me, storm the embassy and demand my return? Really, Marcus, I can take care of myself, and cope with both the princess and the count."

"I'm not sure of that, but I will be around tomorrow at noon to hear all about it, and then we might have luncheon at Gunter's," he coaxed, hoping to persuade her into a more amiable mood.

"That would be lovely. I will see you then." Leslie gave every evidence that the interview had concluded and Marcus had to leave reluctantly.

He left behind a very pleased Leslie, who believed she

had brushed through this meeting quite well, neither up-braiding him like a frightened virgin, nor acting like an abused shrew. Their friendship seemed to be progressing beyond the bounds of professional cooperation and she wondered if she was wise in reading into his concern a deeper feeling. She put aside the thought as highly un-likely and settled down to her letters.

Chapter Seven

The Esterhazys were a noble Hungarian family of Magyar descent who traced their ancestry back to the thirteenth century. Prince Paul, the current holder of the title, had won the approval of Francis II, the Hapsburg emperor of the Austro-Hungarian Empire, by abandoning his own claims to the Hungarian throne and loyally supporting the weak Hapsburg ruler. He had spent his life in the diplomatic corps, serving in Dresden, Rome and Paris but his favorite post was London, where he and his wife had become leading figures in the haute monde. Proud, distinguished and promiscuous, both the Esterhazys were extremely popular and both could claim close ties to Metternich, the Austrian premier, whose influence in European circles after the defeat of Napoleon was paramount.

Leslie, arriving for the requested interview with the princess, tried not to be overawed by the flunkies, dressed so formally, their arrogance as pronounced as their master's, who received her and indicated that she must wait upon the princess' pleasure. Escorted across the wide marble hall, whose niches held priceless statuary, into an imposing reception salon, she perched on a French satin covered chair, uneasy and defiant. She realized that her hostess, born Princess Theresa of Thurn and Taxis, an old German title, would not hurry to oblige a person of low rank. If she were starving she would not accept a post in this intimidating environment, but recalling, belatedly, that she was a journalist not a supplicant, she steeled herself for whatever condescension would be offered.

After a suitable period, at least a half an hour, Leslie was led up the grand staircase to the princess' boudoir.

"Ah, good morning, Miss Dansforth," Princess Ester-hazy, although gowned elaborately and wearing several thousand pounds of jewelry, was not an especially impos-ing figure. Small, round shouldered, with black hair and narrow dark eyes with a spiteful gleam, she cast an as-sessing eye over Miss Dansforth.

Indicating with a regal wave that her visitor should be seated, she continued to favor Leslie with a rather un-nerving stare.

Leslie thought it wise to leave the first questions to the princess.

"I understand that circumstances, the death of your fa-ther, have left you in rather impecunious circumstances?" the princess said. Her English was good but Leslie found the slight guttural accent unattractive.

"That is so, princess."

"Count von Ronberg assures me you would be well up to coping with the duties of a social secretary. Naturally, the prince and I do a great deal of entertaining and are fre-quent guests in the best English society. And as you might know, I am a patroness of Almack's," she said with icy hauteur.

If Leslie wondered at the advisability of a German aristocrat presiding over one of London's most favored institutions she did not voice her misgivings.

"I believe it would not be beyond me, princess," Leslie offered in German. Then, determined to make herself clear. "But I am not at all certain that I would suit the position."

"Really," the princess sniffed. She wondered why Felix was so determined to seduce this young woman. She had no idea of protocol. How dare she infer that the post might not be to her liking. She should be thrilled that she might even be considered for such an honor.

"Not that I am unversed in European affairs. My father and I lived in Vienna for some time." Leslie wondered how she could broach the subject of Metternich. Marcus had given her little hint on how to go on.

Well, she must just use a little imagination and skill. After all she had watched her father exercise his limited talents on ministers and diplomats. She had learned tact and the ability to conceal her own feelings.

"We were privileged to meet Count Metternich, a most unusual and impressive statesman," Leslie offered with suitable subservience.

"A good friend. He relies on us to explain his provisions for the peace of Europe to your majesty's government," the princess explained, unable to resist boasting of her influence.

"I'm sure you and your husband are brilliant advocates of his requirements," Leslie agreed, having difficulty keeping her tone humble.

"Unfortunately your government is hampered by Parliament from meaningful cooperation with our emperor and the tsar," the princess countered, making her opinion of England's untidy method of governing plain. So much easier in an autocratic land where the citizens had little redress for their wrongs. And then, as if angered by the thought of England's obduracy, she went on ill-advisedly. "And the duke can be difficult. Unfortunate that he is a hero."

Leslie, concentrating so as not to miss a word, knew she could only be referring to Wellington. So he was in disfavor with the Russians and Austrians. That was no surprise since he refused to sign the tsar's fanciful Holy Alliance.

The princess, often indiscreet and careless, suddenly realized she was discussing diplomatic business with an underling.

"You seem to have a grasp of our problems. I believe we could deal well together so I offer you the post," she invited magnanimously.

"That is very kind of you, princess, but I am afraid I must refuse. It would not be in my best interests to accept."

"You are an impertinent and ungrateful girl. You will regret this. I would never reconsider. You are dismissed." The princess spoke in her best grande dame manner but beneath the patronage and spite lay a certain puzzlement that Leslie sensed. As she withdrew from the regal presence, escorted on either side of a silent footman, to make sure she did not try to steal the silver, perhaps, she thought whimsically, she wondered why the princess had considered her for the post in the first place. The count had recommended her, but even so, the princess appeared powerful enough not to have been under the spell of von Ronberg. Could he have some special influence over the Austrian ambassador's wife that compelled her to do his bidding? The more she learned about the count the more she realized her first impression of the man was right. He was both a libertine and an autocrat with motives that might bear investigation.

* * *

If Leslie could have listened to the interview Felix von Ronberg was conducting at that very moment in a rather low tavern in Spittalfields she might not have been surprised but she would certainly have been appalled. His companions were rough types, accustomed to all kinds of devilry and violence, but even they reacted with some reluctance to what the count demanded of them. The leader of the trio, a burly dark man with a low brow above beetling eyebrows, and small beady brown eyes, objected to his assignment.

"Not sure, sir, we want to take on this caper. It's the noose if we're caught," he growled.

Von Ronberg quelled him with a steely stare. "You will be well paid, five hundred guineas among the three of you. And that's my last offer. Don't think you can hold out for more."

"It's all very well for you, sir. You ain't chancing your arm," whined another member of the trio.

"What's the rub?" sneered the count. "You don't like the fool, and the country would be well rid of him."

"He's English, like we are, and we don't fancy some foreign bloke coming in and taking matters into his own hands," the leader of the group insisted. Jack Poole bowed his head to no man, but there was something about this cove that made him watch his step.

"Well, if you won't do it, there are plenty who will. Make your choice," the count shrugged as if indifferent to what the three villains decided.

Greed overcame patriotism and Jack Poole after a whispered colloquy with his confederates finally nodded. "We'll do it. How do we get in touch?"

"You don't. I will contact you here through the tavern keeper." The count was wary of these three but time was pressing. He had taken all precautions. All they knew was that he was a foreigner with enough gold to satisfy them. Whatever inhibitions they had about the job the money would persuade them. Giving them a curt nod, he picked up his cane, gloves and hat and sauntered out of the tavern.

When the door had closed behind him, Jack Poole scratched his grizzled head and muttered, "Don't trust that one, he's downy, not telling us his name nor nothin'. Still, it's a lot of blunt. Set us up for some time, uh boys?"

He looked at his cronies, hoping for some sign of reassurance, but Bob and Bert Hooker, brothers, always left such decisions to Jack, their leader. And their dull features brightened at the thought of the women and grog they could enjoy with their share of the swag. Their lives had been spent in petty thievery, fights, brutality of every sort. They had neither the conscience nor the intelligence to wonder at what they had taken on. Jack Poole, a cashiered sergeant major in the army, knew better but he put his misgivings behind him. It was better than starving and that's all the blasted government had left him unless he turned to crime. Calling for three tankards, he settled down to some heavy drinking hoping to banish the uncomfortable notion that he had promised to engage in a killing that could very well end in his own death.

The count, hurrying to put the stench and dirt of Spittalfields behind him, strode quickly away from the scene of his villainous plotting. He had not taken his carriage because he wanted no one, even his trusted coachman, to know his destination. Metternich had persuaded him to take on this distasteful task, with the promise of preferment and a suitable monetary reward if he succeeded.

The preferment mattered more than the money, for the count was not popular in Vienna circles. His reputation, even in that sophisticated society, had a certain odor. He had little need of money, but like most wealthy men, he never scorned the idea of gaining more, and his tastes were expensive, greedy women, fast horses, and unmentionable vices. But if he pulled this off Metternich would be grateful and he would have a certain hold over that wily intriguer. Not that Metternich himself had made the scandalous suggestion or enlisted the count's aid, but von Ronberg had quickly discovered he was the real author of the plot.

That knowledge would serve him well if the murder failed. As he strolled along Piccadilly he looked at ease with the world, the only small measure of discontent his failure to lure Leslie Dansforth into his bed. But he had a plan for that, too, and might even be forced to employ Poole and his confederates again if they were successful in their present assignment. But he hoped to avoid such drastic measures. He had every confidence that Leslie would see the advantages in a liaison. In his over-weening conceit it never occurred to him she would do otherwise. He did not take her professions of virtue seriously and his experience had led him to think all women had a price. Even Princess Esterhazy could be persuaded, one way or the other. He rather enjoyed having that haughty lady in his toils, and as he remembered the fearful look she had quickly masked in their last encounter, he smiled. Yes, matters were falling out just as he wanted. He had never expected otherwise.

Marcus was waiting in the hall when Leslie returned from her meeting with Princess Esterhazy, lounging against the wall.

"The estimable Mrs. Gorey refused to allow me to wait in your sitting room. I think she believes me capable of ravaging your virtue, and she is determined to guard you against any attempt on my part to take liberties," he offered with a cheeky smile.

"She is a good woman, and it's reassuring to know she has my best interests at heart," Leslie replied, repressing a smile.

Before Leslie could invite Marcus to her rooms, Mrs. Gorey appeared as if she had been waiting beyond the door to the kitchen quarters.

"Ah, there you are, Miss Dansforth. Mr. Kingsley wanted to wait upstairs, but I thought it best not," she said giving him a reproving glance. Mrs. Gorey was convinced that it was her duty to protect Leslie from all male advances. She often told her cook, Mrs. Watkins, a fat jolly matron with red cheeks and a fondness for ale, that Miss Dansforth was at the mercy of predatory men now that her father had died and she felt a responsibility to chaperone the poor girl.

"Lawks a mercy, Mrs. Gorey, if the poor dear wants a bit of a fling she will get it no matter what you do," Mrs. Watkins protested, thinking Mrs. Gorey was a bit of a spoil sport. Her own morals were far more flexible. In fact the Mrs. before her name did not reveal her true position. She had adopted it to lend respectability and was even now not above enjoying a passing intimacy with the butcher, the drayman or whatever other likely male crossed her path.

"Miss Dansforth is a respectable girl, and her father told me before he passed, poor man, that she has titled relations," Mrs. Gorey reproved. "So let us hear no more of these scandalous suggestions."

She had not quite made up her mind if Mr. Kingsley was

an honorable gentleman or one with illicit designs on Miss Dansforth and until she had decided she would do her best to see that he did not step beyond the bounds of propriety. Marcus had a very good idea of her opinion of him, and conceded with a rueful sigh, she had every reason to view him with a suspicious eye.

Having soothed Mrs. Gorey and repaired the ravages of her trip from the embassy, Leslie rejoined Marcus in the hall and they set off in a hackney for Gunter's, that fashionable cafe whose ices and cakes attracted a high class clientele.

"Now, Leslie, tell all," Marcus commanded once their orders were taken.

"Well, the princess is a short dark lady with a spiteful nature and a haughty air. She became quite friendly when we discussed her rapport with Metternich, almost indiscreet, I would say, but in the end she dismissed me as an ungrateful chit no better than I should be."

"And what did you learn about Metternich?" Marcus asked, his sense sharpened by her hint that she really had gathered some important clue to the Austrian's intentions.

"That he relies on the Esterhazys to put his views before his majesty's government, which after all, is the ambassador's task, and that Metternich confides in them and trusts them utterly, which I doubt. Also, that the Tsar of Russia and Metternich are quite unhappy about Parliament's refusal to sign the Holy Alliance. And she places all the blame on Wellington. But you certainly knew all this."

"Yes, but I had no real proof. I would not put it beyond Metternich to try to remove the duke, one way or the other. These tyrants despise our ministers and Parliament, and believe we have given too much power to the people."

"I wonder how a foreigner like the princess, who seems to despise us so, has reached such a pinnacle of social influence?" Leslie wondered.

"A patroness of Almack's may have a certain cachet among the ton, but no real influence on his majesty's government. Foreigners never really understand the intricacies of our way of life. Was she very rude to you?" Marcus asked, hoping Leslie had not been humiliated by the interview.

"I suppose she treats all underlings with a certain condescension. What surprises me is why she needs a secretary. There must be rafts of Austrians about the embassy who could fulfill those demands. I believe she is afraid of the count. Just an impression I had. She would never have decided on employing me without his urging, I am convinced. I would dearly like to know what hold he has on her."

"And I would like to know what his real purpose here might be. His rank is too exalted for him to serve in any mundane office at the Embassy, such as first secretary or charge d' affairs, and anyway, those posts are filled. No, he is here for some special reason, probably at the request of Metternich. And the princess is beholden to him," Marcus explained, marshaling his thoughts.

"The count is a very determined man," Leslie agreed, thinking of his efforts to attract her.

"And a nasty fellow into the bargain. Not content with your refusal, he blackmailed the princess into persuading you. But why did she agree?"

"Well, it's all settled now. She wouldn't have me even if I changed my mind, as she told me quite emphatically. And I am sure the count has no option but to forget about me and pursue some other luckless girl," Leslie said with satisfaction.

"You are not so easy to forget, Leslie," Marcus objected only half mockingly.

"Nonsense, I am nothing exceptional."

"I will not pander to your conceit by arguing the point, but few women in your circumstances would be able to embark on a journalistic career, do it successfully, if anonymously," Marcus argued with all sincerity.

"I'm happy to hear that. And you must admit how few newspapers would hire a woman, even anonymously. I am very grateful for the job, Marcus," she assured him, all seriousness.

"You do it well, except for a certain lapse with your participles," he teased, unwilling to listen to Leslie's professions of gratitude. Somehow he did not want her to feel she must be grateful to him. He wanted a different emotion, but just what he was not entirely clear.

They parted at last, having extended the luncheon into the late afternoon, so animated was their conversation and exchange of views, but Leslie repelled any attempts on Marcus' part to return the conversation to more personal matters.

Having restored her to the guardianship of Mrs. Gorey he dismissed the hackney and decided to walk back to Printing House Square. He had a great deal to think about and not much of it concerned *The Times*.

Chapter Eight

Despite her best intentions Dinah Darcy had avidly pursued the agony column in *The Times* daily, and at last found the answer to her plaintive cry for help from Pythius.

Dear Worried,
    When a gentleman tires there is not a great deal to prevent him from leaving. Men are easily bored, and not of a faithful nature. I suggest you look about for another protector since I think you are not about to abandon your present way of life. Cut your losses, my dear.

Dinah sighed unhappily. It was as she suspected. Marcus had found a new mistress, younger, smarter and probably of the first stare. Since she was not prepared to abandon the only way of life she knew she must look about for another protector. Marcus had not been near her in more than a week. Perhaps the press of his duties at the paper kept him occupied, but from her experience of him, she doubted that was the excuse, much as she would like to think so. He was a man of passionate needs, accustomed to women's company both in bed and out. She had always realized that she was only a convenience, but not being of a sensitive nature she had not been offended, accepting that was just the way of the world. Men were in control and if women wanted to lead a comfortable life with them they must adapt. Dinah, if nothing else, was adaptable.

Perhaps she thought, not liking to be sad, she was jumping to the wrong conclusions, could possibly hold him if she were patient and made no demands. He was generous, too, and would not just leave her without some token of his past affection. Dinah might be limited in some ways, but she was both practical and determined. She would be foolish to look about for another man to support her if there was any hope he might still be willing to provide the comfort she needed. Having made up her mind not to act in a hasty fashion she decided to confide in an old friend, Gertie Flowers, who had been wise enough to save her money and jewelry and retire to a small flat in Russell Street, where she lived content and alone, aside from occasional lapses.

Gertie welcomed her with enthusiasm. She did not have many visitors, just the occasional gentleman who appreciated her rather blowzy charms and was not put off by her dedication to wine. Dressed in a soiled wrapper and scuffed slippers she was not at all embarrassed by Dinah surprising her in such dishabille.

"How nice, ducks, of you to drop by. How about a little drink?" she offered hospitably.

"No, thank you, Gertie. I was just passing and realized it had been ages since I had seen you," Dinah lied, wondering if there was any advice Gertie could offer her that would be of any use. Dinah was quite dismayed at the deterioration of her old friend. Some years ago the two had been bosom bows, dancing in the chorus together, and then, when Gertie had been forced to retire by a management that felt she was beyond it, Dinah had still enjoyed her company. Gertie, fond of the theatrical life, had stayed at Covent Garden as a dresser and confidant of the girls whom she viewed in a motherly and uncritical fashion. It was Gertie who had warned Dinah, then nineteen, at the peak of her charm, not to take up with Lord Michelson, whose sexual appetites were sadistic and unnatural. She had quite approved of Marcus.

"Not a toff, that one, but a kind man, with normal desires. You can't go wrong with him, ducks," had been Gertie's advice, and it had proved true until now. Now she asked kindly after Marcus.

"Actually, that is what I came to see you about, Gertie," Dinah confessed deciding to give up the pretense that this was a purely social call.

"Is he misbehavin'? Never would have thought it. He seemed a proper gent," Gertie said, although not surprised. The vagaries of gentlemen were not unknown to her and she accepted them with stoic resignation. A generous, kindhearted woman, if a bit lazy, she had never expected much from the various protectors she had known so she was rarely disappointed when they left her for younger Cyprians.

"No, that is, he is fine when he is around. The trouble is he hasn't been around much," Dinah sighed. "I think he's tiring."

"Could be, they will do it. But make sure you get some healthy token of his esteem, dearie, before he flies the coop. Have to pay for their pleasure, these gents," Gertie insisted. Then, realizing that Dinah might be in some more serious trouble, she asked bluntly, "Hasn't put you in the pod, has he?"

"Oh, no, nothing like that," Dinah assured her, a bit shocked by Gertie's coarseness.

"Well, how are you fixed. Rent paid?" Gertie was not one to mince words when it was a question of survival.

"Until the quarter day," Dinah said, aware of the direction of Gertie's thoughts.

"Well, ducks, hold on as long as you can, then if he pays you off, you'll need to find another obliging gentleman. You've still got your looks. Would you go back to the chorus? It's a hard life," Gertie asked. Then adding shrewdly. "I don't suppose you've saved much."

"No, I just never thought Marcus would go off me," Dinah admitted sorrowfully.

"Well, you don't know he has. Might be thinking of marriage, setting up his nursery. Not that natural way of things should put an end to your company."

"But what should I do, Gertie?" wailed Dinah, now thoroughly worried. Her visit to Gertie, instead of solacing her, had given her an unhappy vision of her own future, if she could not manage to find either employment or a new protector. She could see herself drifting ever lower in the scale of demimondaines, losing her looks, having to accept casual trade. The vision frightened her.

"Wait, duck. That's all you can do. Whatever, don't chivvy the man, ask him a load of questions. If worse comes to worse you can move in here with me for a time, until you get yourself situated." Gertie might be common and coarse but she was also goodhearted and lonely. She would welcome the company. "And I might be able to put you in the way of some lucky opportunity."

Grateful for Gertie's support, but shuddering at the

thought of what that opportunity might be, Dinah gave her friend a hug, thanked her for the offer, and was on her way, not sure that the visit had been a wise one, as her worries seemed more frightening than before.

Dinah's letter was not the only one of that type that Leslie had received, and she wished she had some concrete help to offer these women. Unlike her respectable sisters she felt only pity not disgust for their plight. Few of them achieved the dizzying heights of Harriet Wilson, and even she would some day lose her popularity and appeal. Marriage for most of them was not an option, nor was any respectable employment. Having come close to desperation herself Leslie did not regard the muslin company scornfully.

Nor could she entirely fault the men who took advantage of them. It was just the way society abused the most vulnerable of its members. What a cynic I have become, Leslie reproved herself. But her current job did not inspire optimism about the condition of the world.

As she sat at her desk, thumbing through the current batch of letters after her luncheon with Marcus, she was reminded that Marcus, himself, although she owed him a great deal, represented a threat. He might yet claim some more tangible reward for his magnanimity. And she was not sure she had the strength to refuse him. Facing the problem with her usual honesty she accepted that she found him attractive, exciting, in a way that poor Jonathan, for all his kindness and admiration, had never been able to inspire. In a weak moment she might succumb to any offer Marcus might make. And that would be disaster, for what would just be a passing diversion to him could destroy her new found security. She could lose her heart and then her job, her home and her self respect. It did not bear contemplating. But what a widgeon she was. Marcus might lightly bestow the idle caress but he had no real interest in her. Jonathan had hinted that he had a member of the muslin company in keeping that satisfied his needs. She was no rival to such a woman, and did not choose to be. Having settled the matter with her customary objectivity, Leslie returned to her letters, refusing to admit that the affair of Marcus could not so tidily be docketed under finished business.

One of the submissions in the current pile of letters, growing each week, caught her interest. Now, somewhat hardened to her reader's various plights, she selected either unusual, humorous or genuinely tragic plights. This letter, written on thick creamy paper, with the engraved address obviously cut off to hide the identity of the correspondent, was not unique. Often readers appealed for assistance in locating family members, but this missive struck some sort of feeling in Leslie.

Dear Pythius,

Some years ago I quarreled with a cousin who was in financial difficulties due, I fear, to intemperate habits. I refused to help him as I have strict standards about such excesses. I regret now that I was not more tolerant for I have lost touch with my cousin, who had a child, a boon denied to me. As I grow older I feel the need of the company of some relations. Could you advise me as to how to locate my cousin or his child without revealing my identity?

A Lonely Man

Leslie wondered why a man, literate, and probably well off needed the advice of a newspaper oracle to go about the business of finding his relative. Surely, it was a simple matter to have his solicitor advertise in the personal column. There were several of these requests published each week, appeals to contact some Chancery Lane address where the supplicant might learn information that would benefit him. Was his position so exalted he feared exposure? Of course, even his man of business might not be able to protect him from charlatans, even the obvious ones, and he was reluctant to trust any solicitor with this delicate business. She would have to give the matter some thought. This was not a case where she could quickly compose a sensible reply.

Somewhat to Leslie's annoyance, just as she was finishing her morning's work, Mrs. Gorey announced that Mr. Stirling had arrived. Her landlady considered Jonathan a proper visitor, and favored him with her best smile. Leslie had warned Mrs. Gorey that she was not at home to the Count von Ronberg if he should call, explaining quite plainly that the Austrian peer was neither respectable nor honorable despite his wealth and manner. Jonathan, on the other hand, had managed to get around Mrs. Gorey and was quite a favorite. To Leslie's amusement she noticed that her landlady's opinion of Marcus was still undecided. She approved of him as Miss Dansforth's employer, who enabled her to pay the rent and afford a few luxuries, but she was not so convinced his more personal attentions were acceptable.

"Good morning, Leslie. A gorgeous morning, and you should be out enjoying it," Jonathan insisted, breezing in and tossing his hat carelessly on a chair.

"You are certainly in good spirits, and I suppose have the leisure to enjoy the weather since Parliament is in recess, but alas, I must struggle on. The pile of letters grows ever larger, the advice seekers ever more urgent," she sighed.

"This is a June morning that inspires the poets. And I have good news. You will receive your father's quarterly allowance as provided by his will. Fortunately, it was tied up tightly by your grandfather and despite that rogue of a solicitor, and your father's best efforts, it has stayed safely invested in the funds. I have a friend, an honest solicitor, who has taken over the business from your father's chap, who he says is a shifty type, and you will be asked to sign some papers and then the funds will be paid. I'm rather pleased with myself at successfully concluding this little bit of business for you," Jonathan said smiling at her.

She crossed the room and gave him a sisterly buss on the cheek, "Oh, Jonathan, you are a darling. I was quite at sea about the mess, and never expected to see a penny."

"I suppose such exertions on your behalf don't deserve more than that little peck on the cheek," Jonathan moaned, only half in jest. Then, thinking that he sounded churlish and mean, hurried on. "Forget I said that. I don't want your gratitude only your love, and alas, I see little hope of that."

"Dear Jon, in a way I do love you, or at least feel enormous affection for you, and probably if I had any sense would reward your devotion by becoming your wife. But, somehow I cannot sacrifice my independence for a convenient marriage." Leslie felt chagrined. She had already gone over this ground with Jonathan, and although she was, indeed, grateful to him, for securing her inheritance, meager as it was, that did not entitle him to her hand.

Jonathan, sensitive to her moods, sensed that he had sounded the wrong chord. He wondered if she was already involved with another man. It seemed unlikely as the only

men she saw were Marcus and himself. He had sudden uneasy feelings that Marcus might have made overtures toward her, and knowing his friend, they were not honorable,
Jonathan suspected. But he could hardly come out and ask
Leslie if that were the case. She would rightfully turn him
out of the house, horrified and embarrassed, no matter
whether she had surrendered to Marcus or repulsed him.
Look at how offended she had been by that Austrian count.
He did not want to be treated so cavalierly. If he could stand
on no other terms with Leslie, he at least wanted to keep
his status as a dear friend.

"Let us forget all these sordid business affairs, and stroll
out into this rare June morning. Perhaps I might hire a
hackney and drive you to Richmond. Does that sound acceptable as a celebration?" Jonathan invited coaxingly.

"It sounds wonderful, and if you promise to behave, and
not badger me about marriage, I will get my bonnet and
we will be on our way," Leslie agreed, deciding that
Jonathan's undemanding company was just what she
needed, and having warned him that any talk of marriage
would vex her, she knew his natural consideration would
force him to obey. And as a friend he was great company,
witty, informed, and treating her opinions with gravity.

Having settled the terms on which the outing would proceed, the pair set off under the indulgent eye of Mrs. Gorey,
who hoped that the nice Mr. Stirling would make some
progress toward his heart's desire that day.

Jonathan and Leslie, walking briskly toward Piccadilly
where he suggested they might more easily find a hackney,
did not notice an unobtrusive figure lounging against the
house opposite, his hat tipped over eyes which followed
the pair intently as they walked away. Then, making a
small entry in the notebook he carried, he strolled after

them, keeping well behind, but not losing sight of his quarry.

News of Leslie and Jonathan's departure on a pleasure excursion was received with irritation by Marcus, who called not a quarter of an hour after they had left. Mrs. Gorey took a certain delight in informing him that Miss Leslie and "that nice Mr. Stirling" had decided to go to Richmond as the day was so fine. Marcus did not give Mrs. Gorey the satisfaction of showing his disappointment, thanked her and returned to Printing House Square.

Idly toying with the papers on his desk, despite the urgency of some of these dispatches, Marcus examined his disappointment. How unfair of him to expect Leslie to be at his beck and call just because he employed her to write a column for his newspaper. Did he want more from her than an employer-employee relationship? And if he did, on what terms.

And then there was Dinah. With a shock he realized he had not seen her in nearly a fortnight. Well, he would remedy that omission this very evening. What was the use of supporting a mistress if he failed to enjoy her favors, he thought crossly. And an evening with Dinah would put this whole affair of Leslie in its proper perspective. Shaking off a feeling that he had made a disastrous decision, Marcus settled to work. His irritation and disquiet over his personal problems made him scratch angrily across a quite sensible article on the repeal of the Corn Laws, a stance he had always favored, but today found pretentious and unreasoned. Marcus, in a welter of confused emotions, was far from his normal self, and could not imagine what had brought him to such a pass.

Chapter Nine

The evening with Dinah that Marcus had thought might prove soothing and distract him from his malaise turned out to be uncomfortable. Dinah had been delighted to see him. He could not blame her for the disaster that followed.

"It's been so long, Marcus, I thought you had forgotten me," Dinah complained. Seeing by Marcus' frown that was not the wisest opening gambit, she did her best to retrieve the situation. "Of course I know how busy you are with all your new duties."

"Let's not discuss the paper, Dinah. It has been a difficult week or so." Marcus threw himself down in a chair and stared moodily at his feet, aware that he was behaving badly.

"Well, let us have some nice supper, and I have a burgundy that you will like," Dinah proposed, trying to cheer him up.

"Not hungry. Let's go to bed," Marcus countered, thinking that might banish his demons.

If Dinah was disappointed at this brusque demand she did not show it, appearing more than happy to oblige. She wanted desperately to ask Marcus if he had tired of her, and this was the end of the relationship, but she realized that would be foolish. Perhaps if she exerted her several skills he would forget whatever had made him so morose, and even that he had lost his desire for her. She did her best but the coupling was not a success. Marcus rose and dressed hurriedly, longing to be gone and filled with disgust at himself for using Dinah so badly. Far from being eased he felt frustrated, baffled and restless.

Staring down at the her in the tousled bed he wondered why he had ever thought she was desirable. Her conversation was vapid, her tastes unformed, her interests frivolous and even her beauty seemed a bit tarnished. Although there was no denying she had remarkable skills in bed and a gusty sexual appetite, these former attributes no longer appealed to him. You could not spend all your time in bed, and as a companion over the supper table Marcus found Dinah's prattling boring. What was the matter with him? For two years he had found Dinah soothing, comfortable, even exciting at times. Should he break off the affair? It was costing him a pretty penny and if he no longer was enjoying her, it would be best to end it. Marcus could be ruthless when it came to a professional decision, but in personal matters he shrank from inflicting pain. Perhaps his feeling about Dinah was only temporary. He would be both foolish and unkind to dismiss her just because this evening he could not settle into their usual relationship

"Forgive me, Dinah. I have a lot of matters on my mind. I had best leave, but I will be in touch," he promised, and left the room as if all the devils in hell were after him.

Dinah rolled over, sobbing lustily. It was true, he was tired of her, just too kind to tell her. But he would and she must be prepared. Neither Gertie nor *The Times* had helped her. She must trust to her own resources and they were not very encouraging. She was about to lose her lover, her income, her home and her peace of mind. Despite her sexual skills, her enjoyment of the pleasures of the bed, Dinah was not really a passionate woman, nor a confident one. She quite liked Marcus, but she certainly did not love him with any overwhelming emotion. His defection was a blow to her pride as much as any other emotion. And it was a reflection on her abilities. She had never expected marriage, but she had hoped they could rub along happily for some years. Not a provident type she had given little thought to the future, but now she would have to make some plans. She would have to find another protector and provider. And she could not afford to be too choosy. Sighing unhappily Dinah dragged herself from the bed and wandered over to the mirror where she gazed with mounting dissatisfaction at her reflected figure. What was it about herself Marcus suddenly found so unsatisfactory? If she knew she might correct it. It never occurred to her that it was her intellectual failings he suddenly found so dispiriting.

Marcus, sitting in his office the following day and staring off into the distance, could not concentrate. That Dinah had been becoming an annoying encumbrance suddenly confused him. He had never demanded much from her and she had filled a necessary role in his life. Most men, who could afford them, had mistresses, and they certainly did not select them for their brains. Women were not expected to have intellects that rivaled those of their brothers, husbands and fathers. They should be attractive, obliging and submissive. That a man could want more, a companionable, respected and intelligent female, even as a wife, would be considered nonsensical. Of course, there were such women, but they were rare, and usually of mature years, not sexual objects.

Marcus' position on women had not deviated much from the normal view until now, but his association with Leslie had radically changed his thinking even if he were not aware of it. All he did realize was that he found her company stimulating, he wanted to see more of her, and women like Dinah had lost their attraction.

My God, Marcus thought, jerking upright from his moody slouch over his desk, jumping to his feet and striding about the cluttered office. Has Leslie Dansforth become so important to me? He was convinced that what he felt for her was not love, but only the respectful admiration of an employer for a valued and contributing employee. And friendship, of course. Could a man have a platonic relationship with a woman? Rare, but not impossible. He should be able to conduct just such a relationship with Leslie, and for any other needs he had Dinah. His temporary disenchantment with her would pass. Having settled the situation to his satisfaction, he thought, he returned to his desk and began to read his current leader on the education bill that was causing so much animosity.

Marcus prided himself on being a radical Whig, a severe critic of Liverpool's Tory government. He believed the Tories were rigid, authoritarian, uncaring of the poor, and too supportive of the landed gentry and aristocrats. Henry Brougham headed a committee to look into education, the disposal of income of property left to trustees for the benefit of the poor, primarily for education. Marcus was a firm adherent of Brougham's principles. So that it was with great cordiality that he greeted the member of Parliament for Camelford when Brougham called upon him that morning to discuss the pending education bill.

Son of a Westmoreland squire, Brougham had been born and brought up in Edinburgh and educated at the university there. Tall, thin with dark hair, deep set eyes, a sensitive mouth and a square determined chin, his most prominent feature was his long bumpy nose that became the target of caricaturists. A brilliant lawyer and philosophic thinker, he had made a tremendous impact on London intellectual and political life when he took his seat in Parliament some seven years ago. More important to Marcus, Brougham was a firm friend of the press, realizing its importance as an ally in his legislative program.

"Good morning, Marcus. I hope I am not interrupting some vital work on tomorrow's leader," he greeted his friend and sank down in the chair opposite Marcus' desk as if exhausted.

"I am trying to write a fervent plea for your education bill," Marcus informed him with a smile.

"Good, good, we need all the help we can get to bring those thieving trustees to book, but that was not what I came to see you about. It's the Prince Regent."

"What has poor Prinny been about now?" Marcus asked.

"The usual, profligate, notorious and exceedingly unpopular with the people, dangerously so, I might add. He is spending thousands of guineas on that Brighton monstrosity while deserving Englishmen starve."

"Quite as usual," Marcus agreed with a cynicism that was his standard reaction to the Prince Regent.

"Yes, but his actions are endangering any reform. That abortive attack on him alarmed the government which insists on strengthening a whole list of punitive laws, and is reluctant to grant any relief to the poor."

"Do you really think his life is in danger?"

"Yes, I do. If not from local malcontents, from foreign agitators. Metternich for one would like to get rid of him."

"He wouldn't dare."

"I have heard rumors that there may be another attempt on his life," Brougham insisted with a gravity that forced Marcus to take him seriously.

"So what can we do?"

"Keep your ear to the ground. You must have sources far better than mine."

"I doubt that, Henry, but I will take the affair seriously, I promise. Ever since the French Revolution our leaders have behaved as if a revolt here was imminent, and instead of introducing needed reforms, all they do is pass stricter laws to repress the people."

"Well, have a care," Brougham warned and then went on to discuss his plans for the education bill.

Despite Brougham's budget of bad news Marcus found that his hour-long interview with Brougham had cheered him. He believed no man in London was more perceptive, intelligent and forceful than Brougham and his visit had been a tonic. He bent to his writing with renewed energy and all personal thoughts were banished for the moment.

Dinah had no work to distract her from her problems the morning after Marcus' disappointing visit so she was pleased if puzzled when her little maid announced with awe that a very distinguished foreign gentleman had called to see her mistress.

"A count, ma'am," she said, holding out an engraved card to Dinah, being unable to read it herself. All she had caught was the title when Felix von Ronberg had called. But she had seen the elegant coach outside the door, and was impressed by the Austrian's fine clothes and jeweled watch fob and ring.

Dinah, although surprised, was elated. Perhaps this meant her fortunes were improving, for she believed gentlemen had only one interest in her. Loyal as she was to Marcus, she had her own future to consider, and until now that had looked rather bleak.

"Show him in, Abby," she instructed the maid. She crossed to the mirror above her sitting room's mantel piece and looked at herself critically. Not too bad, no red rimmed eyes, or wan cheeks as a result of her troubled night. She turned with a smile to greet the imposing aristocrat who entered behind her maid.

"Good morning, Miss Darcy. I hope this is not an inconvenient hour to call," Count von Ronberg greeted her, bowing and kissing her hand, a tribute Dinah found very welcome.

"Not at all, sir. Perhaps I can offer you some refreshment," Dinah offered in what she hoped was a suitable grand manner, as if she were accustomed to entertaining such noblemen every day.

"Not just now, thank you. Perhaps when we have completed our business," he suggested, sitting down in the chair Dinah indicated after she had sunk back onto a nearby settee.

"And what would that be?" Dinah asked archly, although she had a suspicion that she knew only too well.

Von Ronberg hesitated. This would be a delicate matter. Since Marcus had made such an unpleasant incursion into his life he had made it his business to institute inquiries about that young brash journalist. And among his discoveries was that Dinah had been in Kingsley's keeping for two years, but that lately he had seemed to tire of her. In the count's experience spurned ladies could serve a useful purpose in revenging him on his enemies.

"It has come to my attention that your long time connection with Mr. Kingsley may be drawing to an end. I am sure that an attractive lady such as yourself will have no difficulty in securing another well intentioned man to provide you with the luxuries you deserve." The count showed every sign of finding Dinah attractive and she preened under his knowing stare, not at all insulted by his insinuation. After Marcus' brusque treatment this approach by a titled and wealthy nobleman was a great balm. If she might have wondered why the count, who must have access to the most dashing members of the muslin company, should have sought her out it was just a momentary question.

"That is kind of you, sir. Of course, Mr. Kingsley has made no definite sign that he means to leave me," she admitted with an honesty that was rather endearing, if the count had been the type of man to appreciate it. Loyalty was among Dinah's most appealing qualities.

"But you think he might be?" the count insinuated.

"Oh, sir, you seem to know a great deal about my situation," Dinah said with a sad little moue.

"Let us just say, that I find it inexcusable that a lovely lady, with your indubitable talents, should be treated so cavalierly."

If Dinah did not exactly understand his allusion she was soothed by his description of her, and she waited with a rising feeling of excitement for his next suggestion.

Seeing that he had laid the ground well, and realizing he was not dealing with an astute nor particularly intelligent woman, the count wasted no more time.

"I would be delighted to take on the responsibility for your well-being. And before you can raise your objections just let me say I do not require that you abandon Mr. Kingsley entirely. I commend your loyalty to him and realize you feel you owe him a great deal. My own requirement, and that is a stringent one, is that you not tell him that you have made arrangements with a new protector."

Dinah, fascinated and relieved, wondered why this obliging man should wish to share her with Marcus, but on the whole was not inclined to quarrel with his demand. She could keep Marcus on a string and if he decided to cut all ties with her, she would have this grand gentleman in reserve.

With grateful enthusiasm she agreed, not seeing that the relationship the count suggested had any drawbacks. Whatever happened, she thought, she would not be the loser. That the count's motives might be more devious than he said never occurred to her. She was thinking only that her worries were over. It might behoove her to make the break with Marcus herself. But she did not offer that suggestion to the count, sensing that he, for some reason, would not find it agreeable. Thinking that the count would want to seal their bargain with a tangible sign of her agreement, she delicately indicated they might adjourn to the bedroom.

"How sensible of you, dear lady, but not this morning. I will call in the evening. But I will be sure not to embarrass you by intruding when you are entertaining Mr. Kingsley," he promised, leaving Dinah with a certain uneasiness, that was banished immediately when the count took a great wad of bank notes from his pocket and deposited them on a nearby table. He made no reference to this contribution, but bowed again over her hand, kissed it lingeringly, and strolled nonchalantly from the room.

As soon as the door closed Dinah rushed to count the notes. At least fifty guineas, she discovered. If she had second thoughts about the path on which she was embarking and any questions about the count's unusual request the bank notes soothed her qualms. What a fortunate girl she was. Two distinguished gentlemen on her string. Her future looked quite bright.

She might not have been so sanguine if she had seen the cruel expression on the count's face as he rode away from her lodgings. He had given this matter much thought. He needed to have a conduit to Marcus' life and what could be better than his mistress, of whom he appeared to be tiring. Probably because he was interested in the delectable Miss Dansforth. The count had several objects in pursuing Marcus' downfall. He still smarted from that young man's interference in his pursuit of Leslie, and he had a suspicion that the editor of *The Times* could throw a rub into his other plans of a more important, if not so enjoyable, nature. The count believed in covering all eventualities in any endeavor he undertook. Then there was the bonus of Miss Darcy herself, quite a common girl, but not without a certain charm. A practiced womanizer the count recognized unabashed sensuality when he met it and in Dinah he felt he had secured an acceptable partner for his lust until he could secure the very much more intriguing Miss Dansforth. All in all he was very satisfied with his morning's work.

Chapter Ten

Determined to put his new resolution to the test, Marcus called on Leslie the following day, committed to discussing the column and avoiding any indication of personal emotion. He walked briskly into her sitting room, having declined Mrs. Gorey's intention of announcing him with a curt refusal.

"Good afternoon, Leslie. Nasty day out there," he remarked, placing his parcel of material on her desk, and waiting a bit warily to see what her attitude might be.

"What do you know about Bow Street Runners, Marcus?" was her only acknowledgment of his presence.

Taken aback by this singular greeting, when he had been prepared for a far warmer reception, he frowned and looked at her in astonishment.

"Now why would you want to know about Bow Street? Are you thinking of hiring one of the Runners for some mysterious task. Not that I wish to pry into your private affairs but it does seem an odd question."

Leslie turned away from the window where she had been staring with a calculating eye at some distant prospect. Looking at Marcus with exasperation she said carefully as if explaining the obvious to a man of limited intellect, "I want to know about Bow Street because I have heard the men there are not the honest protectors of the peace, and the valiant defenders of victims, that I had been led to expect."

"Quite true, I fear. The poor devils are in it for the money, for they are only paid a pittance, a guinea a week, I believe."

Marcus was not sure that he liked Leslie's very businesslike approach to a problem that was occupying her mind far more than his presence.

"What a shame. Surely they are not all corrupt. Some of them must be dedicated to solving crime and not amenable to bribes."

She appeared entirely absorbed by this far from fascinating subject. Marcus having steeled himself to take an aloof approach to Leslie at their next meeting, very much on his dignity as her employer, was annoyed to discover she hardly heeded his arrival, evidently in some brown study that certainly did not concern him. If he had feared she might be reading some deeper emotion into their relationship he should be relieved to discover that his fears had no foundation, but contrarily he was irritated.

Deciding he was reacting in a churlish fashion, he threw himself into a chair, and indicated he was prepared to give her a potted history of the Bow Street Runners, not at all what he had envisioned when he called.

"Well," she urged impatiently, settling opposite him on the edge of her chair.

"The Bow Street Runners were founded about seventeen fifty by Henry Fielding, the author, and also a magistrate. He found it appalling that the only police force in London were the ancient bumbling Charlies, little more than night watchmen, who did little to protect the populace. He organized a private force, that had no writ from Parliament, and encouraged the public to report crime to his residence in Bow Street. It has been largely a successful experiment although there are often instances of Runners bearing false witness against the thieves they apprehend for the reward. But I think this is rare, most of them seem honest fellows committed to nabbing crooks, to put it vulgarly."

"And private citizens can hire them to catch villains who have robbed or attacked them, or to investigate other matters," Leslie asked, furrowing her brow. She had two reasons for these searching questions, one personal, one professional.

"Yes, since only private citizens can prosecute criminals, this practice often leads to settlement out of court and possibly to some graft. It's a hideous system. England is the only civilized country without a police force. The Whigs have been pressing for one as part of their program for social reform but little has been done."

"Stop pontificating. Could I hire a Bow Street Runner to investigate a matter for me?"

Ignoring her brusque complaint with a long suffering sigh, he answered, "Yes, of course, although why you would want to baffles me." He waited, thinking that most women would be unable to resist the chance to confide in a sympathetic man, but Leslie, in this as so much else, was far different from most of her sex.

Realizing she had perhaps been both abrupt and even shrewish in her catechism of Marcus, who after all was owed some courtesy as her employer, she smiled, leaned back and relaxed as she tried to offer a convincing reason for her queries.

"I'm sorry if I sounded peevish. It's just that I have been

wondering whether to advise one of my correspondents if he should hire a Runner to solve his problem. He appears to be both educated and respectable, even well-to-do, and why he should need advice to locate a missing relative puzzles me. Surely the man has a solicitor, a family man of business. But I must give the poor dear an answer."

"How do you know he's a poor dear," Marcus asked, fascinated despite himself by this analysis of a man just from his writing paper.

Leslie crossed to her desk, located the letter and handed it to him wordlessly. He read it rapidly and then looked up with raised eyebrows. Snatching the letter from his hand she scanned it again and turning said to him impatiently, as if explaining to a backward child, "Well, the paper is heavy, good rag, and the engraving of what must be a prestigious direction, has been snipped from the top. The language is educated, and from the tone I believe he is elderly and lonely, and regretting some past breach with a family member."

Marcus shook his head in wonder. "You really would make quite a good detective yourself, Leslie, reading all that from a letter, but now that you explain it so concisely to this poor bumbling male, I quite grasp it."

"Don't sneer and condescend, Marcus, it does not become you," Leslie reproved, then had to laugh as she saw Marcus throw up his hands in a disclaimer against such a criticism.

"You must beg to excuse me, Marcus, I sound just like a vinegary school mistress. But I have been brooding over this letter for some time and I must write an answer today. But there is an air of mystery about the whole business and I want to get to the bottom of it."

"Yes, it does seem peculiar, that is if this gentleman has

the resources and certainly a solicitor to advise him, that he should feel it necessary to write to us." Having settled the matter, Marcus realized he was not satisfied. He sensed that Leslie had another reason for her interest in the Bow Street Runners and he wanted to discover it.

"I'm not sure you are telling me the whole business," Marcus insisted with a perception that shook Leslie from her abstraction.

Should she confide in him about her current suspicion or would he just laugh and dismiss her idea as a female's silly fancy? That would be Jonathan's reaction she knew, and she had said nothing to him about her conviction that she was being watched.

Saying nothing, she walked to the window, drew aside the drapery and looked across the street. Yes, the man was there, leaning idly against the railing.

"Come here, Marcus," she ordered, and he obeyed, joining her at the window.

"See that man across the street, with the brown cap and the ugly boots."

Marcus had no trouble in identifying the man she indicated. "Well, what about it?"

"He has been just there for the past few days, and when I go out, to the shops, or for a walk in the park, he follows me, or at least I think he does," Leslie blurted out, rather ashamed, as she professed to be an independent woman, well able to take care of herself.

Marcus although tempted to doubt her tale, then remembered the count. That libertine would be capable of any villainy. But would it be prudent to mention his suspicion to Leslie? It might be well to warn her that the brown-capped man could be in the hire of von Ronberg so that she could protect herself. But he might be arousing her fear unnecessarily. Marcus, rarely at a loss, hesitated.

But Leslie seemed to read his mind. "Could that man be some minion of the dreadful count?" she asked, her brow wrinkling in distaste.

"He might be. That would seem to be a bit outré even for the count. I know the man has a penchant for you. Still, hiring some rogue to keep you under surveillance goes beyond all reason."

"You mean I am not worth the effort," Leslie suggested with a laugh, determined not to give much credence to the matter.

"Not at all. I can quite see a man obsessed by desire for you," Marcus returned crossing to her side, and staring down at her with an expression in his eyes that brought a blush to her cheek.

"Don't be ridiculous, Marcus. I was only funning. I cannot believe the count would be so lost to all propriety as to have a man spy on me just to satisfy some warped perversion."

Marcus took a deep breath. He did not want to alarm her but she must be warned. "You have a rather modest appreciation of your charms, Leslie. And a rather casual attitude toward the count. Granted you have rebuffed him decidedly, but that may only have increased his determination to have you one way or another."

"Nonsense. There are plenty of available and willing women out there. I can't believe I am the only one to satisfy his lust," she said boldly, as usual not mincing her words.

"You are exasperating, Leslie. How do you plan to protect yourself from some determined villain?" Marcus' concern over her indifference to her danger was rising. He could understand the count's determination to possess Leslie. He was in some danger of succumbing to an unholy desire to teach her a lesson. And before she could understand what he was about, he took her in his arms and kissed her with a drugging thoroughness, ignoring her struggles. She admitted later that after her first shock she found the sensation not unpleasant. Nor did she react with the anger and disgust he had half expected.

"Did that make you feel better, to show a man's ability to dominate a woman by brute strength?" she mocked, to hide her reaction. It would never do to encourage Marcus. Before she knew it his blandishments might lure her into an even more unhappy situation than any danger the count could offer.

"If you want me to apologize again for behaving in a rag-mannered fashion, I refuse. You are not above the normal impulses of a woman, Leslie. Do you expect to go through your life without love or affection?" Marcus retorted, vexed by her ability to turn off any suggestion of softer emotions.

"Not at all. I expect someday to find a remarkable man who will return my feelings. Then we will settle down in domestic harmony to raise a family. But I doubt you are that man, Marcus. Your inclinations, from what I observe, do not lie in the direction of fidelity. I would be a ninny hammer to take a few reckless kisses as any sign other than that you were amusing yourself."

"You really have a most jaundiced opinion of me, don't you?" Marcus asked, more chagrined than he wanted to admit to himself.

"Not at all. I respect your talent, your skill at directing the paper and I am grateful to you for giving me employment. It would be the height of foolishness for me to en-

gage in any intimate alliance with you that might threaten
our good working relationship," she argued sensibly, although she hoped Marcus did not realize how disturbed she
had been by his kiss.

"You have this uncanny ability to make me feel as much
of a cad as the odious count," he said, only half in jest.

"Not a cad, Marcus, just unable to resist an opportunity.
Probably the same quality that makes you such a good
journalist. Now, shall we forget your momentary lapse and
go over the column."

"If you insist. I take it any light diversion is not welcome."

"Quite right." Leslie gathered up some foolscap and
pointed out to him a letter that she considered might be too
risqué for the column and they settled down to business.

About a half an hour later Marcus left. His intention to
ask Leslie out for a drive, firmly relegated to the back of
his mind. She had made it clear that any amorous ideas he
might have about her would be discouraged. Somehow
this depressed him exceedingly. He had decided not to
press his attentions on her and at the first temptation had
thrown away all caution. What did he really want from
Leslie? It was clear she would entertain no intimacies outside the bounds of matrimony, and Marcus was not about
to put himself in the parson's mousetrap. Marriage held no
attraction for him even if he sensed that Leslie would make
a provocative and satisfying wife. If that was what she
was holding out for she would be disappointed, he muttered
to himself as he walked rapidly away from her lodgings.

But he was not so lost to his surroundings that he did not
take a careful look at the brown-capped man still loitering
across the street. The man appeared to realize Marcus' interest in him and slunk away, turning the corner before

Marcus could make up his mind to approach him and ask his business. Scurvy fellow, Marcus thought, and up to no good. It would behoove him to keep an eye out for the man, in case his mysterious watch on Leslie might lead to unhappy results. But, perhaps, they were both imagining his interest in her.

The man might be just a casual loiterer, looking out for an easy mark. Pickpockets abounded in this area of London, but there was little fear of more violent crime such as would be found in Seven Dials, for example. However Marcus was filled with an uneasy foreboding as he hurried back to his office. His interview with Leslie had been badly managed, and his own behavior puzzled him. She was becoming a real irritant to him. He wanted her but he could not agree to surrender his liberty to any woman, even such a one as Leslie. Let Jonathan Stirling have her. She would make him an exceptional wife and Jonathan would return her loyalty and affection two-fold. Why this picture further exacerbated Marcus he did not understand, but he was in a nasty mood for the rest of the day and the members of his staff tiptoed cautiously around him, wondering what transgression they had committed.

Leslie, even more confused than Marcus, settled down to write to the man appealing for aid in locating his lost relative. She suggested hiring a Bow Street Runner but reminded the man that a solicitor should fulfill his needs. She had a peculiar reaction to this plea, sensing some strange yet wistful appeal from the lonely gentleman. Not for the first time she wished her correspondents did not have to remain shadowy anonymous figures and that she could meet and talk to them.

Finally she finished her work and decided that she had time before tea to take a brisk walk that would banish all her disquiet. The rain and wind that had darkened the morning had disappeared she noticed, and so had the man lurking across from her lodgings. She was rather ashamed at pointing him out to Marcus. He must think she was some timorous, vaporizing female, to imagine that someone was spying on her, the result of a feverish fancy. Surely even the count would not dare any outrageous action, and certainly there was no other she could think of who would want her watched.

In far off Wiltshire the Earl of Rothfield received his copy of *The Times,* a day late, and about four days after Leslie had answered his request for advice. He read the letter with deep interest, not at all surprised that Pythius had suggested he rely on his man of business. The earl, for all his ill health, loneliness and reclusive life, was an astute man. Normally that would have been his resolution of the problem of his missing cousin. He had been brusque and critical when Sir Alan had approached him, asking for financial help, for he believed that Sir Alan would have squandered the money on drink or gambling. A man of temperate, almost puritanical habits himself, he disliked excess of any kind. In his disgust he had never bothered to inquire as to the sex of the child on whose behalf Sir Alan had pleaded. All he knew was that the child's mother had recently died, that Sir Alan found it difficult to rear the child on his own and needed money.

The Earl had pointed out to him that he had a suitable income if he would manage to exercise some restraint, and he did not believe in subsidizing lechery and drunkenness. This led to harsh words being exchanged and the earl had banished the miscreant from his door.

He had meant it at the time but wiser counsels had prevailed. In the fifteen years that had intervened he had come to regret his precipitate action. At the time of Alan's death he had been laid low with one of his reoccurring attacks of fever and had not seen the modest obituary in *The Times,* which mentioned Dansforth's only survivor, a daughter. Later his solicitor had notified him of Sir Alan's death while discussing some other business. The earl had not confided in Oswald Orphington because he had come to distrust him. With his health partially restored he had gone over his affairs carefully and discovered that Orphington, with the aid of the earl's bailiff, had been milking the estate of its assets, gouging the tenants and pocketing a percentage of their rents. He had dismissed the bailiff, and frightened Orphington with court proceedings. Now he was searching for a new man of business, and perhaps if he could find one that was reliable he would turn over this matter of locating his lost relative to him, but for the moment, the idea of the Bow Street Runner appealed to him. He would put the matter in hand on the morrow.

The Earl of Rothfield did not realize how decisive his decision would be, not only for Leslie, but for his own peace of mind.

Chapter Eleven

Leslie was beginning to regret that she had mentioned the lurking watcher to Marcus. Since pointing him out to Marcus she had seen nothing more of the man. Could she have imagined the whole strange business? But her suspicions were to be unhappily confirmed a week later when Count von Ronberg appeared. He had timed his call cleverly, in mid-morning when the ubiquitous Mrs. Gorey was out shopping, and the maid-of-all-work, Aggie, had been forced to answer the door, a duty that always threw her into a nervous sniveling spasm. If Mrs. Gorey had told her not to admit the count she had forgotten, and in any case was in no state to refuse such an august personage.

"Good morning, Miss Dansforth," the count greeted her, ignoring her moue of displeasure.

"Is it, count? I suppose you forced your way in here. Poor Aggie could not deny you, although I have left definite instructions not to admit you. We have nothing to say to each other."

"On the contrary, I have a great deal to say to you, my dear. You are a clever puss, deceiving us all, and especially the great English reading public," he said, placing his hat and cane on the table and settling, without being invited into a chair. "I see you are busily at work on your Pythius letters."

Appalled, Leslie stared at him, wondering how in the world he had unmasked her identity. She took refuge in silence as her best defense. She had no doubt the count intended to use his information in a manner she would find repugnant.

"Really, I am quite impressed with your ingenuity in procuring such employment. I suppose you have charmed that rather brash and vulgar young man who has undertaken the direction of *The Times* to hire you for this unsuitable task." The count did not seem one whit abashed by Leslie's expression of anger and outrage. He continued, "I knew there must be some compelling reason for your refusing my attractive offer of a situation with Princess Esterhazy. And now, I quite understand that becoming a journalist has a certain cachet."

His tone may have been suave, but Leslie could not miss the ugly light in his eye. He had not called just to inform her he had learned her secret. She expected some attempt at blackmail, and had a very good idea of what he intended. She neither denied nor agreed as to the truth of his information.

Evidently neither her silence, nor her look of disdain, deterred him from the purpose of his visit. He went on just as if she had spoken. "I suggest it would not be in your best interest for this news to become public knowledge. Your editor would be ridiculed and his newspaper attacked."

"Do you think so? How peculiar. Possibly that might be true in your less progressive country, count, but women here are not just regarded as objects. There are many successful women writers," Leslie countered, trying to assume a mantle of indifference.

Ignoring her allusion to Austria as a hidebound autocracy, the count pressed on with his offer. "Nevertheless I am sure your editor would find it in his best interests to dismiss you, which would leave you in a precarious financial situation."

"Really. Your information, however you obtained it, is not accurate. And is really none of your business, count."

"Ah, since we share so much I do believe you could call me Felix."

I know what I would like to call you—cad, bounder, a slimy toad, Leslie thought and could not repress a smile at her description, although she was wise enough to bite back the actual words. But the look she flashed at von Ronberg left him in no doubt about her reaction.

"I do regret placing you in this position, but certainly you must see that it would be in your best interests to be more conciliatory," the count said, refusing to show any anger although he promised himself she would pay for such insolence once she was securely in his power. In that he misjudged his victim.

"My best interests would be to call a constable and a solicitor to accuse you of trying to blackmail me into your bed," Leslie stormed tired of this fencing.

"How crass, my dear. I am only suggesting that it behooves you to treat my generous offer to provide for you in return for a few favors, to which I am sure you are not a stranger. I see no occasion for this pretense that you are offended by my suggestion."

"Hardly a suggestion, more of a demand. If I had any doubt about your character, your morals, or your perverted behavior this confirms my opinion that you are all I thought and worse." Leslie had decided that only frank words would serve, besides she had thoroughly lost her temper in her disgust.

"You are willing to take the consequences, unpleasant although they may be," the count said, his tone harsh and his pale face reddening under her attack. He was not accustomed to having his arrangements turned down so summarily, nor his character impugned in such a decided manner. The stupid chit should be grateful for his interest instead of treating him like some monster.

"Please leave. This conversation is leading nowhere. If your intention is to broadcast my identity to the world if I refuse to surrender to your disgusting demands, you must seek your revenge. But I might say that your own actions in the past bear some scrutiny. In Austria you had a reputation for chicanery and even murder. Just how did your late wife meet her death?" Leslie was shocked at her effrontery in countering his proposal with such threats. She knew only too well that a man of the count's prestige could easily discount any rumors spread about London society. It was only women who suffered exile and obloquy from wicked gossip. It might be unfair but it was a realistic view of the inequality of the sexes, no matter how much Leslie decried it.

"You are an ungrateful, spiteful shrew. I hope you suffer what you deserve."

"I probably will. Now, if you have no more odious suggestions I think there is no point in your remaining." Leslie stood up to emphasize her words, and walked to the door. If he would not leave she would have to seek help in ejecting him and she was at a loss as quite how to do that. But he evidently realized he had exhausted his options, and taking up his hat and cane, pushed by her without a word, only giving her a burning glance that promised retaliation. She heard with relief his steps hurrying down the stairs.

Returning to her sitting room, shutting the door firmly on any intrusion, she considered what she should do. Of course, she must contact Marcus and let him know that their well-kept secret would be revealed to an avid public and to his eager competitors. He would be furious. For a moment Leslie felt she would like to damn them both and leave them to their fate. She could take her few pence and retire to some country hamlet where she could live in peace and anonymity, becoming the village spinster, renowned for good works and pitied for her manless state.

She laughed despite her anger and worry at this glum picture. No, she would not be defeated by the count and his wicked actions. Then her sense of humor, never in abeyance, surfaced. She must now consider herself a femme fatale, the object of an aristocrat's lust and a good man's honorable proposal. The count and Jonathan, two so opposing personalities. But where did this leave Marcus? Would he now wash his hands of her, deciding her meager talents were not worth all the trouble to his beloved newspaper.

Of course the count would not behave so crudely as to personally accuse her of writing the Pythius column. He would insinuate some scandalous relationship between Marcus and the writer, using Princess Esterhazy, a notorious rumor monger, to spread the idea. Then he would let it be known that Pythius was Miss Dansforth. Well, there was little she could do in rebuttal. She was not in a position, beyond the ton's intimate circle, to counter with equally nasty gossip about the count, and it would avail her little in any case. Still, she must contact Marcus. He was not expected until two days hence and she could hardly

wait for his expected appearance to notify him of this disaster. Nor could she boldly walk into *The Times* office and
request an interview. How long would it take the count to
make good on his promise to reveal the identity of Pythius?

That he would not let it rest there crossed her mind fleetingly and she dismissed the idea as the nonsensical notions
of a spineless coward. He could hardly force her into his
bed if she were unwilling. That was why he had tried this
ploy, threatening her with unmasking if she did not allow
him to seduce her. What kind of a man wanted a woman
in those circumstances?

For all her continental experience and her belief that she
understood men's motives, Leslie had no conception of the
type of man with which she was dealing. On first emerging from Leslie's lodgings, his face contorted with fury, the
count had been in the grip of his passions, determined to
force Leslie's surrender at any cost. But having tooled his
curricle at a reckless pace to the Austrian Embassy, his rage
began to give way to calculated planning. Leslie's refusal
to be cowed by his threats had only increased his determination to have her one way or the other. And he really enjoyed putting a rub in the way of that bumptious young man
who had spoiled his initial approach to her, then thwarted
his effort to get her into the embassy. However, he must
plot his strategy carefully. He could not take the chance of
endangering the real reason for his sojourn in London.

Meanwhile Leslie left alone and prey to the fears the
count had raised, decided she must contact Marcus no matter how brazen she appeared. Dressing in her plainest dark

garb she walked hurriedly to Printing House Square, the exercise bringing a glow to her cheeks. In her reticule lay a message for Marcus. The walk gave her time for reflection. Just what could he do to stop the count from revealing their secret?

At the same time she felt her irritation rising. It was not as if she were engaged in some scandalous activity. Surely being gainfully employed at a respectable newspaper should not place her reputation in jeopardy. Nevertheless she could not deny that if it were revealed that Pythius was a young woman there would be an outcry. No legal recourse was available.

And what would Marcus' reaction to the count's threat be? He might want to abandon her to her fate. But no, his pride was involved. By the time she reached the newspaper building she still had not decided how to cope with this latest threat to her security and reputation.

Although she had passed *The Times* on several occasions she had never entered its portals. The grimy stone building with its high arched windows looked rather intimidating, but she refused to be turned off by its imposing facade. Entering the reception area, crossing the marble floor toward the desk, manned by a burley porter, she could not entirely repress a tremor. But the man, accustomed to much tougher invaders, smiled encouragingly at her.

"Can I help you, madam?" he asked, raking her with an experienced glance. This was no light skirt off the street even if she was not chaperoned, he decided.

"Good morning. Could you deliver this message to Mr. Kingsley, please," Leslie asked in a small voice, expecting a rebuff. "It's quite important."

"Certainly, madam. Will you wait for a reply," the man

agreed, ringing a large bell at his desk, no doubt to summon some minion.

"No, that will not be necessary," Leslie said with a sigh, and, before he could question her further, darted away.

She only hoped he would not decide she was some mischief maker, and disregard her letter.

In that suspicion she did John Hughes an injustice. He had been instructed by Marcus in very decided terms to be both polite and cooperative with the public. It was as much as his job was worth to behave haughtily, no matter what the provocation. Certainly Leslie offered none. Hughes had dealt firmly in the past with trouble makers, and learned to recognize them with one experienced stare. Leslie turned at the door and noticed a young boy, in a page's uniform scurry to take her precious letter, and was satisfied.

A few minutes later Marcus took the letter from the page's hand, muttering at the interruption, and laid it to one side of his desk. He had endured a difficult meeting with the printers earlier and was behind in his work. Whatever was in the message, on the crisp cream paper, could wait until he had composed the final paragraph of his daily leader. Finally, with a sigh, he wrote the last sentence with a flourish and leaned back with a satisfied sigh.

That should make Liverpool and his ministers, "Mouldy & Co.", as his Whig rivals had dubbed his cabinet, sit up and take notice. Marcus was genuinely disturbed about the state of the country, its unrest, its economy, and labor conditions. And he feared Liverpool's reaction was to tighten the screws instead of opting for reform, and so he had stated in the leader. The Tories would be after his blood, he thought with satisfaction.

He looked from his window to discover the sun shining

bravely through its rather smudged panes, and wished for a moment he could abandon his responsibilities and take Leslie for a jaunt to the country. Alas, that was not possible, but he might just drop in to see her later today. Turning fretfully back to his desk, a bit ashamed at the direction of his musings, he noticed the letter again, and the distinctive script "Mr. Kingsley" across the envelope, with a feeling of familiarity. Hurriedly he slit it open with his paper knife, and glanced first at the signature. Yes, it was from Leslie. Then he read what she had written:

> Marcus,
>   Count von Ronberg has discovered our deception and is making nasty threats. I don't know what you can do but I think we must meet soon and discuss it.
>   Pythius.

Marcus had no difficulty interpreting this laconic note. That dastardly Austrian had somehow learned that Leslie was the author of the agony column and had made demands upon her. Marcus had a very good idea what those demands entailed and his anger rose. Well, he would settle the villain for once and all. How dare he try to blackmail Leslie and by inference *The Times*. Ringing for his clerk, he looked fierce, and when the young man entered his sanctum, he paled somewhat at the sight of his employer's angry face, and only hoped he was not the culprit who had inspired the fury. Marcus, when aroused, could be truly formidable as his staff had learned.

"Henry, I have an urgent appointment, and will probably not be back today. Take the leader to the printers, and be sure you record any messages," Marcus ordered on his way out the door, not stopping to hear if Henry had un-

derstood, nor caring much if he protested. Henry, who had
scheduled an appointment with a junior secretary from the
Home Office for later in the day, realized this was not
the moment to remind Marcus of the folly of treating the
Crown's servant in such a cavalier fashion, and only nodded to Marcus' retreating back.

Marcus, in a fever of impatience, hailed a hackney, and
was at Leslie's door almost before she had removed her hat
from her own journey. Mrs. Gorey, returned from her shopping, and hearing from a scared Aggie, of the count's visit,
was not inclined to look favorably on Marcus' arrival,
sensing that he brought trouble in his wake. But she was
no match for the determined young man, and barely scurried before him up the stairs to announce his arrival to
Miss Dansforth.

Leslie, taking one look at his flushed and angry face, was
having second thoughts about her frantic trip to seek his
aid. Before she could utter a word of greeting or explanation Marcus crossed to her, throwing his hat on the divan,
and took her by the shoulders and then into a comforting
caress.

"You are not to allow that bounder to worry you, Leslie.
I won't have it."

Touched, and lightly amused by Marcus' fierce cham-
pionship, Leslie disengaged herself and motioned Marcus
to a chair.

"Let us sit down and discuss this calmly. I sense that you
are far too angry to behave sensibly just now, but we must
confer on what this means to my continued employment
at *The Times,*" she said, intent on keeping the meeting on
an unemotional level.

Marcus barked out a rather bitter laugh. "You know,

Leslie, you are unique. Most women would be wailing and behaving like scared rabbits in your situation."

"What would that avail me?" she asked with a shrug.

"Nothing, but few would realize that."

"Do you want my resignation. I feel you have every right to demand it."

"Certainly not. Now that I have had a few moments to reflect without anger, as you so rightly suggested, it occurs to me, that the brown-capped man we noticed the other day was hired by the count to investigate you, and by assiduous attention to his duty has discovered our alliance, and reported to his master."

"Probably. But that does not answer the question of what we do next."

"Well, I don't intend to ignore the count's threats. I suppose he made you an infamous offer. Become his mistress and he will not bruit this shocking information about London."

If Leslie was embarrassed by Marcus' frankness, she showed no evidence of it. "Quite right," she agreed with his analysis.

"I regret I was not on hand to give the cad the facer he deserves," Marcus said, surprised at how angry he was by the count's infamous suggestion.

"Well, it came as no surprise. We know the man is capable of any betise."

"I wonder what he is really up to in London, aside from trying to seduce you." Marcus' journalistic curiosity was aroused by the idea that the count had some devious motive for his anomalous position at the embassy.

Leslie smiled, understanding exactly what he was thinking and not at all annoyed that he should suspect the count of some political maneuver in addition to seducing her, "The question is what we should do about it?"

"What did you tell him?"

"I'm afraid I did not handle the business as coolly as I might have. But I did tell him to do his worse, that I had no intention of submitting to his scandalous blackmail."

"Of course. I have an idea I might spike his guns with an anonymous suggestion in our Talk of Town article that a certain foreign nobleman, attached to a reputed embassy, is up to some nefarious plot. As long as no names are mentioned he would have little recourse. I suspect his own method of revenging himself on you, and me, for that matter, will involve spreading the tale of Pythius about the ton. I'm tempted to call him out. The man is a coward and a poltroon and should be brought to account."

A sudden fear shook Leslie. "You would not challenge him to a duel."

"I might. I have no intention of submitting to his blackmail. Of course, if you feel endangered, that is another story."

"Won't the news that a woman is writing the agony column cause you some embarrassment, even humiliation. I would not want that, after all your kindness to me, Marcus." Leslie was disturbed, not wanting to place Marcus in a situation where he would be ridiculed or worse.

"I have had threats of every kind since becoming editor of *The Times*. I discount them, for the most part. But I do not want you endangered by the man's vengeful nature, nor do I want you the target of his vile intentions."

"Thank you, Marcus. But might it not be best for me to give up the column, even leave London."

Marcus realized that he could not contemplate Leslie removing herself from his orbit. The thought of her absence

was almost painful to him, and if that give him pause, now
was not the time to examine his emotions. "Certainly not
We cannot give in to the villain. We must go on the offense
I am certain there is more to the count than his role as a
vile seducer, and I will discover it. He is a tool of Metter
nich and I believe is here on some mysterious mission fo
that wily intriguer. But, Leslie, you must take care. He is
not above abducting you or luring you into some secre
assignation." Marcus was clearly worried that the coun
represented a real threat to her.

"I am not so foolish as to ignore the danger. If you are
certain that my continuing in my job will not cause you
grief, Marcus, I will go on. And I cannot tell you what your
confidence in me means. Not many men would take the
risk."

"Not many men have such a clever and strong willed co-
conspirator. Eventually we will triumph, Leslie." He took
both her hands in his, tempted by the gratitude in her eyes,
to give her a more intimate expression of his faith in her,
but he sensed she would not be receptive to any caress, especially after her exposure to the count's advances.

"Let us just try to carry on as if he had not threatened
you. And let me know immediately if he tries any ploy. I
do wish you were not so alone, without any protection."

For a moment Leslie, half afraid, half excited, wondered
if he was to offer his own protection with all that implied,
but then she chided herself for being so foolish. But she
wondered what her answer would have been if he had suggested their relationship progress to a more intimate level.
What a wanton she was, and what a ninny. To become Marcus' mistress would only complicate the situation and involve her in even more peril, this time to her heart.

Marcus, watching her expression, had no idea where

her turbulent thoughts were leading, but he sensed a with-
drawal and hurried to reassure her.

"Just go on with the work, and try to put the count from
your mind. Not easy, I know, especially since you must be
vigilant for any more attempts to lure you into some kind
of nasty situation. I will keep in close touch, and now I
must return to the office. I'm afraid I rudely canceled a
meeting with an important minister when I received your
message. I will have to make my peace with him."

He leaned over and kissed her on the forehead, a brief
salute of comfort, and with a hasty farewell left her to
wonder just what Marcus really thought of her, musing
about that complex skein successfully banished all
thoughts of the count for the rest of the day.

Chapter Twelve

Leslie tried conscientiously to follow Marcus' advice. Whenever she went out, to the British Museum, to the library, to the shops, she found herself constantly looking behind, searching for some watcher, some anonymous man dogging her steps. She saw no sign of the brown-capped man, but she suspected that he might have been replaced by a less obvious figure. The whole business made every outing a trial. Jonathan escorted her on a few jaunts, and she felt secure in his company, although he noticed that she was far from relaxed, and finally asked her what was causing her so much concern.

They were strolling in the park on a fine June day when he broached the question.

"Leslie, I know something is bothering you. You seem unusually nervous, always looking about as if you expect some trouble. Can't you tell me about it. I might help," Jonathan urged, unhappy over her distress.

"Oh, Jonathan, you are such a comfort, always trying to ease my path, never creating problems. I wish I could love you as you deserve instead of being so unaccomodating." Leslie looked at his kind, open countenance and wondered

why she could not return his love. She did feel overwhelming affection for him, but knew that was not the
emotion he craved.

"Perhaps I would have a better chance with you if I behaved like a cad," he teased.

"I can't imagine you ever resorting such actions, no
matter how sorely you were tried. I'm sorry to be such bad
company."

"You are never that, Leslie, and I respect your feelings.
You are too honest and forthright to pretend to something
you don't feel. But don't avoid my question. You behave
as if you expected to be spirited away by some unknown
person."

"Well, that is about it. Come, let us sit down here on this
convenient bench and I will tell you all about it, if you
promise not to vow vengeance or embroil yourself with my
persecutor."

Jonathan shook his head in sorrow. "It will be an effort
but I promise to behave with all circumspection."

Leslie, comforted by having a sympathetic audience for
her dilemma, gave Jonathan a concise report of the count's
discoveries and threats. She tried to downplay his attempt
at blackmailing her into his bed, but Jonathan at once
grasped what the Austrian intended. She hesitantly mentioned Marcus' threat to challenge the count to a duel, and
he was secretly appalled as well as wondering if this reaction meant that Marcus really cared for Leslie. If he did he
thought it put an end to his own hopes of winning her.

Jonathan, modest and unassuming, believed that he had
little to offer compared to Marcus' charm, power and
worldly goods. Not that he suspected that Leslie was a female who valued wealth and position, but she and Marcus
shared a good deal and propinquity was a great aid to ro-

mance. He thought briefly of telling her about Dinah Darcy, but could not bring himself to act so shabbily. Marcus was his friend and he would do nothing to put a rub in his way if Marcus truly loved Leslie and wanted to marry her. However, his experience of his friends' amatory career did not augur well for Leslie if she returned his love. Of far more importance was this threat to her livelihood, her peace of mind, her safety. He was truly worried about her, unprotected as she was.

While Leslie and Jonathan discussed what the count's threats might produce, unbeknownst to them another actor was entering the drama.

The Earl of Rothfield, impatient at the lack of results from his search for his only surviving relative, had decided to come to London, where he was convinced the mystery could be solved. After installing himself in his somewhat gloomy mansion on Bruton Place off Berkeley Square, he contacted the Bow Street Runners and put his problem before their chief, Sir Nathaniel Conant, who assigned one of his best investigators to the case.

Harry Weems was an oddity in the service, a former gentleman, down on his luck, with an ingratiating manner and a certain suave appearance that enabled him to take his place among the toffs without exciting comment. Tall, well built, with a pair of bold, merry blue eyes and fashionably styled brown hair, he did not at first appear capable of holding his own with villains. But beneath his well cut coat and trim breeches was a strong body and allied to his quick mind, he was a formidable opponent as many a thief and rogue had discovered. His past jobs had mostly concerned banks, who were often victims of robbery, and in tracking down the miscreants and their loot he had been extremely successful.

His interview with the earl had established respect on both sides. Harry's first job was to interview Oswald Orphington, the earl's unsavory solicitor, in his offices off Chancery Lane. Orphington had not been cooperative, sensing that this Bow Street fellow threatened his position viz a viz the Earl of Rothfield.

A weedy unlikeable man, his waistcoat stained with snuff, with close-set eyes and thinning hair, Oswald did not inspire confidence. He had inherited the practice from his upright father, Henry, a far different type, and had managed to alienate most of his father's better clients. The earl remained his sole eminent one and he had managed to soothe that gentleman's complaints as long as the earl remained in seclusion in Wiltshire. At the same time he had been most skillful in hiding his manipulations of the earl's funds, directing a goodly sum into his own pockets, while assuring his noble client that all was well. He adopted a superior pose when confronted by Harry Weems, not liking the fellow's manner.

"My firm has conducted the earl's affairs for some years without any complaints. I resent this suggestion that the earl is not satisfied with my direction of his business," he said.

His lofty air did not deceive Harry for a moment. "Yes, that may well be, but the earl is not satisfied now, and has come to London to look into his situation more closely. Also, he has been disappointed that you have done little to increase his holdings. In fact, they seem to have dissipated in the past four years, he tells me," Harry said. He was convinced the solicitor had been milking the earl's resources for some time. The old man probably had so much money, and his wants were so limited, that he had hardly been aware of what was happening.

Of course, Harry had no proof, but his investigator's nose led him to believe that Oswald was a downy one. The earl had not given Oswald the assignment of locating his missing relative, and that in itself, showed that he no longer trusted the man. Harry would warn the earl that his man of business was not acting in his best interests.

"Orphington, I am empowered by the earl to make an investigation for him, and I am beginning with you." He paused noticing a flicker of fear in the man's eyes. He intended to go on and ask him about the earl's relatives, but before he could launch into those questions, Oswald, sputtering a bit, was quick to absolve himself of any wrong doing. He ignored the letter Harry placed on his desk from the earl requesting that he give Harry any assistance he could, and launched into a spirited defense of his custodianship.

"If the earl is unhappy with my conduct of his affairs he should have requested my presence so that I can give him an account of matters, not sent some Bow Street rogue to badger me with unfounded accusations."

Harry, now completely convinced the man was a charlatan, ignored Oswald's words, and continued with his questions.

"What do you know about Sir Alan Dansforth?"

"That libertine. He tried to gouge money from the earl and was deservedly turned away with a flea in his ear," Orphington said, adopting a puritanical manner, not at all justified by his own ethics Harry decided.

"Yes, I know about that. But Sir Alan is dead. The most cursory investigation had assured me of that. Why did you not inform the earl?"

"I doubted he would be interested."

"Nonsense. The man had a child, and naturally the earl wants to locate this survivor."

Oswald, who worried that an heir to the earl's estate, would demand a strict accounting of his business, had omitted telling the earl of Sir Alan's daughter for that very reason. And he was not at all happy at this Bow Street chap ferreting around in his affairs. But, of course, he would never admit such a fear.

"I see no reason for the earl to hire one of you people to make inquires. My resources are much better. He had only to ask for my assistance," Oswald said, returning to his aggrieved stance of injury.

Harry, impatient and disgusted with the man's attempts to justify himself, countered quickly. "The earl does not have faith in you, and I expect will be transferring his affairs to a more reputable solicitor before too long. If you are refusing to give me information, I will report it to him, and that will reinforce his suspicions of you."

Oswald blanched. This would never do. "Surely that drastic action is unnecessary," he confided. "Of course, I will cooperate in any way with your investigations."

The upshot of this inconclusive chat was that Harry Weems left Orphington's office no wiser than when he came, except for his conviction the man was a thief and unreliable. Oswald had no information about Sir Alan's child, and would no doubt obstruct any further investigations while pretending to help. He must be dismissed immediately.

Harry left to report to the earl, determined to urge just such an action on the old gentleman, who had been gulled by the very man who should have been protecting him. Wise in the ways of the world, but not cynical, for all that,

Harry felt sorry for the earl, and looked forward to finding this heir, banishing Oswald and bringing the earl some happiness.

What is the role of a certain foreign noble-man attached to his Embassy? Surely he is not just enjoying the amenities of our fair town. Suspicions have been aroused and your columnist wonders at this gentleman's real motives in visiting us.

The count, who had a perfect grasp of English, and read *The Times* assiduously, mostly to keep track of various statesmen in whom he was interested, was not pleased by this item in the Talk of the Town column. He was furious, and blamed Leslie for the innuendo. Well, that settled it. He would take retaliatory measures immediately. But before he could put his plan into action he was requested to pay a visit to Prince Esterhazy in that ambassador's office. Although the message was conveyed with all due respect and utmost politeness, the count astutely accepted that he had best accept.

Prince Esterhazy had received a smooth communication from Metternich requesting he offer all hospitality to the count, and the prince knew better than oppose his head of state, but he had no love for the devious nobleman. He knew too much of his dubious past and believed every story he had heard. It placed him in a delicate position, but he could not ignore the allusion in *The Times*. He was convinced it referred to von Ronberg, and he was determined to learn exactly what the count was up to.

The two noble Austrians greeted each other with a false show of cordiality. Both were adept at such maneuvers.

"I hope your stay with us has been an enjoyable one." Esterhazy opened the proceedings in a bland tone.

"You and the princess have been most hospitable, and I am very grateful for your welcome." The count would not be undone by flattering inanities.

"I don't wish to seem inquisitive, but there seems to be some mystery about your visit to us. Metternich has written to insist that we give you every cooperation, but he has failed to mention in what manner we may assist you," the prince continued in his most diplomatic manner. If the fellow was unwilling to confide the real purpose of his trip to London, and the prince doubted it was purely social, he intended to discover it.

"Not at all, Esterhazy. Unfortunately I am not at liberty to reveal my instructions from Metternich," von Ronberg said in a manner that repelled any further presumptuous questions. But the count was not dealing with an underling now. The prince had the ear of Metternich and was much respected both at the Austrian court and in vital political and social circles in London. A skilled diplomat he could also be quite ruthless in protecting his own interests.

"I understand that, von Ronberg, but our hosts might not be quite so tolerant. There is a rather strange item in today's *Times,* which might refer to you. Of course, on the other hand so much intrigue is usual in the milieu which we inhabit that the allusion could refer to any number of our colleagues. But it is rather unusual for the British, so thick skinned and convinced of their superiority, to suspect any deviltry on their home ground so to speak."

"Since we both are concerned, first of all with the interests of our country, I know you will understand that I can say nothing about my business here. I, too, saw the item to which you refer, but it was so nebulous, so vague, I cannot believe that it refers to me. Of course, if you believe that it does you might make diplomatic objections to Liverpool," the count suggested, knowing full well that the prince would do no such thing, since that would infer he realized the reference concerned his titled guest.

Esterhazy, angry that he was being both challenged and fobbed off with specious reasoning, showed no sign of his displeasure. "That would be most unwise. The British pride themselves on their freedoms. They would not look kindly on any attempt by a foreign government to try to muzzle their newspapers. They might take action themselves. In fact, I remember quite a famous libel case concerning the Prince Regent, but certainly we cannot take that type of action."

"In our country such behavior by the gutter press would be immediately punished," the count said.

"Yes, but the British are not so fortunate in their government." The prince paused. He believed he had made his position clear, but perhaps he might go further.

"Whatever your mission here, count, I do not want the Embassy involved, nor will I be a participant in any illegal action. My worth to Austria is my popularity in England. I will do nothing to jeopardize that by appearing to join any conspiracy against our hosts."

Von Ronberg, equally irate, had enough sense to control himself but he intended to have the last word. "That may well be, prince, but Metternich does not share your view and we both owe him, and of course, our revered sovereign our allegiance." Having delivered these quelling words in his haughtiest tones, he stood up, gave a formal bow. "And now you must excuse me. I have a pressing appointment." He left without further ceremony.

The prince, frustrated, brooded for a moment and then

frowned. It was as he had suspected. Von Ronberg had been sent here to conduct some conspiracy against the British government or one of its statesmen, perhaps Liverpool, or Wellington. Who knew which one Metternich had decided would best be disgraced, removed from power, even assassinated? The prince would put none of these options beyond Metternich. With casual cynicism he had no moral revulsion from such tactics but he worried that he might suffer any recriminations if the count failed in his nasty task. His own political and diplomatic survival was always utmost in Esterhazy's mind. He could not take the obvious step of appealing to Liverpool to have von Ronberg labeled *persona non grata* and deported. Whatever his own reactions to the man, the count was an Austrian, an ally of Metternich's, and in a position to do the prince a great deal of harm. So Esterhazy must keep his own counsel, although he might just put his fears before the princess, an astute woman who had helped him before in delicate maneuvers.

The count, calling brusquely for his carriage, thought he had handled the interview with the prince quite well. The man might have illustrious ancestors and be a favorite of the Austrian monarch but he lacked a certain ruthlessness that the count always admired in his adversaries. Too long in this decadent English environment where he had been insidiously influenced by those fools who prated about freedom and democratic principles. None of that nonsense at home, thank God. And when he had completed his assignment here the Hanoverians might not be so amenable to these foolish principles either. The count rode off to his appointment feeling quite pleased with himself, an emotion he often entertained, not supposing for a moment that any man could best him.

But it appeared a woman might, and as he rode along he reminded himself that the unfinished business with Leslie Dansforth still had to be settled. He was convinced she was responsible for the item in *The Times* and would pay the penalty, not only for that insolent insult, but for her rejection of him. When he had done with her she would only be fit for a brothel. His plans were almost completed, and there was no way she would escape him this time.

Chapter Thirteen

Dinah Darcy was beginning to wish she had never made her infamous bargain with the count. Much as she enjoyed the luxuries of life as a kept woman, she did not find the count an easy protector. He was a brutal lover, not caring for her satisfaction, only his own, and it was not only in bed that he was difficult. He kept quizzing her about Marcus, and she had little information for him.

Marcus had only visited her once in the past fortnight, and today she had received a message from him saying he would be around this evening and had an important matter to discuss with her. She wondered fleetingly if he had discovered that he would be sharing her favors with the count. Not that he would care, she decided, a bit bitterly. No, he probably wanted to bring an end to their relationship.

That posed two problems for her. The count would be angry, might withdraw his support, because she no longer had news of Marcus to offer him, although why he wanted it puzzled her.

Of much more immediate concern was Marcus' intention to abandon her. Why had he tired? Her limited mind

went over and over any evidence that had caused his in
difference. Of course he might have discovered her rela
tionship with the count, but she doubted he had, or that h
cared enough to object. Still, he might use that as an ex
cuse to rid himself of her. Dinah, brooding and unhappy
wondered how she could find out if Marcus was interested
in another woman. Her resources were limited but she had
an idea. She would prevail on his friend, that kind Jonathan
Stirling, to tell her. Perhaps if she promised him a suitable
reward, several hours in her bed, he would cooperate.

However, before she could plan how to approach
Jonathan, she received a visit from Count von Ronberg that
changed her mind. After a mannerless and brief coupling
in the bedroom, the count ordered Dinah to get dressed. He
required her to perform another service for him. She did
not like the expression on his face when he brusquely made
his wishes known. Dinah, pulling on a gown and stockings
hastily, and pushing her feet into shoes, decided that what
ever he asked of her was certain to be unpleasant.

"Well, here I am, count, at your pleasure," she said with
an insouciant air as she entered the sitting room where von
Ronberg was gazing with intensity out of the window.

When he turned to face her Dinah wondered if her read
ing of his character had been unfair. He smiled as if he
found her charming and his silken words reinforced this
impression.

"My dear Dinah, you are really a very talented woman
I am more than satisfied with our arrangement on that
score, but I believe we must now extend your services."

Dinah felt a sudden apprehension but stoutly suppressed
it. After all the man was laying out good money and all he

had received for it so far were a few tumbles. She had known from the beginning he would demand more, and she was convinced that additional demand would concern Marcus.

"When do you expect Mr. Kingsley to call upon you again? He appears very dilatory in his attentions from what you tell me. That is if you are not lying." And then he continued in a voice laden with menace. "And I would not like to think you are untruthful, my dear. Ladies who try that ploy on me soon find themselves in unhappy circumstances."

Dinah could well believe it, but she had a certain obstinate courage that had served her well in the past. She was no faint-hearted miss, liable to quail beneath threats and intimidation. This was not yet the time to challenge the count, perhaps, but she would not allow him to think she was completely under his thumb.

"I don't like being threatened, sir, and can not imagine what I have done to deserve such treatment. I have agreed to tell you of Marcus' visits, and have done so. It just happens he has not been to see me for some time." She had not decided whether to inform the count of tonight's appointment.

Poor Dinah was in a perilous position. The protector she preferred, with whom she had enjoyed the most pleasant relations, she sensed was about to leave her, and she was left with this unsavory foreigner, whose pockets might be deep, but whose intentions were unknown. He had offered his protection for other reasons than the usual ones, and Dinah was beginning to think his money was not worth it. If she failed to tell him of Marcus' visit this evening and he discovered that she had omitted this vital news just what revenge would he wreak upon her? She would tell him but that would not be the end of it.

Whatever nasty plans the count had involving Marcus she could at least warn him that he was in danger. And she would be quite honest about her reasons for allowing the count the freedom of her bedroom. Dinah had some vague idea that she has assumed a role in an intrigue for which she was ill-suited but might end up paying a heavy price in her desire for security.

"As a matter of fact he has sent a note that he plans to visit me tonight," Dinah said with a casual air, as if she saw nothing peculiar in the count's desire for such information.

"Fine, excellent." In a moment the count's manner had changed and he assumed the charming pose he could adopt when the occasion demanded it.

But Dinah, although relieved by his affability, was not deceived. He planned some mischief and she realized she would be a part of it, not a position she liked at all. Boldly she made her objections known.

"Our arrangement, count, was that I would inform you of Marcus' visits, as well as providing certain favors. I did not agree to take part in any scheme that would lead to violence or trouble." Dinah admired her choice of words, and strengthened her spine. She expected the count to threaten her again and was surprised when he smiled at her.

"Of course, my dear. I would not want you involved in any unpleasantness. You must just trust me that the situation between Mr. Kingsley and myself is a personal one, a disagreement of a casual nature, that need not trouble you in the slightest." Then he settled the matter by kissing her hand, pressing into it some notes, and took his farewell, leaving behind a perplexed Dinah.

The whole conversation had left her very uneasy. Still,

she was not such a ninny that she did not realize the count was plotting against Marcus, and she suspected that it involved a woman. Jonathan would be able to tell her. Unlike Leslie she had no compunction about calling on Jonathan at *The Times,* although she must manage it so that Marcus did not learn of her visit. She could not contact Marcus and warn him of the count's interest in his affairs in case Marcus' ended their arrangement on the spot.

The Earl of Rothfield was extremely grateful to Pythius, that sage advice columnist in the *Times,* and commended his good sense in suggesting the Bow Street Runners. He found Harry Weems a delightful fellow, polite, personable and awake on all suits. Harry had reported to the earl about his interview with Oswald Orphington and strongly urged the earl to get rid of the man, remove his affairs from the solicitor immediately.

"It's none of my business, sir, of course, and you did not hire me to give my opinion of the man, but to quiz him about Sir Alan Dansforth's missing child. But I found his manner suspicious and I doubt very much that he told me the truth about the Dansforth matter as well as showing definite signs of agitation. He is hiding something and I greatly fear it concerns your estate, your moneys. I cannot understand how a gentleman of your position let his affairs be managed by such a one." Harry had grasped immediately that the earl would not be offended by such frank talk.

"Of course it's your business, my boy. You have been hired to find my missing relative and if on the way you discover maleficence in the handling of my affairs you are only doing your duty in informing me of it." The earl hesitated and then seeing Harry's sympathetic expression engaged in confidences he had long suppressed.

The poor old man has no one to talk to, Harry thought, and settled down to listen.

"You see, Weems, this chap's father had handled the Rothfield affairs for donkey's ages, and his father before him. They originally hailed from Wiltshire, had an office in Salisbury, and were well respected. When old Orphington died, this fellow moved to London, thought it a step up, I imagine, and since the firm had always been satisfactory I just continued with him. Too lazy to change, I suppose. Very remiss of me, and I will certainly make other arrangements now. Do you think he has been embezzling money from me." He paused and then shook his head. "Of course he has, and I am a fool not to have noticed, but my income far exceeds my needs, you know, and I have never worried about money, a careless attitude, I am sure you think," the earl said with an air of engaging candor and as if he thoroughly expected to be reproved.

But Harry was too canny to venture into those waters, and returned to the matter that concerned him.

"You see, sir, I think he has not only been siphoning off money from your estate, but has deceived you about the whereabouts of Sir Alan's child. I mean he would not want a possible heir rooting about in estate matters. His chicanery would be immediately discovered."

"You are a downy one, my boy. Should have brought you into the affair months ago. Now, what is our next move?"

Harry could see that the earl believed this was some sort of game in which together they would track and then expose villains. The old boy probably bored to death. In that he misjudged the earl, who surprised him with his next words.

"I feel guilty about Sir Alan's child. I behaved in a rag-mannered fashion toward him when he appealed to me. He was a bit of a bounder, and a weakling, but his wife was a fine woman, and there is no reason his child should suffer for his sins, even the Bible tells us that."

Harry, touched by the earl's sincerity and kindliness, promised to pursue his inquires with all diligence and emphasized again that a change of solicitors was vital to the earl's interests. The earl agreed. They shared a glass of Madeira and parted on the most satisfactory terms.

While this varied cast of characters were pursuing their ploys, Leslie and Marcus remained impervious to the intrigues that would soon alter their lives. Marcus, genuinely worried about the count, realized that the man was moving behind the scenes to cause Marcus and *The Times* as much embarrassment as possible. No doubt the count was responsible for the derisive piece today in *The Gazette* about the sex of Pythius. An even more scurrilous item appeared in *The Advertizer* about the effrontery of Marcus in hiring a woman to edit personal and advice columns and then hiding her identity from the public. Marcus had already received several letters commenting on this shocking affair, all of course from hide-bound males who resented the elevation of a mere woman to such a position on a newspaper that claimed to be serious and objective. Marcus discovered in his reaction to these critics that his own opinions about women had been dramatically changed by his association with Leslie, almost without him being aware of the alteration. Respect for her ability, enjoyment of her company and an unaccountable desire to protect her from whatever obloquy she might suffer from the count's revelations all combined to lead him to view her in a new light.

Astute and perceptive, Marcus realized his relationship with Leslie had influenced his feelings toward Dinah. He no longer wanted to continue the arrangement that had satisfied him for some time. The whole business appeared tawdry. He had decided to end it, and had written Dinah, not without some compunction, advising her he had a serious matter to discuss with her. Certainly she must be aware of what he meant to say. He had virtually ignored her for the past few weeks. Still, he was unhappy about the coming interview. He meant to give her a lavish gift in recompense for ending their affair, but even so he felt some guilt at his shabby treatment of a girl to whom he owed affection and support. His conscience began to nag him, and he could not settle to his work.

Throwing down his quill in disgust, he walked to the window and looked out on the square. It was useless. He felt a sudden longing to see Leslie, to reinforce his decision. Picking up his hat he strode briskly from his office, pausing only to tell his clerk that he would be away until the afternoon. As he hurried from Printing House Square, intent on his decision and his destination, he just missed the arrival of Dinah, who glimpsed him rounding the corner as she approached the entrance to *The Times*. Sighing with relief, she approached John Hughes, ensconced in all his majesty behind the reception desk, and asked for Mr. Stirling. Hughes, casting an experienced eye over Dinah, smiled inwardly. Who would have thought the proper and somewhat staid Mr. Stirling would be involved with this bold little madam. Quite an expensive article, too, Hughes decided, while asking her politely to take a seat.

Dinah settled into one of the chairs lining the hall, next

to a likely looking fellow who might be obliging. She always preferred the company of men and took advantage of any opportunity to attract any who came her way.

Harry Weems, waiting to see a clerk who might help him search through past obituaries in search of some mention of Sir Alan's death and his survivors, was not adverse to chatting with such a luscious lady, although he judged that she was of the muslin company. They quickly became acquainted and each found the other entertaining, although both of them were careful not to reveal the object of their visit to *The Times*.

Harry was all too soon called away by a clerk who escorted him to the cellar where the files were stored. Before leaving he managed to learn Dinah's name but not her direction. She was too canny to reveal that but he promised himself he would track her down without too much difficulty, just from the few clues she had dropped.

Dinah sighed as she watched him march away jauntily. She would have enjoyed more of the fellow's company. Not of the first stare, perhaps, but certainly a gentleman who knew how to treat a girl, a pleasant interlude after the count. She wondered idly what his business could be. Perhaps he was seeking employment, although he seemed reasonably well set-up, not in need of a guinea.

Dinah's musings were interrupted by the arrival of Jonathan, who greeted her kindly, and suggested they have their talk at a cafe on the square. He had little doubt that she wanted advice from him about Marcus and he dreaded answering her questions. He had to be honest with Dinah, whom he had always liked in a casual fashion, although not approving of Marcus' arrangement with her. He suspected, as did Dinah, that Marcus had formed a new attachment and that both he and Dinah would suffer from it.

Chapter Fourteen

As he neared Leslie's lodgings Marcus searched the neighborhood for any suspicious characters lurking about. He was not convinced that the count had abandoned his designs on Leslie. He might have replaced the brown-capped man with a less obtrusive watcher. But Marcus could see no persons not on lawful business. Answering the door, Mrs. Gorey gave him her usual disapproving stare. Despite his best efforts he could not improve Leslie's landlady's opinion of him. He knew she preferred Jonathan as a possible suitor. Usually this assessment of his intentions toward her favorite lodger amused him but today it added to his irritation.

"No need to announce me, Mrs. Gorey," he said and marched up the stairs quickly. She sniffed, but made no attempt to prevent him, muttering under her breath as she scurried into her own quarters.

Marcus knocked on the door with force, calling out at the same time. "Leslie, it's me, Marcus."

She opened the door, surprised to find her frowning employer on the threshold.

"What's wrong, Marcus?" she greeted him, pleased but a bit disturbed by his obvious anger.

He strode to the middle of the room, throwing his hat carelessly on a chair and answered her. "I wish you would tell that watchdog of yours that every time I call I am not intending rape. That woman annoys me."

Leslie laughed. "She's really very kind, just trying to protect me."

"Well, I know she doesn't receive Jonathan in that starchy manner."

"Yes, but she thinks Jonathan's intentions are strictly honorable."

"And she has decided that mine are not. Perhaps she's right." He smiled, seeing the humor in the situation.

"She knows you are my employer. Otherwise I fear she would not admit you at all," Leslie explained, quite heartened by Marcus' attitude. And she wondered not for the first time what her response would be if he really meant to seduce her. Dangerous thoughts indeed, and she pushed the idea from her resolutely.

"I hope she is as diligent in protecting you from the count."

"Well, she is torn. She is most impressed by his title and his obvious prestige. But she doesn't trust foreigners, so she is truly caught in a dilemma. But sit down and stop glowering. I assure you that she is aware of my opinion of that villain. Still, it's comforting to believe you are concerned for my welfare," she said, and reproved herself for sounding like a simpering flirt.

Somewhat mollified, but not entirely approving of Leslie's cavalier treatment of his objections, Marcus threw himself in a chair.

"And why am I being honored with this unexpected visit?" Leslie asked, seating herself across from him.

Not wanting to admit his sudden desperate wish to see her, Marcus hesitated, then said in an offhand voice, "I wanted to report to you on the results of the count's rumor mongering. We have had quite a few letters castigating us for employing you."

Leslie sighed, expecting he wanted to end her role as Pythius. "You have decided that I am not worth the fuss."

"Not at all. I am not so in thrall to my readers that they influence my decisions. But I wondered if you had been bothered, although I don't believe you have been unmasked. The readers know you are a woman, but not your identity. I hope that mysterious reference to the count in the Talk of the Town will give him pause, and force him to see the dangers of going any further."

"Then I am to continue," Leslie asked, relieved that she was not to be dismissed. She enjoyed her work, but more important she needed it, not only for the income but to keep her busy.

"Of course. I am convinced the count is up to some skullduggery and it does not just concern you."

"But what could it be?" Leslie was determined not to show her disappointment. Somehow she had hoped that Marcus' first concern was her welfare, but it seemed he saw her as a possible lure to draw out the count's real purpose in London.

"Some villainous attack on our government, I think. He is not here just because of you, I am sure. But you are an additional attraction."

"A distraction, rather. Oh dear, I suppose I, too, am proud of my conquests. You have put me in my place."

"Stop angling for compliments. And flirting with me. That is not your style."

Now that he was sparring with Leslie all his good humor had returned. She might be funning she had him firmly in her toils, and he rather enjoyed his capture. He relaxed and smiled at her, his eyes softening as he looked at the woman who was fast dominating his life. How could Dinah compete with Leslie's charms? No wonder he wanted to break with his mistress, even if there was no chance of Leslie supplanting her in his bed. But what a temptation she was.

He had just enough control not to suggest such an outrageous idea to her, but it was all he could do to keep his hands off her. He had enough sense to know that if he made any overtures that she would treat him with scorn, and all their pleasant companionship could vanish in a moment. She did not trust him, and she had every reason to doubt his intentions. Why could he not offer the honorable proposal she deserved? Well, he was not prepared to give up his freedom, even for Leslie.

Disturbed by the uncomfortable silence that had fallen, Leslie returned to the problem posed by the count, feeling on safer ground. Marcus' effect on her was unsettling, and she sensed he would make a move if he received the slightest encouragement.

"How do you mean to thwart the count, if he really means to commit some attack on the government?"

"I haven't the smallest notion, but I will set my spies onto an investigation. The man is a thorn in my side. I feel he is dangerous, an opportunist rather than a patriot. I hear that he is not well liked in Vienna. He has a shady past and a problematical future. He is fortunate in Metternich's friendship, but he must have some hold over Prince Esterhazy. I don't think the Austrian ambassador likes him. Just a suggestion I have picked up from my sources."

"Interesting. However, if he is here to cause trouble of some sort at least that will keep him busy and I need no longer worry," Leslie said. She did not really think the count would continue his pursuit of her after the rebuffs she had delivered.

"The man has neither morals nor conscience. He is capable of the most heinous actions. Don't relax your guard. You have seen no more suspicious characters lurking about, I hope."

"No, but sometimes when I go out I have a feeling that someone is following me. Mere nerves, I guess. If he did attempt an abduction, and it failed, he would be *persona non grata* in London and have to return to Vienna. That would abort his purpose if what you suspect is true. I can't believe he would be that foolish."

"I'm not so sure. Just continue to be vigilant."

Eager to change the subject, Leslie told him she had finally received her quarterly funds from her father's estate. Jonathan had arranged a new solicitor for her and he had expedited matters.

"None of my business, of course, but where do these funds come from?" Marcus asked, willing to follow her lead. No good would come of exciting her apprehensions about the count any further.

"I'm not quite sure. From his mother, I think. She was a Rothfield, I believe, and I understand the current earl is rich as Croesus."

"He should do something for you." Marcus frowned, not liking the thought of Leslie suffering from her father's sins.

"Why? He and father had a falling out, and I regret it, but I am sure the earl had every reason to cut him off. I loved my father but I would be less than honest if I did not admit he was feckless," Leslie said sighing as she thought of her wayward parent.

"You need protection, my girl. You are not the stalwart soul you pretend to be," Marcus rose and lifted Leslie from her chair. "You have no resources against a determined male." And despite himself he dragged her into his arms and began a thorough assault on her senses.

Because she found herself responding to his kisses, Leslie struggled to release herself, disgusted that Marcus, like the count, found her fair game.

Wresting herself from his arms she faced him with flushed cheeks and a righteous anger.

"Stop this, Marcus. You have proved your point, that you can dominate me with your greater strength. You would not dare commit such liberties if I were under the aegis of the Earl of Rothfield. Perhaps I should appeal to him." Leslie was rather ashamed at behaving like a heroine in a gothic novel but she could not have Marcus kissing her whenever he wanted, out of boredom, or just because she was some sort of challenge.

"I think you protest too much, my dear," he drawled in a hateful tone. But he was feeling chagrined that he had so lost command of himself that he had transgressed beyond the limits he had set himself.

"Do you really believe that every woman you meet must fall victim to your charms? Conceited oaf," she stormed, disappointment as well as anger spurring her to words she would later regret. She should have laughed off the whole encounter. That would have served her far better in her amatory duel with Marcus.

"Not at all, but I don't think you are completely impervious to my so-called charms. I apologize yet again if that is what you want. You have no idea of your power, Leslie. You would tempt a saint, and I am no saint."

"You certainly are not, more like a devil. You want to enjoy women without taking any responsibility for the havoc you raise."

Marcus grinned. "I am delighted to raise havoc in you, Leslie. But come let us have a truce. I will take you to Gunter's for cream cakes and in such a respectable environment we can have a civilized conversation and you will be safe from my advances."

Leslie glared at him, but could not resist the invitation. She so rarely had treats of that sort and wanted to spend some time in Marcus' company, no matter how badly he behaved. Weak-minded of her, but she was honest enough to admit that despite using her for amusement she found him stimulating and exciting. When he wasn't working his flirtatious wiles, meaningless as they were, she conceded, she enjoyed their tilts.

"On my best behavior, I promise. Now get your bonnet and we will be off," Marcus invited, buoyed by her forgiveness but a bit nettled that she found his attentions so annoying. He could have gone on making love to her all afternoon, but instead he would be drinking tea and making idle chat. Somehow he had to win her trust, and he thought ruefully, if every time he saw her he attacked her, that might be difficult. She was no light skirt and he had been in danger of treating her as one. He would do well to remind himself that Leslie was not to be approached so carelessly.

While Marcus and Leslie were regaling themselves with tea and cakes at Gunter's, Dinah Darcy and Jonathan were partaking of refreshments in a much humbler establishment. Jonathan felt compassion for Dinah, a woman he had always found cheerful and comfortable if not overburdened with intellect. He could quite understand her attraction for Marcus, who probably enjoyed her unchallenging manner as well as the sexual relief she offered. But he had always known the relationship could not be an enduring one. Marcus would become bored and exposure to Leslie had shown him what he was missing in a female companion. It was not Dinah's fault she could not compete on a level she could never understand.

"You are blooming, Dinah," Jonathan said, hoping to put off for as long as possible any discussion of Marcus' defection, for he suspected his friend had been ignoring his mistress lately in favor of more stimulating company.

For once Dinah was not concerned with her looks, which were as ripe and provocative as usual. She was wearing a cherry silk gown that showed off her abundant figure, and her blond curls framed a round smooth face from which her blue eyes normally sparkling, looked out on a world suddenly threatening.

"Jonathan, I won't beat about the bush. I know you will tell me the truth. Has Marcus tired of me?" she appealed.

"He rarely discusses you with me, Dinah," Jonathan equivocated.

"But you know all about us. He has had me in his keeping for two years," Dinah said bluntly, not at all embarrassed by stating what she considered a very normal situation. "Of course I never expected marriage, but then Marcus is not a marrying man, and even if he was, I would not be his choice," she concluded without any sign of animosity.

"Most men would envy him. You are a delightful girl," Jonathan complimented her, dreading what he realized she wanted from him, some sign that Marcus had not tired of her, and in all honesty he could not give her that assurance.

"Has he found another mistress? He wrote to me today saying he had a matter he wanted to discuss, sounded most serious and quite decided in his mind," Dinah revealed, sipping distastefully at the chocolate the small cafe had provided.

Jonathan, who was not an accomplished dissembler, hesitated. He did not want to mention Leslie. The two women were poles apart, in character, background, interests and in every other conceivable way, except they were both extremely attractive and appealing in different ways. But Jonathan, who had been completely captivated by Leslie, could see why Dinah, by comparison, had lost Marcus.

"He has not found another mistress, Dinah. I fear he has discovered a woman who would not consent to such an arrangement."

"Too respectable, I bet. She'd be pretty disgusted if she knew about me, I fancy," Dinah said without any signs of rancor.

"Not disgusted, more disappointed. But why should she learn about you?" Jonathan asked, not liking the direction of the conversation.

"Oh, I'm no spoilsport, not the jealous kind, either. I will admit I have another cove in sight myself. I prefer Marcus. But a girl has to look after herself. Can't always have it the way she wants," Dinah agreed accustomed to taking the rough with the smooth in life. "I quite liked Marcus. It's a shame."

"You're a good girl, Dinah, and I hope it all works out to your benefit." Jonathan was vastly relieved at her sensible attitude, although not surprised. He had always thought Dinah looked upon Marcus as a provider rather

han a lover. In her situation what else could she do? She
might be passionate but she was also a realist.

"I don't suppose you'd be interested in taking me on,"
Dinah suggested with a roguish glint in her big blue eyes.

"Sorry, Dinah, I doubt if I could afford you. I do not have
Marcus' income." Jonathan smiled. He could not but ad-
mire her pragmatic views, and her acceptance of what she
could not change. His deeper concern was Leslie, for he
did not believe Marcus intended to offer her marriage.

"Have another cup of chocolate," he suggested, but before she could either agree or disagree, they were interrupted by a tallish chap with merry eyes, and a cheeky
smile.

"Sorry to interrupt, but I recognized this delightful lady
from our recent encounter at *The Times*. Harry Weems is
the name," he offered, not expecting a rebuff. Harry rarely
met rejection, his engaging personality winning even the
crustiest types.

Jonathan obligingly made the introductions and asked
Harry to join them. After a few moments idle conversation
in which he failed to discover much about Harry except that
he was an entertaining chap, not quite out of the top drawer,
perhaps, but witty and well-mannered. Jonathan, experienced in interviewing all kinds of people, found him easy
to talk to and obviously quite intrigued with Dinah. It
seemed he could safely leave her in the fellow's company,
and after a half an hour bid them both good-bye.

Walking back to the paper he wondered just how determined Marcus was to break with Dinah and if the impetus
to do so was his relationship with Leslie. This troubled him
more than a bit, and he completely forgot Dinah's reference to having another protector ready to assume Marcus'
role in her life.

Chapter Fifteen

After leaving Leslie late in the afternoon, Marcus returned to the newspaper and tried to settle the arrears of work he had found so impossible earlier. His meeting with Leslie had strengthened his resolve to end the liaison with Dinah, but he dreaded the coming interview. He was quite convinced that his mistress had outlived her attraction to him, but he knew that telling Dinah of his decision would be painful to them both. Of course he would settle a good sum on her. She deserved no less. When he tried to examine his reasons for ending the affair he realized that exposure to Leslie had shown Dinah for what she was, a lively partner in bed but a woman of limited assets. He had always sensed this but she had satisfied his basic needs and before meeting Leslie he had not seen how tawdry the association with Dinah really was. He had rather carelessly taken her up, having liked her looks and her temperament and until recently had not accepted the shallowness of the relationship. But he did not want Dinah to suffer from his rejection. He was fond of her. He eased his conscience by deciding she would quickly attract a new protector.

Having secured a draft from his banker, he arrived at

Dinah's lodgings about nine o'clock. She received him warily. He realized she had some notion of what he meant to tell her.

"Good evening, Marcus. It's been a lovely June day, hasn't it?" she greeted him, hoping for the best but sure that he had come to tell her that their affair was over.

"Yes, and you are looking in fine fettle," he complimented her. A rather awkward silence followed and he walked to the window turning his back on her. This business was proving more difficult than he had expected. He took a deep breath and plunged into the unhappy subject, thinking there was no point in drawing out the news he must give her.

"You must have noticed, Dinah, that I have not been very attentive lately. I admit I have treated you shabbily, not coming around often, and not informing you that I have other interests."

"Yes, Marcus, I have noticed. I suppose you are thinking of marriage. You are at the age and in a position when men want a respectable settled life, and I am in the way of that. I always expected you would get married some day, only I hoped not quite yet," she answered, trying to behave with some dignity.

Marcus, touched by her efforts to make his task easier, faced her with a weak smile. "I don't know that I am thinking of marriage."

"But you have met a woman who would suit as a wife," Dinah insisted, accepting the inevitable but trying to repress her disappointment. "I know I am not smart enough to keep you. And now you have this big job as editor of *The Times,* you must have a wife who can entertain your literary friends, politicians and all those important nobs."

She sighed remembering when his tastes were not so austere.

"I am very occupied with my position as editor, that's true, but not entirely the whole story," Marcus admitted carefully choosing his words. He did not want to deceive Dinah that he was thinking of marriage, although she was allowing him this acceptable explanation of breaking off their affair.

"You have found some nice respectable girl who is also up to your weight, I vow."

Marcus did not want to discuss Leslie with Dinah. He knew she would not understand his obsession with Leslie. He didn't understand it himself.

"Well, yes. There is a woman I have met in the last few months who shares my interests. But, Dinah, I don't want you to think that you have done anything wrong, anything to annoy me. I am entirely at fault for allowing this situation to go on so long. And I do not want you to lose by your loyalty and devotion to me. I only wish I could explain this to you so you will not think too badly of me." He waited for some recriminations. Somehow her anger would make this disagreeable business easier.

"I don't think badly of you, Marcus. We have had some wonderful times," Dinah said, a bit wistful as she recalled happier days.

"I realize that you depend on me for support, and although I want to end our association I don't want you to be in want. Here is a draft on my bank that should see you safely through the next month or so while you make other arrangements," he explained with specious tact, while proffering the draft.

Too practical not to accept this token of his sympathy and guilt, Dinah looked at it, her eyes widening at the amount, and a satisfied sigh escaping her. "This is very generous, Marcus."

"I could not bear for you to be in need, Dinah. I hope, too, if you need help at any time, you will call on me," Marcus insisted with a sigh of relief. She was taking the whole business much better than he had expected and he wondered idly if she already had an eye on a new protector. Dinah was realistic, aware that her charms would not endure forever, and that she must provide for her future.

"Thank you, Marcus. I will miss you, but I have no complaint. You have always been fair with me." Dinah had her own guilt to deal with and almost blurted out the news of the count's offer.

"Well, there is no purpose in prolonging this. I will take my leave," Marcus said, now eager to get away.

"Of course. But do keep in touch. I will always welcome a visit," Dinah said with an effort to be cheerful. She could not yet accept that this was the end of their two year affair.

"I will, and you too. Thank you for all you have been and done. I have the best of memories," Marcus said and took up his hat in preparation for departure. He only hoped she would not suggest a final supper, unwilling to let him go.

But Dinah was as eager for him to leave as he was himself and made no such suggestion. He walked over to her, took her by the shoulders and looked searchingly into her eyes. Relieved at what he saw there he kissed her warmly on the cheek and walked out of her life.

As the door closed on him Dinah allowed a few tears to trickle down her cheeks, rather enjoying the melodrama of the situation and resolutely turned away from the window.

* * *

Lost in thought Marcus had not noticed the ruffians who surrounded him until it was too late, and he was no match for their brutality. One of them coshed him on the head, and as he fell to the ground the trio picked him up and hustled him into a carriage they had hidden around the corner. The whole wretched kidnapping had only taken a few minutes and no one in the neighborhood noticed the abduction on this slightly-less-than respectable street where householders minded their own business not that of others. In only minutes the shrouded carriage rode off into the deepening night and the street returned to its usual silence.

When Marcus did not arrive at his office the following morning, his clerk was annoyed but not particularly disturbed. He was often indefinite in his movements, although the clerk, Henry Bolt, had expected him as he had an appointment with an official from the War Office that morning. As the hour neared for the interview and there was no sign or message from Marcus, Mr. Bolt, a steady pedestrian type of man with a well developed nose for the proprieties, sent off a lackey to the gentleman in question postponing the interview. No doubt, Mr. Kingsley had been called away on some urgent business he decided, although it was unlike him not to inform Mr. Bolt of such a matter.

As the day wore on, Henry Bolt's uneasiness increased. He knew that Marcus had received threats. Editors always were the focus of malcontents and people who felt ill-used by the newspaper. Perhaps he should mention the matter to someone. He disliked taking responsibility and dithered. But just as he thought he must take action, Jonathan arrived at the door of Marcus' office. The afternoon was well advanced and Jonathan had thought of inviting Marcus for a drink as the paper had now been put to bed.

"He's not here, Mr. Stirling, hasn't been in all day. I can't imagine what has happened. So unlike Mr. Kingsley to be so thoughtless," Mr. Bolt complained, beginning to feel ill-used and eager to lodge his worries on Jonathan's broader shoulders.

"That's odd. He said nothing to me about going out of town," Jonathan frowned. A sudden premonition of trouble surfaced. Could Marcus have lured Leslie into escaping with him for an illicit weekend, for today was Friday and decidedly warm in London? But Jonathan wanted to believe that Leslie would not so easily be seduced. Bolt, here, obviously had suspicions. He must calm them.

"He did say he might be going away for the weekend, now that I remember, but it was too bad of him not to tell you. Don't worry, Bolt. I will discover where Mr. Kingsley is," he said with more confidence than he felt. Still, he must calm Bolt's worries. The man was not only a fusser, but he might gossip. He did not want rumors that Marcus was unreliable to reach the proprietor.

"Thank you, Mr. Stirling. I will leave it all in your hands," Bolt said, pulling on his gloves. He was late for his supper and only too happy to shove his responsibilities onto Jonathan, "Good night, then."

He departed leaving a puzzled Jonathan, who did not quite know what his next move should be. Perhaps he would walk around to Leslie's lodgings and see if she were at home. Despite his effort to throw off his sense of trouble looming, he determined not to act hastily. There must be some reasonable explanation for Marcus' untoward behavior.

Leslie received him with her usual gracious welcome, but not unaware that Jonathan seemed disturbed.

"Good afternoon, Jonathan. How nice to see you."

"Leslie, do you know where Marcus is?" Jonathan blurted out, now somewhat shamefaced that he could have accused Leslie of scandalous cooperation in any scheme of Marcus' to seduce her.

"I imagine he's at the paper, but of course, you would not be searching for him if you hadn't tried *The Times* first," she said, sensing his concern.

"He never turned up all day, so unlike him. Where could he be?" Jonathan asked, not expecting an answer.

"I have no idea. I am not Marcus' keeper," Leslie answered, a bit annoyed at Jonathan's assumption that she was living in Marcus' pocket.

"Don't get your hackles up, Leslie. This could be serious. It's most unlike Marcus to wander off without giving the office his direction, and his clerk tells me he had an important appointment. The poor man had to make up some lame excuse for the dignitary when Marcus failed to appear."

"Do you think he has met with an accident?" Leslie asked, now as worried as Jonathan. She realized that if any danger had befallen Marcus she would be frantic. He could not have been injured. A constable or someone would have notified the paper. After all he was a well-known figure. Then she remembered how long it had taken before she had heard of her father's death. Marcus could be lying in some darkened doorway in pain, victim of some attack. Leslie's normal good sense was swamped by unwarranted fears and anxiety. She made a terrific effort to think rationally.

"Have you tried his lodgings?" she asked Jonathan.

"No, how stupid of me. He lives in the Albany, and has a man. Surely he would have informed us if Marcus had suddenly taken ill? But I will go around there immediately." Jonathan said.

"Should I come with you?" Leslie desperately wanted to take some practical action, but even before Jonathan objected she knew what she was asking was foolish.

"Women are not welcome at the Albany," Jonathan admitted, wanting her support, but realized the unsuitability of her accompanying him.

"Yes, of course, but whatever you discover, please return here right away and let me know. I have grave fears that Marcus has suffered some dreadful fate."

She must care for him more than I thought, Jonathan said to himself, and hurried to calm her fears, although his own had surfaced under her questioning. "I'll be off then, and return as soon as possible," he promised.

Leslie watched him go, feeling helpless and worried almost beyond bearing. She, too, knew that Marcus had received threats, but it was only after Jonathan's departure that she remembered the count. Could that wretched man have committed some horrid maneuver, lured Marcus into a trap. She threw open the door, intent on calling after Jonathan, but he had disappeared. She could hardly restrain herself from rushing down the street after him, but realized the foolishness of some feckless behavior. She must just wait to learn what Jonathan discovered, and if he returned with no news, confess her suspicions to him and decide what to do.

Jonathan had no luck at the Albany. Marcus' man, Roberts, was as puzzled as they all were. He admitted his master had not come home the evening before, but had not worried, as he explained diplomatically that sometimes Marcus visited a lady and remained for the night.

Of course, Dinah. Jonathan reproved himself for not thinking of her. Thanking the man and trying to pass off his inquiry with a casual air, he turned to leave, intent on reaching Dinah. On the street he met Harry Weems, much to his surprise, and a growing suspicion.

"Weems, you are an ubiquitous fellow. Are you looking for Mr. Kingsley?"

Harry grinned, "Good afternoon, or should I say evening, Mr. Stirling. Yes, as a matter of fact, I had some business to discuss with him, but you say he is not available. Too bad. I don't want to postpone this affair."

Jonathan, determined to keep an eye on Weems and discover his business with Marcus, decided to risk it. "I believe he might be with Miss Darcy. I am just on my way there now. Why not come with me and we can both settle our business with Marcus." His voice held a question. Would Weems tell him why he wanted to see Marcus and settle his doubts?

"That's a good idea. But you could probably help me just as well," he confided as they walked along at a brisk pace.

Jonathan, distracted, and looking for a hackney, barely registered what Weems had said, only absently nodding.

"I am trying to find a relative for a client. I don't believe I told you the other day that I am a Bow Street Runner. And I have been employed by the Earl of Rothfield to look for the offspring of a Sir Alan Dansforth."

Jonathan stopped, stunned by this news. The earl was searching for Leslie. What could that mean? And was Weems telling the truth. His story could all be a hum, to allay Jonathan's fears and he could really be planning some villainy. Looking at Weems with a stern mien, Jonathan examined him, trying to read behind that engaging facade.

"I might be able to solve your difficulties, but first I must find Marcus." Just then a hackney appeared and Jonathan hailed it, relieved not to have to make further explanations

until he had considered matters more fully. He was not a
man prone to rash action.

As Harry climbed into the carriage after Jonathan, he
thought, this man is a cagey one. What is so mysterious
about the earl's relative?

"Any lead you give me would be most appreciated. In
the meantime I would be happy to accompany you to call
on Miss Darcy, a delightful girl, I thought when we met
yesterday," he said, eager to disarm Jonathan.

Jonathan did not reply, deep in thought and considering
this new development. Could the earl be seeking Leslie to
acknowledge her? He might have repented at his harsh
treatment of her father, and now the man was dead, had decided Leslie deserved some assistance. On the other hand,
Weems could be spinning him a tale, might even be in the
employ of the count. But in that case he would know all
about Leslie and would not be seeking his help. It was a
dilemma. He wished the man would confide fully in him,
but why should he expect that when he was not yet ready
to return the compliment. If Weems was really a Bow
Street Runner he was a rare type, not like any of that crew
Jonathan had met before. The Runners could be respectable, but many of them were as corrupt as the thieves
they apprehended. He would bide his time before revealing Leslie's name and direction.

In a short time the two men arrived at Dinah's lodgings
and hurried up the steps, Jonathan's concern quite evident
to Harry. There was some odd twist to his affair, Harry
thought with the shrewdness that had served him well in
his profession. Stirling was worried about Marcus Kingsley. Why would that be?

Dinah greeted both men happily. She had been bored,
and she admitted, a bit uneasy. She had heard nothing from

the count, and now began to think that he had won an admission from her that might rebound to Marcus' danger. She would hate to think she had been responsible for any harm coming to her former protector.

"How nice to see you Jonathan, and you, too, Mr. Weems." She greeted them, and indicated they should be seated.

"Dinah, has Marcus been here today?" Jonathan asked, having peered around and seeing no sign of his friend.

"No, he was here last evening, to tell me, as we discussed, Jonathan, that our affair was ended." Dinah had no false pretension about her place in Marcus' life, and if Harry was surprised at her candor he did not show it. He had taken Dinah's mettle when they met and suspected that she was a member of the muslin company. Such an attractive girl, if not of the first stare, would naturally be in some fortunate cove's keeping, he thought. He smiled sympathetically at Dinah, to let her know he was not shocked.

"Well, he seems to have disappeared, and caused no little amount of consternation at the paper," Jonathan said. In his concern he ignored the wisdom of blurting out this news before Harry.

"Had the chap any enemies?" Harry asked. In his experience it was not unusual for well-set up gentlemen to be the target of some villain.

"Oh, no," Dinah wailed. "What have I done?"

In moments they had the whole story of the count from her. If Harry was confused by her somewhat incoherent tale, he made no interruption, nor did he press for further explanations. He realized he had stumbled into a situation he did not understand and until he had more information he would hold his peace. But he wondered if this Marcus fellow could be involved in his own case.

"Well, Dinah, I won't rake you up and down for falling for the count's wicked ploys. You were only trying to protect your future since you sensed your association with Marcus was ended. But you have delivered him into the hands of a real rogue," Jonathan informed her, his stern air causing her to break out in a new flood of tears.

"I wish the man had never come near me," she wailed. Then, "And I will have nothing more to do with him."

"Oh, yes you will. You are our only hope to rescue Marcus," Jonathan reproved her, thoroughly alarmed at what could have befallen his friend.

"Does this have anything to do with my case?" Harry asked, determined to pursue his own interests. But he smiled at Dinah and gave her a pat on the shoulder as if to say, "I don't blame you, my girl, whatever this chap feels."

"Perhaps," said Jonathan. "And I might hire you to find Marcus. You wouldn't turn down the job, would you?"

Harry hesitated. He had enough to worry him with this Dansforth business, but it appeared he must find Marcus Kingsley for the answers to his questions, and Stirling was a factor. He obviously knew more than he was saying about Dansforth, whom Harry had learned from his forays at *The Times,* had once worked for the paper, and probably for Kingsley.

"I will be glad to take it on, as long as it does not conflict with the earl's case," he said after a moment's deliberation.

"Good. We must first determine if anyone saw Marcus after he left here."

"I will take that on," Harry said.

In his turn Jonathan hesitated. He wanted to return to Leslie, but he was not sure he wanted to tell Weems his quest of Sir Alan's offspring had been answered. Leslie might not want to be questioned by Harry.

"Look, Weems, *The Times* will pay a reward for locating Marcus. He's a very important man, I assure you. If he has come to any harm there will be hell to pay."

"So I understand. Well, I had best get on with it, but are you sure you can't or won't tell me what I want to know about the Dansforth business."

"I have to consider that. But here is my address. I will be there later this evening and you can report if you have any news. I might be able to tell you what you want to know then," Jonathan said, feeling he was rapidly getting out of his depth. But he owed his first loyalty to Leslie. He would not put her in the way of danger, if that would result from his confiding in this fellow. He would check out his credentials in the meantime.

Bidding Dinah and Harry a hurried farewell, Jonathan went on his way to face Leslie with what he knew she would regard as bad news.

Chapter Sixteen

Marcus came slowly to his senses, groggy and fuddled from the blow on the head. His eyes flickered and closed again. He realized he had been abducted by some thugs and taken to some hiding place. And he was aware, by gingerly flexing his legs, that he was lying on a straw pallet. The room was dim. As his mind cleared he heard the growling of voices from a shadowed recess where his captors appeared to be arguing and drinking.

"I don't like this caper, Jack. This cove looks a toff. All very well to take the blunt but he could recognize us if he ever gets free and tells a magistrate. I don't reckon to end my days on some conscript ship," Bert Hooker paused in his complaints to take a deep swig of the bottle being companionably passed around the table where Poole and Bert's brother, Bob, sat.

"Don't be so lily-livered, Bert. If you don't like this job you'll have no stomach for the next one, and I could get some better blokes with more fire in their bellies."

"Well, how long do we keep him here?" Bert asked, ignoring the reference to the other blokes.

"Until that foreign gent shows up and tells us what's

next. The man is a deep one. You can bet he has some further ploy."

"No killing. I'll not hang for any man," Bob insisted, not liking the way matters were developing.

"Not this one. But you know what's ahead," Jack warned. He lacked his companions timidity in business where gold was offered. He would kill his mother if the price was right, Bob thought, uneasy at the alliance he and his brother had formed. Events were too complicated and moving too fast for his limited brain to comprehend, but he sensed trouble.

"Now listen here, Bob," Jack Poole began to intimidate his reluctant colleague, not liking the drift of the conversation. He had won his dominance over the brothers through fear and he had no intention of abandoning that weapon. "The foreign gent has been quite generous with his gold and there is more to come. Then you will be on easy street with lots of grog and molls to comfort you. I don't want to hear more jabber from you, get it?"

"Well, if you say it's all right, Jack," Bob backed down, flinching from the ugly glint in his leader's eyes. "But how long do we have to stay here with this cove?"

"Until I say different," Jack said. His own doubts about the wisdom of the course upon which they had set he kept hidden. But the foreign gent had promised to contact them sometime today and he would have some hard words for that jumped-up toff. After all, he had him just where he wanted him. He could blow the gaff if the foreign gent got out of line.

Marcus, who had heard much of this conversation, had his worst suspicions realized. Count von Ronberg had instigated this abduction, leaving Leslie unprotected. Marcus feared that his next move would be against her and he would be powerless to help. He groaned realistically and sat up, his head clearing rapidly under this budget of bad news. Jack Poole looked at him, grinning, and walked over to where Marcus was attempting to rise to his feet.

"Now, cap'n, we don't want no trouble with you. Just rest easy and it will go the better for you," he warned, an expression on his face that brooked no rebellion. Marcus sighed, trying to think what might be the best approach to this brute.

Felix von Ronberg, wanting to check up on his trio of desperadoes, was on the brink of leaving the embassy the afternoon after Marcus' abduction when he received a peremptory summons to Prince Esterhazy's office.

Feeling it behooved him to play his cards carefully, he appeared at the prince's door, but prepared to adopt an air of annoyance at the curtness of the summons.

"Good afternoon, Esterhazy. I understand you wished to see me. Is there some urgency? I have an appointment." the count asked on entering the sanctum, assuming his haughtiest air.

"Yes, there is some urgency. I have just received a dispatch from Metternich, who intends to come here within the week. It seems he has some business to discuss with you, for he asked that I insure you will be on hand when he arrives." The prince's tone was equally haughty for he was beginning to think that von Ronberg's business in London would cause him trouble. He had learned from one of his vast army of spies that the count was seen coming from the direction of the docks, an insalubrious venue for an Austrian aristocrat. Whatever his errand there it could not have been a respectable one. When Metternich arrived he would have some strong words to say about Esterhazy's unwanted guest.

"I will, of course, be available to confer with the prince." If von Ronberg was aware of Esterhazy's hostility he showed no signs of it.

"See that you are. I find your comings and goings quite mysterious, count, and only hope you are not involving this embassy in any mischief."

"How can you think such a thing, Esterhazy? I lead an irreproachable life," the count assured him, meanwhile hiding his worry that Esterhazy may have had him followed and discovered his meetings with Poole.

"I can think it easily. And if I find out that you have brought the wrong sort of attention to the embassy, I shall have no hesitation in asking Metternich to recall you," Esterhazy said in his coolest tones. He was not deceived by von Ronberg's bland protestations. He wanted the man out of London. "That's all, I think," he dismissed his visitor with a quelling air that did not entertain any further argument.

Von Ronberg, furious at being treated like a lackey, was about to voice his own displeasure, but wisdom prevailed, and giving his host a curt nod, he left, slamming the door behind him.

Esterhazy, dissatisfied with the interview, decided that the count bore careful watching and he would put that matter in train immediately. His own opinion of Metternich was that the man was not above any deviltry if it suited him but the prince had the ear and the gratitude of the emperor, and would call on his support if he needed it. Having settled the matter for the moment he turned to other more soothing diplomatic business, but the count would not be forgotten.

After leaving Dinah's, Jonathan had hurried around to Leslie's unhappy at having to give her the results of his fruitless search. He did not mention his call on Dinah, feeling the least he could do was to spare her the knowledge of Marcus' failings in that relationship. He was now convinced that Leslie cared for Marcus, even if she had not admitted it to herself. Jonathan hid his own disappointment. His fear for his friend overcame any jealousy he might have felt. A man whose loyalties were firm and his friendship deep, Jonathan could not rejoice in Marcus' downfall. If he was in trouble and it appeared he was, his instinct was to help in any way he could.

Almost as an afterthought he told her about Harry Weems' search on behalf of the Earl of Rothfield. "Leslie, there is one more troubling matter. A Bow Street Runner has been hired by the Earl of Rothfield to find Sir Alan's child. Weems has approached me for the information since he could not find Marcus whom he first wanted to interview. I will see him later this evening. What should I tell him?"

"My name and direction, of course. I cannot imagine why the earl wants to locate me, but I see no reason to make a mystery of it. I would like to be reconciled to my only relative," she said in a sober tone. Somehow the news that the earl wanted to find her was comforting.

"All right, I will send Weems around. He seems a decent type, a cut above most of these Runners and an amiable chap," Jonathan agreed, wondering what this new development would mean to Leslie's future. He left her with a few comforting words, although he feared they meant little.

That evening, twenty four hours after Marcus' abduction, Harry Weems reported to Jonathan where he was eagerly awaited.

"Any news?" Jonathan asked impatiently almost before Harry had removed his hat and settled into a chair by Jonathan's desk.

"Not too good, I'm afraid. An elderly woman was looking out of her window and noticed a carriage waiting for some time in the street around from Miss Darcy's place. Unfortunately she turned away to eat her supper before seeing the actual abduction, if that was what it was."

"Oh, God. It's what I was afraid of. But who could be behind such a heinous plot?" Jonathan said, although he thought he knew whom to blame.

"I think you have some idea of the instigator," Harry replied. "If you want me to work effectively you will have to take me into your confidence."

"Yes, I know. But first I will tell you what the Earl of Rothfield wants to know. I contracted Miss Dansforth, Sir Alan's daughter, and she has no objection to the earl learning of her direction. She's a fine woman, who has had a difficult time and I would not want her harassed."

"The chance to become the heiress of the Earl of Rothfield is not one any right thinking female would turn down. And the earl is a duck, a genuinely nice old man. She won't come to any harm through him, or me, for that matter." Harry was relieved to have his job so easily solved but he sensed that there was more to the story than he had learned so far. And so it proved to be. After giving Leslie's direction to Harry, Jonathan went on to tell him of the threat posed by the count, whom he suspected of engineering Marcus' abduction in revenge for Marcus' interference in his odious plan to seduce Leslie.

Harry, who had heard some brutal and sordid tales in his

career, was neither shocked nor surprised. He could see that Jonathan was both and surmised that the young man had rather tender feelings for Miss Dansforth. The only information Jonathan did not divulge was Leslie's authorship of the Pythius column. He owed both Leslie and Marcus that reticence. But on the whole he liked and trusted Harry and was grateful for an ally in this nasty business.

"It's quite late or I would call on Miss Dansforth this evening," Harry suggested.

"No, tomorrow might be best, and in the meantime you can contact the earl. I want your full energies devoted to this business of Marcus' abduction," Jonathan agreed, and the men parted with mutual expression of a hopeful outcome.

Harry, walking slowly away from Jonathan's lodgings in Milford Place, had a naggling pricking in his shoulders. This was a sign of trouble, he knew from long experience. He may have made a mistake in delaying his interview with Miss Dansforth. Perhaps, he would just amble by her lodgings and view the lay of the land. If he saw a light, he might call upon the lady.

While Harry and Jonathan were scurrying about trying to discover some clue to Marcus' whereabouts, the count had arrived at the grubby rooms where Poole and his confederates were keeping Marcus. Not wanting Marcus to learn the identity of the man responsible for his predicament until he had achieved his revenge, a particularly diabolical one, the count sent a boy to summon Poole to his hackney in the street.

"I have a further job for you this evening, Poole. I take

it all went well with the abduction of Kingsley," the count ordered when Poole had joined him.

"Of course, sir. I usually does what I plans to do," Poole said, his swaggering air and tone implying that he could accomplish any villainy he wanted. Not impressed with the count's haughty disdain, he only cared about the depth of his employer's pockets, and he would not take on another piece of skullduggery without seeing the color of the count's money.

"I want you and your men to kidnap a young woman," the count said as if this outrageous suggestion was nothing unusual.

"Suppose we can manage that, but not without I see some blunt," Poole insisted. He had no interest at all in the fate the count planned for the woman, but he leered unpleasantly as if he had no doubts of what was in store for the victim.

"Here are some guineas for the Kingsley affair, and a bit in advance for the woman," the count said unwilling to argue. He was ready to pay any amount to achieve his ends.

"When do we do the job?" Poole asked.

"This evening. Here is her direction, near the Strand, and a note you must give her that will lure her into coming without any struggle. If she is suspicious or raises a fuss, you know how to handle that, but I do not want her harmed."

"I'll take Bert with me. Between us we should be able to handle any mort," Poole leered.

"And will Bob be able to handle Kingsley?" the count asked. Part of his revenge was to confront Marcus with the abducted Leslie, showing him that she was in his power.

"Bob is a right old cully. He'll take care of him right and

tight, sir, have no fear of that. If that's all we'll be off on this next caper, then," Poole assured the count with his usual braggadocio.

"See to it, then, man. I will return later tonight to see that all is in train."

The count, his odious business dispatched and the money passed to Poole, dismissed the man as he would any lackey, an attitude Poole for the moment accepted. He did not intend to put up with this foreigner's airs indefinitely. Poole would let him know who was in charge and see that he paid through the nose for his nasty japes.

On arriving back in the rooms where the infamous trio were keeping Marcus, Poole summoned his allies to a hurried conference, conducted out of Marcus' hearing. All he grasped was Poole's final admonition to Bob Hooker.

"Keep him close, Bob, or it will go hardly with you," Poole warned. "You come with me, Bert."

He laid a heavy pistol on a nearby table, and checked an equally vicious weapon that he thrust under his coat. Bob nodded in agreement, but Poole would not have departed with him on his errand with such aplomb if he had realized that Bob Hooker was not so under his thumb as he supposed. Bob was too wary of Poole's temper to dispute his orders, but this whole affair was beginning to trouble him, abducting a toff and now a female without so much as a by-your-leave. Foreigners might behave so in their own primitive lands but Englishmen braved the displeasure of the law more reluctantly. Punishment was severe and Bob had no liking for the direction of affairs.

Marcus, left alone with only one captor, and feeling a bit more the thing, quickly realized that this was his best chance to escape from the rogues who had taken him. At three to one the odds were against him but with only the more malleable Bob to deal with, he might have some opportunity of eluding the man, or threatening him with the probable outcome of his participation in this kidnapping. He waited a significant time for Bob to become uneasy and then launched into his campaign.

Meanwhile Poole and Bert approached Leslie's lodgings skulking carefully about the neighborhood and testing the lie of the land. Realizing that they would have to make a respectable approach to the door of Leslie's lodgings, not arousing the suspicions of the landlord, they conferred over the best plan.

Poole, who could when he wished, assume the role of a retired sergeant, ordered Bert to wait with the horse and carriage until he emerged with the woman. If she gave any sign of trouble, Poole had no doubt he could easily deal with it.

"Keep a sharp eye out for any Charlies," he directed his henchman. Poole viewed them with scorn, but it would be best to avoid any suspicious interest in their business.

Poole saluted sharply when Mrs. Gorey opened the door and gave every appearance of respectability and disapproval.

"Good evening, ma'am," he said in his most obliging tone.

"What do you want, my man. This is no respectable hour to come calling whatever your business," Mrs. Gorey said.

"I have a message to deliver to one of your lodgers, ma'am," Poole said trying to ingratiate himself with this old biddy. He did not want to give her any cause to suspect him of any but the most creditable errand.

"Well, give it to me. I will see that she gets it," Mrs.

Gorey stood her ground, preventing Poole from gaining entrance to her house.

"I was instructed to hand it to the lady herself," Poole insisted adopting a conciliatory manner.

"It must be important," Mrs. Gorey insisted, still not willing to allow the man inside.

"Yes, it is, and quite urgent," Poole said.

"I will just see if she has not retired," Mrs. Gorey allowed grudgingly. "You wait here."

Poole hesitated, watching Mrs. Gorey ascend the stairs. This was proving to be more dodgy than he had expected. He could follow the old woman up the stairs, ignore her objections, and force admittance into Leslie's rooms, but he abandoned that violent course. Much better to see if he could bring off a less suspicious contact with the lady. It was just as well that he waited, for within a few minutes Mrs. Gorey was back, nodding acquiescence to his seeing Miss Dansforth.

While these negotiations were going forward, Bert Hooker was tramping impatiently beside his horse and carriage. He didn't like this havey cavey affair one bit, and thought Poole was taking a good time to get the business done. He looked around nervously, but the dark street held no sign of any observers. Most householders were either abed or minding their own affairs. A few revelers had passed by earlier but they were too intent on their own drink-induced progress to notice him. He patted the restive horse.

Leslie, apprehensive as to Marcus's fate, and not thinking as clearly as she might under other circumstances, let Poole into her rooms and read with some puzzlement a note purporting to come from Marcus requesting that she accompany the messenger immediately.

"What is all this mystery?" Leslie asked Poole.

"I don't know, ma'am. I was only directed to deliver this message," Poole said with an air of stolid unconcern.

Leslie, knowing she must not fail Marcus, whatever the difficulty, decided she must go with this man, who was probably some employee of the paper, and perfectly respectable. She was behaving like a missish grudgeon. Even if there was some danger she would never forgive herself if some action of hers brought further trouble to Marcus.

"All right. Just a moment while I get a shawl and bonnet," she instructed Poole.

Much as he would have liked to snatch her then and there, some remnant of caution urged Poole to wait patiently while she doused her candles, and dressed to leave. He followed her politely down the stairs, hoping that the old biddy would not interrupt with embarrassing questions, but there was no sign of Mrs. Gorey.

Once outside the house, Poole took Leslie's arm in a firm grip and growled with menace. "Now, just come along and don't give any trouble or it will be the worse for you."

He should have kept up his act a bit longer. Before he could drag Leslie around the corner to the waiting carriage and Bert Hooker, a tall man loomed out of the darkness and accosted them.

"Are you Miss Dansforth?" Harry Weems asked Leslie, noting that she was trying to evade the firm grasp of the man holding her.

"Yes, yes, I am. And who are you?" Leslie blurted out, relieved to have some interruption to the journey she now suspected was some sort of ruse.

"Harry Weems, Bow Street Runner, at your service, ma'am," he answered paying no attention to Poole, who did not know exactly how to handle this unforeseen encounter. The words 'Bow Street Runner' impressed him, although he would be loath to admit his healthy respect for these minions of the law.

"Is this man annoying you, Miss Dansforth?" Harry asked quite sure that Poole was trying to abduct Leslie, and not liking the man's threatening stance. He had tackled hard cases before, and despite his somewhat willowy appearance could give a good account of himself in a fight. He hoped it would not come to that.

"Yes, he is." With a violent wrench, Leslie removed herself from Poole's grip, and hurried to Harry's side.

"Well, we can't have that. Best be on your way, my fellow, before you give me cause to hail you up before a magistrate," Harry said, his tone even, but there was a calm assurance in his voice that rather befuddled Poole. Not a great thinker at the best of times, and accustomed to solving his problems with brute force, he stepped forward, as if to attack Harry.

The wily Harry, unwilling to engage in fisticuffs if it could be avoided, did not flinch but calmly drew a whistle from his pocket and blew it. This action startled Poole who swore roundly and backed off, expecting reinforcements.

"You bloody body snatcher. You won't get your hands on me," Poole bragged while backing away and shouting for Bert Hooker.

Leslie, seeing that her rescuer might be in trouble, let out a series of piercing screams, surprising both Poole and Harry with the shrillness of her cries. Almost immediately the door of her lodgings opened and Mrs. Gorey, supported by a large beefy man, peered out to see what the disturbance was. Seeing Leslie, Mrs. Gorey gawked and cried out, "Oh, my dear, what ails you? Are you all right?"

"I am now, Mrs. Gorey," Leslie assured her, rather ashamed of her vulgar screaming. Poole, seeing that he could no longer spirit Leslie away with impunity, began to slink away into the darkness, but Leslie would not have that. "Don't let him get away. That brute is a villain and a kidnapper," she cried, and before Poole could disappear, Mrs. Gorey's escort and Harry had him secured. Like most bullies, when he recognized superior strength, Poole backed down.

"Let me off, you coves. I meant no trouble. The woman mistook me," he pleaded, wishing Bert Hooker would come to his aid, but that canny man, peeking around the corner and seeing the plight of his leader, made no effort to help him. Deciding his best hope was to slip away, abandoning Poole, the horse and carriage, and running as quickly as possible back to his brother.

"I am a Bow Street Runner and wish to apprehend this man for a series of crimes," Harry informed Leslie, Mrs. Gorey and Jim Lowdnes, who turned out to be Mrs. Gorey's gentleman friend, the neighborhood butcher, a man of strong physique and handy with his fives.

"Looks a right villain to me. Take him around to the station, will you. I best come along. He looks a mean cove and could give you trouble," Mr. Lowdnes insisted, happy to participate in this stirring drama.

"You take the lady inside and give her a nip of brandy, eh, love," he ordered Mrs. Gorey, who had stood by watching fascinated, but unable to believe her eyes and ears. That Miss Dansforth would be involved in a street brawl, even if it was not her fault, shocked her. And that a Bow Street Runner should be loitering around her premises as well as this deceiving rogue who had turned out to be criminal was more than she could handle. But she knew her duty.

"You come along with me, Miss Dansforth, and let Mr. Lowdnes and the Runner do their duty. Imagine this all happening in our quiet street," she clucked.

Leslie, having given Harry a heartfelt thank you and a promise of an interview, gratefully allowed Mrs. Gorey to shepherd her into the house. By now the noise, and Leslie's screams, had attracted interested residents, who threw open their windows to look upon the scene.

"I will be back to see you, Miss Dansforth," Harry promised. "And in the meantime take care. Someone wishes you ill fortune."

And with Mr. Lowdnes firmly assisting him, he marched the cursing Poole off into the darkness. The street returned to its usual late night calm, and Leslie and Mrs. Gorey repaired to Leslie's sitting room to recover from the danger and excitement.

Chapter Seventeen

Marcus sat on the edge of his pallet and watched Bob Hooker lolling at the table, drinking deeply from a mug that Marcus concluded must be filled with rum or gin. He could have used a tot himself, although his head had cleared from the results of the blow that had rendered him unconscious. He was convinced that Bob's brother, Bert, and the brutal and commanding Poole had left to kidnap Leslie and deliver her into the hands of the count. Her fate if the two rogues were successful did not bear thinking about. He had to get out of this prison and rescue her. But near Bob's hand lay the pistol that Poole had left for his jailer.

"Could I have a drink of whatever it is you are enjoying, Bob?" Marcus said in his most cajoling voice.

"Why not? You might as well have some. You're not going nowhere," Bob agreed. He swayed over to Marcus and offered a grubby mug filled with the brew.

Marcus thanked him with a grin, signifying he held no grudge and drank deeply. To his surprise it was quite a good rum, not the ruinous gin he had expected. Having made the first overtures he continued in a mild tone, hop-

ing to disarm the increasingly befuddled Bob with friendly
chat, showing no anger for what had befallen him.

"How did you get into such scurvy work, Bob?" he
asked.

"Better than starving," growled Bob, whose limited
brain was becoming clouded by the liquor. He missed the
reassuring presence of his brother and found the waiting
for his next orders tedious. Might as well talk to this cove.
It couldn't cause any harm, and Bob suspected the poor sod
would never live to name him to the constables even if by
some mischance he should escape.

"But wouldn't you like some respectable work? You
look a brave strong chap. I can offer you a much healthier
line of employment," Marcus cajoled.

"Doing what? Carrying out pots in some gent's house,
or digging some rocky land in the country. I didn't come
to London for that," Bob complained. He had grown up on
a tenant farm in Wiltshire, descended from a long line of
farm laborers and had joined the army with his brother to
find military life even more back-breaking and himself at
the mercy of hard commanders. Bob was lazy and had discovered crime demanded only an occasional use of brute
strength, a relief from the grinding routine of the army. He
was by nature a follower and content to obey his brother
and the domineering and far cleverer Jack Poole whose vicious habits both impressed and cowed him.

"Not at all. Working as a loader for my newspaper. Respectable job with a good screw," Marcus insisted. "And
far safer than abducting harmless editors," he added with
a whimsical smile.

"Couldn't leave my brother. And Jack Poole would settle me good," Bob complained.

"Yes, and Jack Poole will probably lead you to jail if not

worse. What's he up to tonight? Another snatch. Eventually he will be taken and he won't worry too much about what happens to you, probably rat on you and your brother if he thinks it will help him."

Bob had little doubt that Poole would abandon him if it suited his purposes. He wondered how he and Bert had been lured into Poole's criminal circle. Indolence and greed were the main factors, but he did not see that, content to obey his brother, and inspired by a certain awe of Poole.

"Poole's all right," he muttered uneasily. Where were Poole and his brother? They should have returned before now. Bob had no idea of time as the rum befuddled him.

"He's a dangerous rogue and cares nothing about you. He has probably been taken up the Charlies by now and left you to get out of this mess as best you can."

"He'd never do that. Bert would see to it." But Bob was beginning to worry, and Marcus sensed his disquiet.

"Do you really think Bert could do that?"

"Sure. Bert's a good 'un," Bob protested.

"They have been gone quite a spell. Must have run into trouble," Marcus offered, seeing that Bob was weakening. "Do you know who I am?"

"Naw. Just some poor bloke who Poole was ordered to bash and carry away," Bob informed him, taking another deep drink.

"I am the editor of *The Times,* the newspaper, and there is probably already a great hue and cry over my disappearance," Marcus said cheerfully, as if he expected to be rescued at any minute.

"I just knows you're a nob who has gotten himself up the backside of this foreign gent. He wants you put out of the way," Bob answered as if this were a sensible method of disposing of one's enemies.

"Quite so, and who will be in the soup if he fails. You and your brother."

Bob appeared to be thinking about this unhappy outcome to their work, but still was not persuaded. Marcus groaned for he heard a door slam and the heavy tread of feet on the steps leading up to his prison. Bert Hooker burst into the room and ignoring Marcus, said tersely to his brother.

"We're in trouble, Bob. The Runners have Jack. He muffed the whole business."

"Ah, Gawd. What happens now?" Bob moaned.

"We get out of here. Old Molly will put us up. Jack doesn't know about her. We'd be safe there for a while till we can get out of town."

"But what about this toff? He'd recognize us, wouldn't he?"

"Let's dump him in the river. He can't talk if he's a goner," Bert insisted with some truth.

"And if we're discovered it's the transport ships for us." Bob appeared to have some idea of what lay in wait for them. "He's some big cove at a newspaper and there will be a real hue and cry."

"Let him go then. He'll never find us." Bert was still shaken by the sight of the indomitable Poole being dragged away to the magistrates. He never thought the authorities would get Poole and his faith in his leader had been badly damaged.

"All right." Bob agreed. Bert turned to Marcus and ordered. "You can go, but you'd better hurry. The foreign gent will be here before long."

"I think we had all better go, then," Marcus said, hiding his impatience. Obviously Leslie was safe and Poole in custody but the count was still a man to be reckoned with.

Bob and Bert ignored him and rushed to the door, clattering down the steps without another word, and Marcus was not slow to follow them. By the time he emerged they were fast disappearing down the street, and Marcus turned away in the opposite direction. Not a moment too soon. As he rounded the corner, a carriage pulled up near the house in which he had been imprisoned. The count had arrived to enjoy his revenge.

Marcus, confused as to his location, tried to get his bearings. Like most newspaper men he had a sound knowledge of London, including the more insalubrious districts. After wandering down a few dark and nasty streets, alive with foot pads and prostitutes, he came out on a broader thoroughfare, Whitechapel Road, and with some strenuous walking soon reached Fleet Street where he secured a hackney to take him to the Albany. The Hookers had rifled his pockets but he was able to persuade the cabby to wait while he sent the porter to pay his fare. His man, waiting in some anxiety for his arrival hailed him with protestations of concern and was sent off immediately to secure a hot bath.

Marcus was eager to contact Leslie but it was now after eleven o'clock and he realized he could not raise Mrs. Gorey's household at this unseemly hour. After a bath and a hurried meal he sat down to consider his next move. Somehow the count must be punished for his temerity in Marcus' kidnapping, and his attempt on Leslie. If the Bow Street Runners had Poole in custody, she, at least, was safe for the moment. He doubted that the count would try to accost her in her lodgings although he might attempt another kidnapping if she went out. But the man must pay for his effrontery. His diplomat's status might protect him, and Marcus knew he had powerful friends. Would Esterhazy shield him from any reprisal? Probably, even if he disliked the man. It would only endanger Esterhazy's own status with the Foreign Office.

It seemed to Marcus that the only alternative was to challenge the count to a duel. Marcus was no coward but he realized that by taking such a step he would be exposing himself not only to danger but to scandal. His proprietor, John Walter, would exceedingly dislike his becoming involved in such an affair. He could lose his position and his income. Not that that was as dire a fate as it might be as he had sufficient funds to live comfortably without his salary and perquisites from *The Times*. But he would hate to give up the editor's chair and all the influence that brought him. But did he have any choice?

The count must be muffled. Who knew what other skullduggery he would be up to and as long as the man operated in London Leslie would be at risk. The count had determined somehow to get his hands on Leslie, and Marcus could not allow that. He realized with a shock that she meant more to him than his prestige as editor of *The Times*. Had he been fairly caught at last in the toils of love, and by a girl who probably felt no more for him than a tepid gratitude for her employment? Well, he would persuade her differently once he had dealt with the count.

Having made his decision Marcus settled into an uneasy sleep, his dreams disturbed by pictures of Leslie struggling in the count's embrace, and being forced into his bed. Ghastly visions of her terror and disgust haunted him, and he awoke early, sweating and confused. His mind went back to his own imprisonment and his anger rose. He could not delay. Calling for his man, he breakfasted hastily and dressed, determined to discover what had happened while had been immured in that slum, and to bring the count to account for his crimes.

Leslie's night had been equally disturbed, worried about Marcus, and exhausted from her near brush with abduction by the odious Jack Poole, she had finally fallen into a deep sleep, aided by the surreptitious tot of brandy Mrs. Gorey had put in her cup of chocolate. Upon awakening Leslie remembered the occurrences of the preceding day and night with a shudder. And then, resolute and practical as she was normally, she rose and dressed, ate quite a good breakfast presided over by Mrs. Gorey, who told her she must eat to keep up her strength and that she needed nourishment after her brush with disaster.

However, alone after her landlady's departure, and her promise to that good guardian not to think of venturing out, she castigated herself for her foolishness. After all she had been warned. She had thoughtlessly dismissed Jonathan and Marcus' warnings about the count. It had been a clever ploy to work on her concern for Marcus with that note. She had gone with that villain so meekly, eager to respond to any plea from Marcus. How credulous she had been—and then not to learn anything about Marcus' whereabouts. Where was he and was he safe? By now he could have suffered some horrible fate, murdered even, by that man Poole, or even by the count himself, whom she realized was capable of any infamy. But how had that Bow Street Runner appeared so fortuitously? Had he been watching her? So many questions and so few answers.

Some of her questions were soon answered when Marcus, himself, arrived to assure her of his safety and tell her what had happened to him during the last thirty six hours.

Mrs. Gorey had shepherded him up, all agog, but her curiosity was not to be satisfied by Marcus, who only said calmly that he had suffered a misadventure but had come about as she could see.

"All very well, sir, but you worried Miss Dansforth to death, and I am sure that scurvy fellow that turned up here last night with some gammon tale was involved."

"So he was, Mrs. Gorey, and I am sure Miss Dansforth will reveal all soon. But now, be a good woman, and let me see her," Marcus insisted, relieved that Leslie's welfare was so important to Mrs. Gorey but not prepared to waste any more time placating her.

"Humpf," Mrs. Gorey snorted, but some quality in Marcus warned her to keep her tongue still and she rapped on Leslie's door and announced, "Here is a caller you will want to see, Miss."

Leslie's surprise and relief when she opened the door, having expected Jonathan, was more than revealing, and Marcus gave a huge sigh. She did care a bit about him, he was convinced and much heartened by it.

"Oh, Marcus," Leslie cried, and disgraced herself by bursting into tears and falling into his arms.

He held her closely, trying to comfort her, and then tried to restore her by saying with smug satisfaction. "I had no idea you would be so worried about me."

Recognizing that she had been within a whisker of revealing just how much she had been worried, and hearing the satisfaction in his voice she composed herself and felt a rising anger.

"Of course we were worried, Jonathan, your office and your friends and employees. What happened to you?" she asked determined to learn the whole story.

Marcus told her about his kidnapping, a heavily edited

version. He was not about to confess he was leaving his mistress's flat when the crime occurred. But Leslie was astute enough to sense he was holding back some vital information. Still, if he did not want her to know what business had sent him to that part of town she would not be so rude as to press him.

"And you are convinced the count was behind the whole affair, your kidnapping and my attempted abduction by this villain Poole?" she concluded having heard Marcus' adventure.

"Who else could the foreign gent be? Although I might have some enemies, due to my position, I doubt that any of them would go so far. And then there is your role in this. I am certain the count intended to ravish you, and then have his revenge by telling me in detail before dispatching me into the Thames or some other nasty place," he said, trying to make light of it. He did not refer to what he feared might have become of Leslie after the count had his way with her. But she was not so squeamish.

"If he didn't intend a like fate for me, he probably had some other, equally distasteful career in mind," she said quite calmly.

Marcus, eager to fend off any questions about what his next move would be, asked her about the Bow Street Runner.

"Could the man have been hired by the count to spy on you, do you suppose?"

"I doubt it. If that were the case he would not have interfered. Jonathan said a Bow Street Runner had been hired by the Earl of Rothfield to locate me. He just happened to be on hand when Poole took me from the house."

"You can't be sure. Whatever am I to do with you, Leslie? You won't take even the most elemental precautions to assure your own safety. I can't stand guard over you all day," Marcus protested.

They were wrangling amicably about the matter when Jonathan arrived some moments later. Mrs. Gorey had told him of Marcus' appearance, and he was fulsome in his relief at finding his friend safe, but full of questions. Only after he had satisfied himself as to the happy outcome of both Marcus' and Leslie's adventures did he turn to the matter of Harry Weems.

"The man approached me because he couldn't find Marcus. The Earl of Rothfield regrets how he treated your father and wants to make some recompense. As well he should."

"I don't see why. He owes me nothing, but if, as you say, he is a worried old man, trying to make peace, I would be the veriest jade to refuse him," Leslie decided. "I suppose this Mr. Weems will contact me, or the earl, once he has sorted out last night's business. I want to thank Mr. Weems for his role. He arrived most providentially."

"He certainly did. I had given him your direction, but suggested it was too late for a call. He must have just wanted to spy out the land, so to speak, and seen that you were being coerced by that brute Poole," Jonathan explained.

"What will happen to Poole?" Leslie asked.

"Well, for one thing, I will call around at Bow Street and lodge a complaint. Not mentioning the count, I think. Suggest that Poole abducted me for ransom. The paper might be expected to take some interest in my life, I suppose." Marcus had decided he would not mention any of his plans to revenge himself on the count, and to remove him from Leslie's orbit once and for all.

"Why not accuse the count? Poole will tell the magistrate he had been hired to abduct you," Leslie protested.

"Somehow I don't think he will," Marcus replied, feeling that Poole would not be believed even if he betrayed the count.

"Will he get a severe sentence?"

"Not more than he deserves. But he served with Wellington on the Peninsula. That might mitigate his crime somewhat."

Leslie wanted to ask Marcus what he was doing on New Albany Street where he was abducted and how the count and his minions knew where to find him, but she was reluctant to quiz Marcus. After all his actions were none of her business, but there was a mystery there. His reticence on this matter not only puzzled her but made her feel that he did not trust her enough to confide in her. There had always been some barrier in her relations with Marcus and she never suspected that it might be his unease about confessing to the relationship with Dinah Darcy.

"If you promise not to engage in any detective work of your own and go wandering off unescorted, at the mercy of who knows what villainy of the count's, I will be off to the magistrates," Marcus said, wanting to tell her of his concern but hesitant, the result of his liaison with Dinah. If he intended to improve his standing with Leslie, to bring her to care for him, he would have to tell her eventually, but now did not seem the appropriate time. In that decision he was woefully wrong, but he could not realize what trouble it would cause.

"I have no intention of going out. I think that Bow Street Runner, Mr. Weems, means to call on me and tell me about the Earl of Rothfield who hired him to find me," Leslie confided sensing that Marcus was not being forthright with her, but unable to understand why that should be.

"Take care and try to avoid trouble," Marcus warned,

looking at her with a gaze she found enigmatic, and then before she could voice her disquiet, he took her in his arms, and kissed her, ignoring Jonathan, who reddened and turned his back. Marcus' calm assumption of possessiveness toward Leslie both disturbed and embarrassed him, and he would like to question his friend about his intentions but sensed now was not the time.

"I will see you at the paper, Marcus," he muttered, and then wishing Leslie a hurried farewell and promise of a future meeting, took his leave.

Leslie, torn between amusement and anger at Marcus' actions barely heeded Jonathan's departure. "There is a great deal more I have to say to you, to ask you, but later," Marcus said, anticipating her questions. "I will catch up Jonathan." And without any more ado fled, leaving Leslie prey to a host of emotions, not the least of which was wonder.

Did that last proprietal embrace mean he had come to feel more than just a friendly affection for her? Had his recent brush with danger caused him to think about the transitory pleasure of his present existence and yearn for some lasting commitment? Was she foolish to believe they might come together in a truly meaningful relationship? Would Marcus ask her to marry him? And if he did what would her answer be?

She remembered how she had felt when she had heard of his disappearance? Did she love him enough to become his wife? Rebuking herself for these idle fancies she turned to her desk. Whatever happened she still had her work, ignored too long. Conscientious and disciplined Leslie soon lost herself in compiling her column, relegating Marcus and her own feelings to the back of her mind. But they were neither of them forgotten.

Chapter Eighteen

Harry Weems had had a busy morning. He had been required by the magistrates to testify as to Poole's attempted abduction of Leslie and his role in her rescue. He was not surprised, having a long and cynical experience of criminals, that Poole denied any such intent and was demanding to be released because of lack of evidence. He insisted he had been merely a messenger, conveying the lady to a Mr. Kingsley, who had requested her presence. Weems vigorously refuted this statement but he could see that the magistrate was dubious. Before the depositions could be completed Marcus arrived and told his own story. If the magistrate, a Mr. Ransom, had been unwilling to accept either Poole's or Harry's version of events, he was more impressed with Marcus. Here was the editor of London's most influential newspaper, an educated prominent man, and a gentleman. Marcus was quite deliberate in describing his abduction by Poole and the villain's proposal to also kidnap Leslie.

"Naturally, Mr. Ransom, it would be distasteful for Miss Dansforth to appear in this court, but if necessary she will testify, I am sure."

Ransom, a grey haired man with a benign appearance but a strong belief in justice and the power of the law, thought for a moment.

"Perhaps, sir, we would admit a written account from the lady, and in any case we have your own testimony that you were going about your lawful business and wrested away by some rogues, incarcerated against your will, and feared for your life at the hands of this villainous trio," Ransom concluded looking down his long nose at Poole with reproof. "And what do you have to say to that, my man?"

"It's all a hum. Just a joke. I was hired by a friend of this toff here to do it. Meant no harm," Poole insisted with an assurance he did not feel. He was wondering if it was to his advantage to mention the count. If he betrayed his master now then he would not be paid, and there was the big job still to do, with a lot of gold promised. It was a dilemma Poole could not solve. After brooding silently for a few moments, he decided that it would serve his interests best to keep any mention of the count to himself.

"And who was this jackanapes that hired you to abduct an upright citizen?" Mr. Ransom asked.

"I don't think I can tell you that. My honor is involved," Poole said in a righteous tone.

"Your honor? I don't think I have much faith in that. You will be remanded for a fortnight while we undertake further investigation," Mr. Ransom concluded, rapping his gavel, and Poole was dragged away by the jailers, muttering obscenities.

After a few words with Harry Weems, Marcus thanked the magistrate and made his way to Printing House Square, where he knew he would be subjected to a round of questions by his staff and by Jonathan. It was the latter he would have difficulty in satisfying, he suspected. Jonathan would quiz him about his feeling for Leslie, and what he meant to do about her. Marcus dreaded depressing his friend's own hopes, but he would be honest with Jonathan about his determination to make Leslie his wife. Jonathan seemed to have appointed himself some sort of guardian for her and would not be fobbed off with a lot of vague suppositions. Well, best to get it over with, Marcus decided and walked briskly to *The Times*.

Weems, in his turn, had a deal of business to conduct. He was in two minds. Should he call on the earl and inform him of the successful end to his search for Miss Dansforth, or visit the lady herself and see how she felt about the matter. Mindful of his fee and his loyalty to his employer he decided to see the earl first. And in the back of his mind he had some notion that he might, later that day, renew his acquaintance with Dinah Darcy, all in all a busy time ahead of him, he thought, and walked jauntily away from the magistrate's court as the next case was called.

The Earl of Rothfield received Harry with some anticipation. And his hopes were quickly satisfied.

"You have located Sir Alan's child, Mr. Weems?" he asked, almost before Harry could settle into the chair before the desk in the Earl's paneled library.

"Yes, sir, I have. She is not a child, but a most attractive young woman of about twenty years, worthy of the Rothfield connection, as you will soon see for yourself."

"Not like her father? I admit I feared she might have inherited his feckless ways. But I know she must be in some want. How is she living?" he queried, now that Weems had accomplished his task the earl was beginning to wonder if he really wanted to meet Sir Alan's daughter. She might be a jade or a loose woman, and the earl's strict notions of propriety would find that unacceptable.

"No, sir. I believe she supports herself with some type of literary activity. She is friendly with the editor of *The Times* and one of his employees. But she lives quite tidily and respectably in lodgings near Shaftesbury." He had decided no purpose would be served by regaling the earl with the tale of Poole's attempted abduction of Miss Dansforth. "I have not called upon her myself yet, but if you wish me to do so, of course, I will."

The earl thought about this for a moment. "Perhaps that would be best. Then you can report on your impression of her. Hearsay is never as effective as a personal encounter," he decided.

"Quite right, sir." Harry waited, wanting to bring up the matter of his fee, but a bit reluctant to break the old man's reverie.

But the earl, lost in the past, had not forgotten what he owed this enterprising young man. He offered him a packet.

"I think this will cover your fee and whatever expenses you have entailed. But report to me as soon as possible about your interview with Miss Dansforth, and there will be an additional amount due you." There was nothing cheese-paring about the earl. Careful as he was with his money, he had a strong sense of justice, and was quite impressed with Harry's quick resolution of the task he had set him.

"I will return this afternoon if possible, sir, after I have seen the lady," Harry promised and took his leave. His own glimpse of Leslie had assured him that she was a respectable female but he had not seen her in the best circumstances. Harry rarely made moral judgments and was prepared to discover that she was all he expected. But if it turned out she was leading a licentious life it behooved him to spare the earl a meeting with Miss Dansforth. He felt sorry for the old man and hoped that he could bring a reconciliation about for he felt the earl needed some young companionship and a relative he could come to care for before he died, lonely and unmourned. The earl had informed him that the title would go to a distant cousin, but Harry knew the old gentleman had vast resources and why should Leslie Dansforth not benefit if she deserved it?

He was received by Mrs. Gorey with some suspicion, that good lady having come to distrust all male callers on her tenant after last night's debacle.

"If you would just send up my name, I would appreciate it. I think she is waiting to see me. I am a Bow Street Runner, you know and not likely to cause her any trouble. On the contrary, I think she will be most pleased with my news," he cajoled, eager to settle Mrs. Gorey's doubts. "If you wish, I can show you my credentials," he urged as a further inducement.

"That might be best. We had some trouble last night with a man who lured Miss Dansforth into the street with false information, and then tried to abduct her. But I believe you were the man who rescued her," Mrs. Gorey decided.

"With the help of your friend, the estimable Mr. Lowndes," Harry insisted, further earning Mrs. Gorey's approval. She simpered and blushed a bit, but allowed as that was true. She inspected the papers he offered and nodded her head.

"Just wait here, then," she invited, persuaded by Harry's winning smile and charm more than the official papers as most women were.

With a few minutes she returned, saying that Miss Dansforth would see him. She longed to ask him the result of last evening's fracas but restrained herself. Harry, liking what he had seen of Mrs. Gorey, sensed her curiosity and promised to see her before he left and tell her the outcome of the arrest of Jack Poole.

Leslie, as well as Mrs. Gorey, had liked what she first saw of Harry Weems. Not a real gentleman she thought but none the less a man of some education and a great deal of address. Inviting him to sit down she looked him over with an astute eye, causing Harry to judge that the attractive Miss Dansforth was a woman of rare quality.

"I believe I owe you a great deal of gratitude for your interference last night in that nasty scene. That brute was trying to force me to accompany him having made false representations to me," Leslie said.

"Poole is a real villain, ma'am. He will pay for his effrontery. But I have to admit I was not up to his weight, and very grateful for the assistance of Mr. Lowndes."

Leslie liked the fact that Harry neither boasted of his prowess nor claimed credit for her rescue. She had no experience with Bow Street Runners but had been led to believe they were only marginally better than the villains they sought. Harry was certainly not what she had expected. "I understand you had been searching for me for a few days," Leslie asked him, having decided he was to be trusted.

"That's true. Your friend Mr. Stirling confirmed your identity once I had told him of my mission and laid any doubts he had. He was concerned about Mr. Kingsley at the time and I offered to help him with that problem." Harry had wondered about the relationship between the two journalists and if there was indeed, a rivalry for the affections of Miss Dansforth in the situation.

"Jonathan is a good friend to us both. But what is this I hear, a garbled account, I fear, about the Earl of Roth-

field?" Leslie asked determined to get to the reason for
Harry Weems' call.

"The earl hired me to locate you, Miss Dansforth. All
the information he had was that your father, Sir Alan, left
a child, and he was most anxious to find you, feeling some
responsibility toward you."

"There is no necessity for him to feel any responsibility
for me. But I would be happy to meet my relative. I have
always regretted the estrangement between the earl and my
father," she explained, unwilling to traduce her dead father.
However, she did feel much of the trouble could be laid at
his door.

"Well, I will report to him that you are willing to meet,"
Harry said, satisfied that not only had he earned his fee but
brought some comfort to the earl as well as possibly ben-
efited Miss Dansforth. Further acquaintance with Leslie
had confirmed his first impression of her as a sensible respectable female—and attractive, too!

But Leslie had some pressing questions about last
evening's debacle she wanted to ask. "It was most provi-
dential that you arrived when you did last night. How did
you come to be in the neighborhood? Mr. Stirling suggested that he had told you of my direction but he expected
that you would wait until a more seemly hour to call,"
Leslie began, determined to discover how Harry Weems
had become involved in the matter of Marcus' abduction.

"I had a notion I would just spy out the land so to speak,"
Harry said, careful not to divulge too much.

"Fortunately," Leslie answered. "And I understand that
Mr. Stirling had also sought your aid in locating Mr. Kingsley?" she ended on a questioning note. "How did you learn
about his disappearance?"

"Well, I happened to run into him when I was making

inquiries at the newspaper. We were introduced by a lady, a friend of Mr. Stirling's, a Miss Dinah Darcy," Harry replied.

The name struck a chord in Leslie's mind, but she could not recall where she had heard it. "And where does Miss Darcy live?" she asked.

"On New Albany Street." Harry was becoming uncomfortable. From his wide experience he sensed that Dinah Darcy had a relationship with Marcus unknown to Leslie. After all he was abducted from around the corner near her lodgings after Kingsley had made a call on the lady. And somehow the count was involved with her, too. He needed to ask that lady some sharp questions before he revealed any more information.

"I wonder what Marcus was doing there?" Leslie mused artlessly, hoping to inveigle the true story from Harry Weems.

But he was too downy a bird to be caught like that. "I have no idea, Miss Dansforth. All I know is that the lady had some connection with that Austrian count, who appears to be an enemy of Mr. Kingsley."

"Well, I hope he will be brought to book as well as his hired thug, Poole," Leslie said. "What is happening to that villain."

"Of course he denies any crime. But he refuses to divulge the name of his employer, really quite unusual for a man of that stamp. There is more to the story than we or the magistrate knows. But Poole has been remanded into custody while further investigations are made, so you have little to fear from another attempt on your safety," Harry assured her.

"I wasn't worried about that," Leslie said in a distracted way. There was a mystery here and Harry Weems appeared reluctant to help her solve it. She wondered why he was being so reticent. Did he owe some special loyalty to Marcus? And this Miss Darcy? What was her role in the affair?

"I will inform the earl you would welcome a visit from him, Miss Dansforth. And now I must be on my way. I have some pressing appointments," Harry said, standing up, eager to avoid any more questions.

"Yes, of course. Thank you again, Mr. Weems, for your timely intervention and your role in finding me for the earl."

After Harry had taken his leave, escorted by Mrs. Gorey, who had been fobbed off with the tale of Harry's discovery of Miss Dansforth as a missing relation of a titled gentleman. Naturally this news excited Mrs. Gorey who rushed back upstairs determined to learn of her favorite lodger's good fortune.

"That Bow Street Runner, Miss Dansforth, he told me all about searching for you for some titled gentleman? Is it true?" she asked, unable to suppress her curiosity. "I always knew you was quality," Mrs. Gorey concluded nodding her head as if in confirmation of her deepest thoughts.

Taking pity on her landlady to whom she felt a certain obligation Leslie gave her a brief sketch of the situation and conceded that she was indeed a cousin to the Earl of Rothfield, who wanted to end the estrangement between their two branches of the family.

"Does that mean you'll be leaving here, going to live in some castle," Mrs. Gorey asked, unhappy at the prospect of losing Miss Dansforth of whom she was genuinely fond and also losing all the excitement such a fascinating lodger had brought into her rather drab life.

"I doubt it, Mrs. Gorey. I would not want to leave your

comfortable rooms, where you take such good care of me,"
Leslie insisted, touched by the woman's concern. She had
not been the recipient of such kindly interest often in her
years with her difficult father. Their roving life had not
leant itself to establishing friends and her constant worry
and care of him had left her little time to develop close re-
lationships. Perhaps the earl would change all that but
Leslie had learned not to rely on any temporary good fortune.

"Do you think this earl has a castle, Miss Leslie?" Mrs.
Gorey pursued the facet of Leslie's new status that interested her the most.

"I don't know, Mrs. Gorey, but no doubt he lives in a
very large and fine home," Leslie explained taking pity on
Mrs. Gorey's avid interest in the earl.

"Well, if I had a chance to live in a castle I wouldn't
bother with these old rooms," Mrs. Gorey sniffed.

"I am very happy and comfortable here, Mrs. Gorey, and
I won't allow you to disparage your accommodations,"
Leslie insisted.

Not exactly sure what disparage meant, Mrs. Gorey,
perforce, had to abandon the conversation and return to her
duties, but pleased that she would have such a budget of
news for Mr. Lowndes when he called later.

Left alone after such a spate of revelations, Leslie wandered over to her desk. Miss Dinah Darcy, she thought. She
began to rifle through the contents of a file holding letters
from those seeking her advice. Of course most correspondents did not sign their requests for help but a nagging suspicion had arisen in Leslie's mind that seemed to fit Harry
Weems' careful description of Dinah Darcy and that somehow brought Marcus into the business. Was she just being
a suspicious shrew? Leslie finally found the letter she was

seeking. Yes, it was as she had suspected, a woman seeking aid in keeping her protector, signed only, "Worried." Why did she associate this letter with Dinah Darcy and with Marcus? And why did the idea that the two could have an association depress her so much?

Surely she did not expect a man of Marcus' assets to have remained unattached. She really knew very little about him, only that he enjoyed the company of several literary men, was admired by Jonathan and had earned the confidence of the proprietor of *The Times* who had such a high opinion of his talents that he appointed him editor at a very young age. However a man could be well regarded by his friends, his employer and his staff and still be false and heartless with women. Was Marcus among that despicable company? Certainly his manner toward her had at times verged on the rakish and ignored her own feelings.

Leslie could not help but feel he would not make the most faithful of husbands if he ever aspired to that role. Her experience with her father had not inclined her to view men as steady reliable companions or partners. Jonathan had done a great deal to dispel her initial distrust even if Marcus had not.

Still, it was Marcus that attracted her and she was a widgeon to think a man in his thirties would not have been involved with women. He probably had a woman in keeping. So many men who could afford it did. After this tortuous reasoning Leslie concluded that Jonathan had tried to warn her that Marcus had a mistress. And she also concluded that for some reason he had been calling on the lady, Dinah Darcy, when he was abducted. And the nefarious count had some contact with the lady also which had enabled him to plan the abduction.

Pleased that she had solved the enigma of Marcus' presence on New Albany Street, Leslie chided herself for the ignoble rise of jealousy that this careful reasoning had evoked. She had no right to criticize Marcus' conduct. But she would ask Jonathan about Miss Darcy. He would not be proof against her plea for information. Leslie realized Jonathan could be manipulated to provide answers to her questions and was rather ashamed of herself for using him so but still determined to test her conclusions.

Jonathan, suspecting that Leslie would quiz him, and more than irritated at being placed in an equivocal position by Marcus decided he had best discover exactly what Marcus intended toward both Dinah and Leslie. Loath to probe into his friend's feelings and actions, only his regard for Leslie enabled him to make the effort. He was quite prepared to put his friendship at risk in order to satisfy himself that Marcus was not pursuing Leslie with dishonorable intentions.

The two friends had said little on their walk to *The Times* and Marcus, upon his arrival, had been inundated with questions from his staff about his disappearance, which he had turned off casually. He admitted that he had been abducted and inferred that his position as editor had been responsible. But later as he cleaned up some arrears of work he realized he would have to explain matters more fully to Jonathan. He owed his friend that at least as well as telling him of his intention to ask Leslie to be his wife. He knew this would cause his friend pain and he regretted it but Jonathan had his chance with Leslie and she had refused his offer. Still, the interview would be an uncomfortable one. Not one to shirk a disagreeable task Marcus called Jonathan into his office and wasted no time.

"Look, Jon, I know you care for Leslie, and cannot view with any enjoyment the fact of a rival for her affections. I

know, too, you think I am a libertine, to have been courting her while keeping Dinah as a mistress. But I promise
you I have broken with Dinah. That was the purpose of my
call upon her. I told her our relationship was at an end. I
fear she has come under the count's influence and was un-
wittingly the source of information to him that enabled him
to hire those villains to apprehend me."

"If you love Leslie and want to marry her, what can I
say? I hope you will deal honestly and faithfully with her,"
Jonathan said, his open face revealing the sorrow this news
had brought him. "I somehow hoped that she might come
to see me as a possible husband, but I know she would
never accept me just because she feels a small fondness for
me."

"Not a small fondness. We both view you as a loyal
friend to whom we owe a great deal. We have shared so
much, I dislike being the cause of your unhappiness. And
I don't even know if she cares a jot for me. I certainly have
given her little reason to trust me," Marcus confided, depressed as he considered his own chance of winning the
lady.

"She was most upset at your disappearance, distraught
even, else she would not have gone off with Poole so heed-
lessly after all our warnings." Jonathan's honesty could not
deny that Leslie had shown every sign of a woman deeply
in love.

"Yes, but she thinks, and with some reason, that I am a
libertine with a bad record concerning women. I have never
told her about Dinah, and I assume you haven't."

"Naturally not. But Leslie is clever. She will be wondering what you were doing on New Albany Street, and by
now, Harry Weems might have revealed Dinah's part in the
plot."

"Yes, I will have to tell her."

"Poor Dinah. I feel for her, too. She never really wanted any harm to come to you. She was just protecting herself when she became involved with the count."

"Yes, but it was regrettable. And I must bring that gentleman to account. He cannot be allowed to escape punishment for his role, not just my abduction, but his intention to seduce Leslie. What a cad the man is!" Marcus said, realizing that he deserved a similar appellation and would probably receive it from Leslie.

"There should be some way to get him declared *persona non grata,*" Jonathan suggested.

"He deserves a nastier fate. And I mean to see that he gets it," Marcus said savagely.

"What will you do?" Jonathan asked, now rather alarmed. Marcus' normal good judgment seemed to be in abeyance when it came to the count and who could blame him. The man looked like he would avoid any retribution for his evil deeds.

"I can challenge him to a duel. Will you act for me? I am sure Leigh Hunt will oblige." Marcus offered this shocking plan calmly, much to Jonathan's dismay.

"He may kill you," Jonathan protested.

"Or I may kill him and have to flee to the continent," Marcus agreed, not at all alarmed by the prospect.

"Don't do it, Marcus. There must be another way," Jonathan urged. The two discussed it for some time but Marcus remained firm in his purpose, only winning a promise from Jonathan not to reveal his intention to Leslie. He left a worried Jonathan, who could only hope that some other method of wreaking vengeance on the count would occur before Marcus took the final step.

Chapter Nineteen

The count, furious that his plans to abduct both Marcus and
Leslie had failed, believed that he had hidden his identity
so well that even if Jack Poole betrayed him he had little
information. All Poole and his two allies knew was that
he was "a foreign gentleman" with deep pockets. Despite
the failure of his attempts on both Marcus and Leslie he
had not given up on his schemes to bring them both under
his power. He would just have to hire some other rogues
to achieve his despicable ends. He was quite convinced that
Marcus was the reason Leslie had refused his proposals,
dishonorable as they were, and for that the arrogant young
man must pay.

As for Leslie, once she had accustomed herself to her
role as his mistress, he expected little trouble from her. His
experience with women had led him to believe that money
and his own attractions would quiet any initial misgivings
about such a relationship. What he did not take into account, his past affairs having always been conducted successfully, was Leslie's determined respectability and her
revulsion toward him. His conceit would not allow him to
entertain either reaction as the cause for her refusal.

For the moment he must postpone any action for Metternich had arrived in London and the count expected to have trouble with that wily and powerful statesman, who would be thoroughly briefed by Esterhazy as to the count's mysterious errands. Of course Metternich would not care at all that the count had designs on an English woman. His chief irritation would be that it distracted the count from his main purpose for coming to London, and he would want to hear that his task had been successfully performed. Metternich had no interest in methods, only in results. This business of Jack Poole's arrest had temporarily altered his assassination assignment, but he had no doubt he could find some other obliging criminals to complete the business for him.

What the count discounted was Prince Esterhazy's real dislike of him. Count von Ronberg did not really understand the English, but Esterhazy did, and the ambassador was convinced that his unwelcome guest was up to some deviltry that would rebound on the embassy and its head. He knew that the count enjoyed some favor with Metternich and he had to tread carefully with the Austrian foreign minister in order to insure his own position. It was a delicate situation so Esterhazy enlisted the services of his wife for whom Metternich had some affection. As eager as her husband to see the count depart, although for not the same reasons, she agreed to use her influence with Metternich.

Austria's foreign minister, cunning, calculating, handsome and suave, had one abiding purpose, to increase the power of Austria, whose role in European affairs had shrunk considerably during the Napoleonic Wars. Metternich had no use for democracy, believing strongly in the divine right of kings, particularly the Hapsburgs, and he thought the British insistence on rights ridiculous. But for all his authoritarian views he was popular in England and Castlereagh approved of him. Metternich did not much care for the Prince Regent, thinking him selfish, wayward and extravagant. He thought Austria could deal more easily with his brothers, Frederick or William. He also believed the English people were frightened of revolution and Parliament could be persuaded to more Draconian measures of repression if the royal house was threatened. He intended to be the master of Europe, to keep the balance of power in his own hands and was not averse to any conspiracy that would insure this result. Few men crossed him and neither Esterhazy nor the count intended to try.

Esterhazy approached Metternich carefully. "I know that Count von Ronberg is on a special mission to London, under your direction, sir," he began.

Metternich frowned. He hoped von Ronberg had not been foolish enough to confide in the Anglophile Esterhazy.

"Just what has the count implied, Esterhazy?" he asked, his eyes stern and his mouth compressed.

"Very little, but he is not above evoking your name when I quizzed him about some undesirable associates," Esterhazy insisted.

"No doubt he is up to his womanizing and debauchery, but Esterhazy, we are both men of the world. We do not judge our friends morals, only their politics," Metternich countered.

"True. But if he gets into trouble it will rebound on the embassy, on me, and on Austria," Esterhazy persisted with unusual courage.

"I will speak to him, but I feel you are seeing trouble where none exists. He is here on a special fact finding mission for me, pursuant to Austria's best interests. That is all I feel free to tell you."

"You don't trust me," Esterhazy said in a mournful voice, his fears increased.

"Not at all, my dear man, but as you know, these intelligence matters are best kept secret. Not to worry. Your own esteemed position in English society will not be affected," Metternich said, understanding that Esterhazy cared chiefly for his own prestige and not finding that human reaction either discreditable nor unusual. Metternich was an excellent psychologist, able to read men's motives and use them to further his own ploys. Feeling that perhaps Esterhazy needed a little soothing he reassured him as to their monarch's regard for him and faith in his abilities. After the interview ended Esterhazy realized that he had learned little and had not solidified his own position. If it were in Metternich's interests to abandon him, he knew his days in London were numbered.

Metternich was much more forthright with the count.

"How are your plans coming over the matter we discussed, von Ronberg? You seem to be taking a long time about it."

"There have been unavoidable delays, but I have a target date for the opening of Parliament," von Ronberg answered.

"You understand that although it is a regrettable fact, only an assassination of one of England's public figures will stir up the populace enough to see that these ridiculous republican sympathies do not prevail. The English are so romantic and stubborn, too, a difficult combination. And most of them are suspicious of foreigners. Look at Wellington, and his refusal to sign the Holy Alliance, for example. The English want to control Europe but stay out of it, and that is an impossible position. They must be forced to see the errors of their ways."

"Of course, I agree, a stiff-necked, arrogant people who must be taught a lesson," the count confirmed Metternich's view.

"We failed with Wellington in France. We must not fail again."

"I assure you I have every confidence it will go off as planned." Von Ronberg did not mention the difficulties involved. That would not please or interest Metternich. If he pulled off this task his own rewards would be great, and his current low standing at the Austrian court and in aristocratic circles would receive a huge boost from Metternich's patronage. Von Ronberg made no pretense in caring about the state of the continent, only his own status concerned him.

"I do not want to know your plot in detail, but I expect success, von Ronberg. I have no use for failure," Metternich warned and left the room before von Ronberg could protest, leaving that gentleman aware that he could expect little support or defense if he failed.

The count had been quite astute in his reading of Jack Poole. That villain had no intention of revealing the name of his employer, and under questioning steadfastly refused to admit he had attempted to abduct Leslie. Despite Marcus' testimony as to his own kidnapping, which Poole also denied, the magistrate felt he could not hold the man indefinitely, although Mr. Ransom was convinced Poole was guilty as sin. It was Marcus' word against Poole's since the Hookers had wisely absented themselves and were not available for testimony which would have damned them as well as Poole. Mr. Ransom, a friend of the reformer William Wilberforce and the radical politician Henry Brougham, jealously guarded the rights of men and the letter of the law. Much as he would have liked to sentence Jack Poole to deportation or a long term in prison could see no way that this could be accomplished without cooperative evidence. Poole's war record spoke in his favor and that wily rogue insisted his captain be called to buttress his character. Ransom believed that the veterans of Wellington's victorious army had been treated shabbily by the government so Poole's standing as a sergeant who had served through the Peninsula campaigns and at Waterloo was a telling factor in his behalf. A clever if shady barrister with the support of an expensive solicitor pressed for his client's freedom and after several days won Poole's release much against Mr. Ransom's instincts and Marcus' furious insistence that he pay for his crime.

"A case of mistaken identity in Mr. Kingsley's case, Your Worship," the barrister said in his oily manner.

"I doubt that, Mr. Wilkie, but I have no choice but to honor the law. *Habeas corpus* demands that I release the plaintiff since there is no compelling evidence to try him. But I will not forget Mr. Poole. I do not doubt I will see him again in my court," he concluded severely.

So Jack Poole was free. After paying the exorbitant fee of his solicitor, and the barrister, he set about locating the Hookers. He was not surprised to discover they had fled, and he was not discouraged for there were many other thugs who could be hired for the task the "foreign gentleman" had set for him. And he intended to raise his price after this temporary inconvenience. He made the usual arrangements to contact the count through an ad in *The Gazette*. His macabre sense of humor would have preferred he used *The Times,* but this method of contact had been established some time past. So he waited impatiently for the "foreign gentleman" to notify him of their next meeting.

It was several days before this was accomplished and Jack Poole holed up in a disreputable lodging near the river while waiting for word from the count. What he did not realize was that Harry Weems had followed him on his release from prison and knew his whereabouts.

Harry, as well as Marcus, was angry that Poole had not paid for his crime, and like the magistrate Mr. Ransom believed the man would pursue his evil ends. Harry was not solely motivated by disgust at Poole's actions, nor his failure to be punished. He believed that he would benefit, amply rewarded by Marcus, if he discovered the villain's next move. He made his intentions known to Marcus who happily agreed on a reward if Harry could come up with some evidence linking the count to Poole. Neither Harry nor Marcus thought that they had heard the last of Jack Poole. During Harry's interview with Marcus he tactfully brought up the matter of Dinah Darcy.

"Naturally, I did not want to involve Miss Darcy in any disagreeable situation which might embarrass her, sir," he said wondering if Marcus would reveal his relationship with the lady.

"Quite right, Weems. I feel a bit guilty about Dinah. Frankly, if I had not decided to end my liaison with her I doubt if she would have agreed to the count's machinations," he admitted.

Neither condoning nor criticizing, Harry suggested that this was the way of the world only suggesting that Miss Darcy was a fine woman and hinting that he had a certain interest in her.

Marcus, who had become quite impressed with this unusual Bow Street Runner, agreed and astutely devised the thrust of Harry's careful inquiries.

"She's a good girl, loyal and not at all greedy. She could benefit from the attentions of a respectable man, Weems, and it would relieve her of applying to a character like the count."

"I understand she has severed her connection with him," Harry said blandly. "She was quite disgusted by the man's use of her."

"Well, see to it she does not suffer from that decision, that's a good chap. She is well provided for during the next few weeks and should not be looking for another protector. At heart Dinah is a domestic soul. She would make a good wife if a man could overlook her past. And I might say that is not as colorful as one would expect. She was in the chorus at Covent Garden when I discovered her and had not had a lot of experience," Marcus confided hoping that Harry would be the answer to Dinah's future.

"My thought, too, Mr. Kingsley," Harry confirmed and the two parted with mutual expressions of esteem and promises to keep in touch.

After Harry's departure Marcus felt a certain lifting of the guilt he had carried about Dinah. She would be safe in that fine chap's hands, he was certain. What he was not so sure of was his own future with Leslie. But his chief priority was bringing the count to book. He doubted that the man would ever have to pay legally for his planned abduction of both Leslie and himself which made it even more imperative that he go ahead with his challenge despite Jonathan's objections.

And he would certainly not tell Leslie of his decision to challenge the count to a duel. He had a far more vital matter to raise with Leslie and he had a real concern that the outcome of that interview would not be in his favor. Postponing the thought of how miserable he would be if she refused his proposal of marriage, he turned instead to the writing of a stiff formal note to the count. Leigh Hunt had agreed to approach the man as one of Marcus' seconds to deliver the challenge. As a man experienced in such matters, Hunt was a better choice than Jonathan who disapproved of the whole business and would only act reluctantly. If Marcus feared the outcome of his meeting the count across the greensward at twenty paces with a pistol in his hand he did not dwell upon it. It had to be done.

So the count was most surprised a day later when he received a visit from a neatly dressed, dark haired gentleman distinguished by a pair of brilliant dark eyes and an observant, kindly manner. The count knew little of Hunt's literary prestige and would only have scorned him as "a dirty scribbler" if he had.

"I am directed to act in Mr. Kingsley's behalf, Count von Ronberg," Hunt said having delivered the challenge. "If you will name your seconds we can get on with the arrangements."

"This is ridiculous, but as a man of honor I cannot refuse. I will direct my friends to contact you. I suppose the weapon will be pistols as I doubt Mr. Kingsley has much experience with the foils," the count sneered.

"As you wish, sir. I will await your friends," Hunt confirmed in his gentle manner. He rarely lost his temper, and his manner hid his aversion to the count, for he was a man of gentle disposition and great tolerance for his fellow's foibles. But the Austrian had not impressed him. He wondered a bit about the woman for whom this duel was being fought, but, of course, her name was never mentioned. He took his leave as politely and quietly as he had appeared, leaving the count in yet another choleric temper.

After leaving Marcus, Harry decided that a call upon Dinah might not come amiss. He knew she felt vulnerable as well as unhappy and dreaded any further encounters with the count. It would be a good opportunity for him to assure her she could rely on his protection.

Despite the more sordid aspects of his career Harry had managed to hold on to his illusions. He really liked people and found most of them repaid his genial attentions, even the felons he apprehended so cheerfully. However, lately he had come to feel a certain lack in his rackety way of casual life.

He was not a moralist nor did he believe that the sins of the flesh should necessarily be confined to males. Women had their temptations and their trials that often led them to make unfortunate choices. He did not condemn Dinah for her association with Marcus, whom he regarded as an upstanding smart fellow although a bit too intellectual for his understanding. And fear of the future had driven her to make her infamous bargain with the count. He could easily forgive her for that misjudgment but he realized she might fall into another relationship equally as disastrous without some guidance. He liked her courage and her matter of fact acceptance of what life had dealt her. He wanted to see more of her and perhaps Marcus was right. A closer bond with Dinah would be to both of their benefits.

He found a sober Dinah, sunk in a depression, which he did his best to alleviate.

"Oh, Harry, I am so glad to see you. I have been sitting here brooding about what my foolishness caused Marcus. I never wanted to cause him harm, but I was scared and angry that he had broken with me," she confided.

"I quite understand, Dinah," Harry said, determined to cheer her up from her doldrums.

Dinah, who always blossomed in the presence of a man, and who found Harry attractive as well as comforting, brightened immediately.

"You haven't taken me in disgust then?" she asked with a pitiful attempt at a smile.

"Of course not. And Mr. Kingsley hasn't either, so set your mind at rest. He does not blame you, only himself for putting you in a position that you felt you needed to give in to the count. He hasn't been near you since the abduction, has he?"

"No, but I am a bit afraid he might and I don't want to see him. There is something quite scary about him."

"Yes, I would say that. And he has yet to pay for his treatment of Mr. Kingsley and you for that matter. You could easily have been in trouble with the law as an abettor of his crime, but I don't think you have to worry about that now."

"But what about that Poole person? Will he try anything again, do you think?" Dinah was recovering her good spirits under Harry's easy handling. She felt Harry's interest and returned it in good measure. And she appealed to him for protection which naturally raised his expectations. She would not disappoint him.

"I think you need some amusement. How about coming to Ranleagh Gardens tonight. It's usually good value," Harry suggested.

"Oh, Harry, I would love that. I have been quite downcast worrying about things." She hesitated, but her generous instincts could not be denied. "It's rather dear. I have a little money, you know. Marcus made a nice settlement."

Harry grinned. What a darling she was. "I think I can afford an evening on the town. I have caught some rather lucrative criminals lately, and am now on a retainer," he informed her proudly.

"I think you are very brave to take on all these scoundrels. I do hope you are careful," Dinah pleaded, not liking the idea of Harry being in danger.

Harry laughed. "Don't you worry your pretty head about me. I'm a survivor. At any rate I don't think I will be a Bow Street Runner much longer. It is losing its charm. I have an idea for a more respectable employment."

Dinah looked impressed, but wisely did not urge him to explain. They made an arrangement to meet later that evening, and Harry took his leave much heartened by her obvious interest and admiration. He intended to make yet another foray by Jack Poole's hideaway for he doubted that gentleman had abandoned his evil ways. Nor did he think that the count had decided not to pursue whatever skullduggery that had brought him to London. All in all he was quite pleased with Dinah, his day's work and a future that had certain interesting possibilities.

Chapter Twenty

Marcus approached Leslie's lodgings later that afternoon with a certain trepidation. He had made up his mind he must confess to her his involvement with Dinah before he proposed, and he knew she would not approve of his past relationship. Who could blame her? It was hardly the best omen for pleading a faithful role as a husband. She might descide to sever all ties with him. And if what Jonathan had told him was true she no longer needed the salary he provided for her work at the newspaper. The Earl of Rothfield was a powerful rival. He could offer her a luxurious home and the support of his name and wealth. Marcus could not aspire to the world in which the earl moved. She might want to assume the role of indulged heiress that the earl could offer.

However, Leslie was a girl with an independent cast of mind, probably not attracted by the idle existence of a society belle. Of course, she would meet other men there who could offer her marriage and an establishment much more to her taste than what Marcus was able to provide. His head awhirl with all these conflicting thoughts as well as the realization that he must make his confession and assume the guise of a betrayer and seducer in her eyes, only confirming her first opinion of him, worried him, too.

And he realized as his steps dragged nearing her lodgings, that he would have a hard time recovering from her rejection. She had come to mean so much to him. Not just because of her attraction nor her clever mind, but for her staunch courage in facing the challenges life had offered her, her loyalty to her father, her sensible attitude toward the vicissitudes she had endured and her ability to cope on her own without the bulwark of a man. All in all he did not weigh his chances as very good. He took a deep breath and mounted the steps, determined to face what was coming no matter what her decision.

For once he seemed to have missed Mrs. Gorey and the young maid, Aggie, admitted him. Unlike her employer Aggie quite admired Marcus, thinking Miss Dansforth fortunate to have such a gent courting her, for her limited experience did not allow any other reason for his frequent calls.

"Thank you, Aggie." he rewarded her with a smile, which sent her heart fluttering. "Such a fine gentleman he is," Aggie confided below stairs where interest in Miss Dansforth's affairs was constant.

Heartened by avoiding Mrs. Gorey, Marcus hoped Aggie's approval would be echoed by Leslie, who, indeed, welcomed him warmly.

"I am so glad to see you, Marcus, and hear what is happening about the case against Poole and the count," she greeted him.

"Unfortunately the magistrate felt there was not enough evidence to hold Poole who did not involve the count. Weems and I did as much as we could to press the charges but the magistrate, a fair minded man, although not believing Poole's plea of mistaken identity, did not feel he could sentence him. But the good news is that Harry, on my instructions and his own initiative, has discovered where Poole is hiding. We will get him yet," he concluded, hoping not to have to spoil her receptive mood.

"That is disappointing. And I suppose you did not want me to testify."

"No point in dragging you into it. Poole insists he was just escorting you to meet me, no more, and a stranger gave him the note. A blatant lie, but one difficult to disprove."

"Well, we can just hope he will commit some other crime and be apprehended. I quite liked Harry Weems who called on me at the behest of the Earl of Rothfield. I have agreed to meet with my relative. Harry spoke most favorably about him."

"A reconciliation with the earl could change your circumstances," Marcus admitted with a wry grin.

"And you don't approve of that," Leslie said, not quite understanding Marcus' reluctance.

"Well, it rather puts a rub in what I wanted to ask you," he said, suddenly wary. He felt like a raw youth encountering his first female, a position to which he was not accustomed.

"And what was that?" Leslie felt a little embarrassment, as if she were behaving like a simpering flirt.

"I want to marry you," Marcus blurted out the words, not the polished address he had planned.

Leslie bit back a gasp. She had not expected such a declaration, and she felt Marcus had forced himself to make the offer, not really wanting to marry her at all.

Marcus waited, feeling equally ill at ease. He was handling this badly. He should have taken her in his arms and confessed to an overwhelming desire to make her his wife, but the business of Dinah was nagging at him.

"Do you really want to be married, Marcus?" Leslie asked, her voice quavering.

"Yes, I do. Any sensible man would want to marry you. You have all the qualities any man with sense desires in a wife."

"And you could not get me any other way," Leslie said, not liking the thought. Marcus had tried to seduce her and she had let him know she was not willing so he had been driven to these lengths. She was not eager to accept on those terms although she was tempted. She loved Marcus, that she had admitted to herself, even if she was not ready to admit it to him, and he had said not one word of love himself. Only that he wanted her and marriage was the price he must pay, reluctantly.

"I realize you think I am a libertine without the values you believe in, and that Jonathan would make you a far better husband," Marcus said, trying to be fair. He should have overridden her doubts by sweeping her into his arms. That was what she was waiting for, but he hesitated. He had a confession to make before he could do that. And he was intimidated by her silence. Well, he would just have to blurt out the details of his past.

"You have some reason to think that. For the past two years I have been keeping a mistress, a nice girl I found in the chorus at Covent Garden. I have recently broken with her because I feel we are no longer suited, and I have come to love and respect you, and want you for my wife. I realized I could not offer for you without confiding this regrettable episode, although I know it darkens my chances." As a confession it lacked skill and the expertise with words that Marcus normally used, but his sincerity was evident.

"Poor girl. What will happen to her?" Leslie's sympathies were engaged, and she discovered that she was not shocked, only disappointed. If Marcus wanted her so badly why didn't he sweep her into his arms and settle her doubts. She could hardly make the first advance herself.

Stupidly Marcus waited, unsure of himself and of Leslie. "Nothing will happen to her. I gave her a suitable parting gift and she has other strings to her bow." As soon as he said that he realized that he had lessened his chances. She would think he was cynical, uncaring.

"Have you come to the time in your life that you feel you need a settled domestic establishment, a wife, even children, and I am a suitable prospect? That is not good enough, Marcus, and I think you have behaved shabbily to this poor girl, who probably cares for you and is devastated."

Too late Marcus acted, dragging Leslie into his arms and kissing her with a fervor he hoped might reassure her. She remained stiff and resisting in his arms, not persuaded by his passion when what she wanted was some token of his real affection. Finally, she tore herself away.

"I have always admitted that your lovemaking stirs me, Marcus, but there is much in your character that disappoints me. I doubt we should deal well together. I could never trust you, for who knows how long this desire for marriage and a legal mate would last," Leslie said, a sad little smile tempering her words.

"Most men are experienced before they marry," Marcus pleaded.

"But they do not want their wives to be," Leslie responded angrily.

"That's the way of the world. I can't change the morality of society, but I do love you and promise to do my best to be a faithful and good husband," he said, desperate that she was refusing him.

"I don't think it's enough, Marcus. How could you treat this poor girl so cavalierly. She depends on you and needs you. If you have had her in keeping so long, you owe her a proposal, not me."

"That's ridiculous. Dinah does not expect marriage. She probably cares for me in a tepid way, but I think is more interested in security than an undying passion," he argued now becoming as angry as Leslie.

"I won't marry you, Marcus, and under the circumstances I don't think we should continue our working relationship," Leslie said with a firmness she did not really feel. If he was so determined to have her as his wife why didn't he show some signs of ardor. The man was a fool to have confided his relationship with Dinah. She might have suspected but she would never have known for certain about his past. Such honesty was mistaken. He wanted to clear his conscience at her expense. She wondered if he really wanted to marry her at all.

"You are behaving like some credulous virgin. I expected better of you, Leslie, and I won't entertain the idea of you abandoning the column. If you don't care for me, say so," he blurted out, angry and mortified at her response.

Taking a deep breath Leslie responded bleakly, "I don't care for you enough to take a chance on your fidelity, Marcus and I won't have a husband who has other women when he tires of domestic ties." The moment the words were out she regretted them.

"You are a shrew and a puritan, a disastrous combination, and I am probably well out of it. But here is something to remember me by." Before she could protest he kissed her with brutal insensitivity, venting his anger and frustration with a series of kisses that were more a punishment than a sign of any love. Before she could struggle away he threw her from him in disgust and stormed out of the room, leaving her in tears and an equal frustration. As she heard his furious footsteps descending the stairs she was tempted to call him back, tell him she didn't mean any of the measured words she had uttered. But her pride prevented her. After a good cry she bathed her face in some cold water and sat down to consider what she could do to retrieve matters. Not much, she conceded, as it was up to the man to make the offer, and Marcus was not the man to take his refusal tamely. He would not propose again, and she viewed the shambles of her life with disgust. Why had she behaved like a shrew and a puritan, damning words he had used? Was she so moral she could deny her feelings for some code that denied her happiness? What had she done?

Marcus reached the street, his temper abating a bit, and disappointment and his own ineptitude replacing anger. He stood for a moment undecided. Should he return and urge her to reconsider?

As he hesitated a crested coach drew up to the door and an elderly gentleman of some distinction emerged and mounted the steps. That decided him. This was undoubtedly the Earl of Rothfield come to offer Leslie a life of ease and luxury among the ton, a rival he could not defeat. The earl was admitted by an awestruck Aggie, and Marcus walked away, his shoulders slumping, feeling of irretrievable loss darkening his features.

Chapter Twenty-One

Marcus was quite right in his belief that the count would escape any immediate retribution for his abduction of him and his attempted kidnapping of Leslie Dansforth. Jack Poole had never learned the count's identity, although he had his suspicions, but as long as "the foreign gentleman's" money kept coming he would keep mum. But his near brush with imprisonment and the defection of the Hooker brothers had not improved his mood. He laid most of the responsibility for the defeat of his plans on the shoulders of the Bow Street Runner, Harry Weems, and vowed to seek his revenge. First he had to wrest some money from the "foreign gentleman" and was waiting impatiently for the count's appearance. That he might be about to commit treason and murder did not disturb him. He might have been less sanguine had he realized that Harry Weems had discovered his bolt hole and was keeping a close eye on the seedy quarters where Poole lodged. Determined not to miss any meeting with the count, Poole never ventured out, relying on a blowzy maid to fulfill all his needs.

Harry had found a convenient room across the street from Poole's lair and by bribing the owner of the building set himself up to watch the comings and goings in Poole's hideaway. His patience was rewarded after several days when he recognized the count making a stealthy approach to Poole's lodgings. Careful not to attract attention, the count arrived on foot near dusk, but Harry spied him immediately.

So the count was still conspiring with that felon, he observed. Marcus Kingsley would be grateful for the information. He only wished he could gain entrance to the rendezvous and discover what the two villains were planning. But perhaps there was a way to manage that. He had noticed that a buxom maid with a certain coarse appeal had been running in and out of the corner pub, bringing foaming tankards of beer back to the house. No doubt to satisfy Jack Poole's thirst. He planned to cultivate her and find out exactly what Poole was planning, and if possible, thwart the rogue's next crime. That the count was involved and intended some wickedness he was now convinced. He would consult Kingsley before making a move. Bow Street Runners had long experience at waiting and collecting evidence and Harry was especially skilled at that job.

Marcus could use some distraction. On returning to the newspaper after seeing the Earl of Rothfield enter Leslie's lodgings he had sunk into a deep depression, castigating himself for handling his proposal to her in such a maladroit fashion. He had not forgotten the count, and was convinced he had not heard the last of that devious aristocrat. He sensed that the count might not have abandoned his attempt to capture Leslie, but more important, he was sure the man had some other evil plot in mind, one that would affect England, and he was determined to defeat it. He had great faith in Harry Weems and believed that enterprising young man would come up with the information he needed. But he could not banish all thoughts of Leslie and wondered what he could do to retrieve his position with her. He might have been cheered if he had realized that Leslie, too, was regretting her cavalier dismissal of Marcus, despite the distraction of the Earl of Rothfield's visit.

Mrs. Gorey had ushered the earl into Leslie's rooms with great ceremony, impressed by his title and manner. And, indeed, he was impressive, tall, a bit stooped, with a shock of white hair and a rather stern appearance. That sternness disappeared upon meeting Leslie.

"My dear, it is so kind of you to receive me," he greeted her, after Mrs. Gorey had departed.

"Not at all, sir. You are my only relation, and I am delighted to meet you," Leslie replied, sitting down and indicating that the earl should do likewise.

"I hope I am not intruding," the earl said diffidently, liking what he saw of Leslie, but not sure how to proceed.

"Not at all," she assured him.

"Let me offer my condolences upon your father's death," he began, and Leslie wisely did not interrupt, only nodding. "I only heard of it by chance, and I regret that former dispute should have closed all communication between us." He hesitated, not wanting to go into that imbroglio. But Leslie, sensing his unhappiness, hurried to set his mind at ease.

"I loved my father but I must confess he was a foolish, reckless man, tempted by gambling and drink. Often I was in despair with him."

"Perhaps I am too puritanical in my ideas," the earl admitted, more than willing to meet her half way.

"Not at all. There was no reason why you should assist

him. He would just have frittered away any money you gave him, and come back for more," Leslie insisted.

"It is kind of you to be so charitable, but I should not have lost touch. I denied myself the pleasure of getting to know you, and I am sure you had some distressing times. I might have helped."

"I have managed fairly well, much better without father to worry me," she admitted with a charming rueful air. "We really have no claim on you."

"I want to make up to you all you have suffered." He looked about the room, noticing the pile of manuscript on the desk but not asking any questions. "Could you possibly forgive a stubborn old man and come to live with me? I am all alone since my dear wife died and have no other relations but a distant cousin who will inherit the place when I go."

Leslie admired his stoicism and felt sorry for his obvious loneliness, but she did not want to surrender her independence. "I hope we can be friends and spend some time together, but I am comfortably situated here and Mrs. Gorey takes very good care of me. Then, there is my writing. I could not give that up," she confided, tempering her refusal with a warm smile.

"Of a literary bent, are you? Splendid. Of course, I would not interfere with any work you have," he pleaded.

Leslie wondered if he would be so acquiescent if he knew the real nature of her writing. Of course, in a fit of temper, she had resigned her job as Pythius with Marcus, but somehow she sensed that was not the end of her career.

"Dear sir, you are all kindness, but I really cannot come to live with you. Don't be angry with me. I am delighted we have met and had this frank discussion, mending the breach father caused, but do try to see my position," she urged.

The earl, disappointed that his plans to treat Leslie as a daughter, to shower her with luxuries and treats, tried not to show his feelings, but he was hurt.

"Is it that you cannot forgive me for abandoning you all these years?" he asked with a plaintive sigh.

"Not at all, sir, it is just that I have managed my life to my satisfaction for some time now, and would not wish to be dependent on another, even as kind a man as you." She frowned. She would not mind one bit giving up a measure of independence for Marcus, but she would not think about that now.

"I suppose I was foolish to hope. No doubt you have several young men who are urging you to the altar, such an attractive girl could not be without suitors," the earl said convinced she preferred marriage to becoming the daughter of the house even to such an august personage as an earl. Although to be fair to him he did not consider himself august, only lonely, and eager to have a closer relationship with this delightful relation.

"I am not thinking of marriage, sir, and I promise that when I do I will bring any prospective husband around for you to meet," she said with a smile.

To meet, not to approve, a very spirited and determined young woman, the earl thought, not at all displeased. Rather unusual, such initiative and self reliance, but very admirable. He realized he could not sway her and put the best face possible upon the situation.

"Well, if you will not come to live with me, I hope you will not be too stubborn to accept a small allowance. Not that you appear to need it, but it would make me feel better," he unfairly pleaded.

"If you insist, sir," she agreed.

"And perhaps you would take pity on an old man and let me escort you to the theater and perhaps supper, some time," he added, sensing she was vulnerable to his appeals.

"Of course, that sounds most enjoyable. The theater is one of my great enjoyments and I cannot think of a better companion."

Having settled on a date for this festivity the earl finally took his leave, but not before giving her his direction, and insisting she call on him at any time if she needed assistance. He mentioned that he would be in town for some weeks yet, but later she might care to visit him at his ancestral seat in Wiltshire just for a break, he cajoled.

Leslie was pleased to oblige and they parted on the warmest terms. No sooner had the earl departed than Mrs. Gorey appeared, all agog, to hear of Miss Dansforth's plans. She was reassured, if a little surprised, that Leslie had no intention of leaving her establishment just yet, but had welcomed the arrival of the earl to mend the family breach.

"I was a-telling Mr. Lowdnes from the day you arrived I knew you was quality," Mrs. Gorey, much heartened by all this excitement, told Leslie.

"That's nice of you, Mrs. Gorey. Now you can tell Mr. Lowdnes, to whom I owe a great deal, all about the earl. He will be taking me to the theater later this week, and I must find a proper gown for the occasion," she confided, knowing Mrs. Gorey was avid for details of her future relationship with the earl. "Although I will not be deserting you I may be visiting my cousin at his seat in Wiltshire late on."

Mrs. Gorey, delighted at Dansforth confidences, would have loved to ask her about her suitors, Marcus and

Jonathan, but even her curiosity was not strong enough to put the question. Later she told Mr. Lowdnes that somehow Miss Dansforth had an air of reserve it was not wise to try and force. "It's 'cause she's a member of the ton, as I always expected. They don't go about gossiping with their underlings," she said in no spirit of animosity, only confirming her good sense.

If Leslie's affairs had taken a turn for the better, for having an imposing relative behind one, could only be comforting, Marcus' affairs seemed muddled and unhappy. All day he brooded about what he could do to mend matters and finally decided that he would appeal to Dinah. He would ask her to intercede with Leslie, explaining the true facts of their former affair. Surely she would see that Dinah represented no threat to their becoming wed. Indeed, she would be assured he had sowed his wild oats and was now eager to settle into domestic bliss. Although, he conceded with a little laugh, marriage with Leslie would probably be a stormy affair, not dull or settled. Still, he had to make some move, and enlisting Dinah might prove disastrous, but then so was the situation as it stood, and he had to change Leslie's mind about his past. That Dinah would not oblige never crossed his mind.

Dinah, having given up all hopes of winning Marcus back into her bed, had turned with a sense of relief to Harry Weems, who was such an easy and admiring caller. She was not sure what he wanted of her, but she enjoyed his company, in many ways far more than she had Marcus', who had always made her feel inadequate beyond the boudoir. Harry had not, up to now, made any advances of a lascivious nature, rather to Dinah's disappointment but in the last few days he had seemed to lose interest. Since he had only mentioned he was much occupied with a case she had at first cheerfully signified that she quite understood. But it had been five days now and she had seen nothing of him. Well, she conceded philosophically, if sadly, that was men for you. You could never depend on them.

At least she had heard nothing from that nasty count, much to her relief, for she sensed that he was an ugly customer. She should never have taken his blunt and caused Marcus harm. Fortunately he had emerged from that horrid situation safely and did not seem to hold her responsible. But she thought she had seen the last of Marcus. But what had she done to put Harry off and what was he doing now?

Dinah would not have been pleased to see Harry that evening in the Fighting Cock, the disreputable tavern at the bottom of the street where Jack Poole lodged. He had struck up an acquaintance with Betsy Plumb, the maid who brought Jack his tankards, by the simple method of buying her a tot of gin. Not averse to the attentions of such a fine gentleman, Betsy was as clay in his hands.

"You work too hard, my dear. I have seen you running back and forth with tankards. Your employer must be a lady with a raging thirst," Harry insisted.

"T'ain't my old lady. 'Tis this new lodger we have, a mean looking cove. I don't fancy him a bit. Doesn't know how to treat a girl. Not like some I could mention. Never a penny for all my serving," she simpered, vastly flattered by Harry's sympathetic air.

"How unkind. He must be a beast, not appreciating your charms," Harry put on a convincing leer, hoping Betsy would fall for his rather obvious ploy.

"A mean josser. It don't pay to cross him," Betsy observed, and as the gin loosened her tongue she confided in her new friend. "There's something queer about him, too He never goes out. Just sits in his room drinking."

"And he never has any visitors?" Harry asked, knowing different.

"Today, he had some smart gent calling on him. Up to no good, the pair of them."

"What do you think they have in mind?" Harry asked.

"Can't tell. They're real secretive. He yelled at me to stay away. And there's sometin' else. See that man over by the fire. He's been hanging about the house. I seen him when I went out several times today."

Harry took a careless glance in the direction she indicated. He saw a trim, neat figure, nursing a cup of ale and appearing quite out of place in this disreputable haunt. Could he be watching Poole too? And if so who employed him? He would bear watching.

"Have another gin, Betsy," he urged.

"Well, just a quick one, then. I better get back or old Mrs. Horn will skin me alive. She doesn't like me having followers," she informed Harry with a coy smile.

Repressing his distaste for Betsy, who had probably not had a bath in a fortnight and whose coarse features left Harry unmoved, he bought her the gin, and promised to meet her again the following night. She rushed away with her tankard for Poole, and Harry sat brooding over the stranger, who appeared not to notice.

*   *   *

The stranger, who was one of Prince Esterhazy's minions, shared Harry's distaste for his surroundings, but he had been ordered by his master to keep a watching brief on the count's actions. He had followed him that evening to Poole's hideaway and noted that the count had spent some time within a house that normally he would never have frequented. Most of the prince's servants disliked the count, whose preemptory manners and obvious disdain for underlings had not endeared him to the Embassy servants. Joe Winters, for that was the man's name, would like to discover something to the count's discredit. Not only because the prince would reward him well but he would like to see the back of that toff. Send him back to that benighted land he came from and leave Englishmen alone, was Joe's analysis. He had planned to question Betsy but that other cove had nabbed her first.

Harry hesitated and then decided that much might be gained by cultivating the stranger. He wandered casually over to where Winters was sitting and offered to buy him a drink. Startled, Winters looked up, and seeing that Harry appeared a cut above most of the Fighting Cock's patrons agreed.

"A pretty frowzy dump, this tavern, wouldn't you agree?" Harry asked after they had settled with their drinks. "I suspect you are not a frequenter here."

Flattered by Harry's astuteness, Winters agreed. "Quite right. Rubbishy place."

Harry, skilled at drawing out both villains and honest men, lost no time in discovering who Winters' employer was, and was clever enough not to ask exactly what Winters was doing in such a low establishment. After several more drinks he heard the whole story. Whatever motive the Austrian ambassador had in ordering this man to shadow his illustrious guest, Harry thought it only confirmed Marcus' belief that the count was up to no good. Realizing that Winters was a man of limited curiosity and intelligence, he decided it might be to his advantage to join forces with the man. Together they might thwart Poole and the count, whatever skullduggery they had in mind.

"I like the cut of your jib, Winters," Harry said. "So I am going to tell you that I, too, am interested in the count. A client of mine wants an eye kept on him, and I could use an ally. No sense in both of us spending every hour hanging about this dreary neighborhood. How about dividing up the job. I will see you don't lose by it. My client has deep pockets."

"That's all right by me. I'd like to get rid of the gent. He's trouble all the way."

"Quite right," Harry agreed and the bargain was made. Harry had been careful not to divulge either the name of his client or his deepest suspicions about the count to the credulous Winters. He had the passing thought that Prince Esterhazy could have chosen a shrewder minion as his spy, but he would not complain. Winters suited him admirably, and he might even be able to relax his surveillance long enough to visit the appealing Miss Darcy, whom he had rather ignored for the past few days. So the two conspirators parted, to meet the next day and pool their information.

Chapter Twenty-Two

Count von Ronberg found himself in an impossible position. His honor demanded he answer Marcus' challenge immediately. But any attempt to enlist seconds, who would necessarily have to come from the embassy, would bring the matter to Esterhazy's ears and from his to Metternich's. The count had no illusions as to how the Austrian minister would view his involvement with a lowly journalist over the attentions of a woman.

Austrian aristocrats did not fight duels with their social inferiors. The benighted English frowned on duels, and if the matter came to the notice of the Prince Regent, von Ronberg would be sent home immediately, his mission unfulfilled.

Of course, he could ignore the challenge as beneath his notice, but that exposed him to a charge of cowardice and he thought Marcus Kingsley would probably air the whole business in *The Times*. Perhaps he could stall his tormentor, explain that he could not answer the challenge while Metternich remained in London. But his chief priority was to take care of the matter that had brought him here in the first place.

The dilemma did not improve his temper, but he decided that killing Marcus across twenty paces on Hampstead Heath would have to wait at least until he had accomplished his nobler purpose, and he was convinced Metternich would not want to be in London when that happened. He would just have to urge Jack Poole to step up his arrangements. To this end he made his way once again to Poole's unsavory lodgings, followed by Esterhazy's minion, Joe Winters.

While the count was urging Poole to get on with his assignment, the Hooker brothers, holed up down river near the docks in the house of a slattern called Molly Bowes, were equally unhappy. Because the attempt to snatch Leslie had failed they had received no money, and their resources were running low. Molly would not keep them without some coins to sweeten her temper. They wracked their limited brains as to where the money could be obtained. Finally after a few days of drinking and brooding, Bert Hooker made a decision. Bob, always content to follow his brother's lead, made no objection, only suggesting they had better be careful not to let themselves be caught by Jack Poole.

"I don't think Poole's worrying about us where he is. Probably on his way to Australia or somewhere by now," Bert said with more assurance than he felt.

"You know that gent we took is a big nob, runs a newspaper," Bert reminded his brother who had confided in him about Marcus' offer of employment.

"Well, what good's that? I ain't working on no scrubby paper," Bob protested.

"Try to use your noggin, Bob. That cove will probably pay for what we know. Papers is always giving rewards for news about villains like Poole. It's our public duty to rat on him."

"More likely get the magistrates to rack us up," Bob mourned, "with the luck we've had lately."

"We'll say we have to have, what's that word, immunity, because what we have to tell is so shocking," Bert insisted.

"I suppose it won't hurt," Bob agreed. "When'll we go?"

"This afternoon, late."

"What if this Kingsley man isn't there?" Bob asked, always fearing the worst.

"Then we'll find him," Bert said with more assurance than he felt, but Bob was always a spoilsport, scared of his own shadow, he admitted silently.

After a sketchy attempt to make themselves look a bit more respectable, Bob and Bert Hooker made their cautious way to Printing House Square, having bought a copy of *The Times* to learn the address. Bert had been taught to read in a country school but Bob had not taken to it, as he said, and relied on his brother to read any necessary documents. He was quite impressed with his brother's skill although he believed all this reading and figuring was of little use. Bob preferred to rely on his own brute strength to answer any problems that arose.

The brothers, neither wanting to admit their fear of Jack Poole, approached *The Times* building with due care, looking behind their backs, and ducking into doorways. They hoped Poole was in jail or on a transport ship, but knowing his prowess, suspected he might have evaded the Charlies and the law. Finally they scurried furtively into the reception hall of *The Times* where they were viewed with much disfavor by John Hughes, who thought them a right pair of villains. He was not inclined to give them access to Marcus, remembering that his employer had been abducted by rogues, probably just like these two. Finally Bert, sweating and nervous, insisted that he could take a message to Marcus and they would see how he received it. Hughes thought about the proposal for long agonizing minutes then agreed to send a boy with a note. Bert scrawled on a piece of paper under Hughes' minatory eye, "If you want to know more about the foreign gent and Jack Poole who snatched you, we have a tale to tell." The construction of the note took some time, and Bert had to borrow a stub of graphite from Hughes and a piece of paper to complete his task.

Finally having composed his message after laborious work, it was sent by Hughes to the upper floor and he ordered the Hookers to stand aside and wait for an answer, which they did with impatience, expecting at any moment to be apprehended either by Poole or a constable. At last Marcus ran lightly down the stairs, accompanied by Jonathan, eager to see if these were indeed his abductors as he suspected.

"Hello, Bob," he greeted his former captor, recognizing him at once. Both the Hookers backed against the wall, not expecting such a cheery greeting, and suspicious.

Jonathan eyed them sternly, thinking he had rarely seen such a stupid and brutal twosome, but Marcus was all good will, determined to discover what they had to tell him. He led the Hookers, eyed with some disgust by Hughes, who wondered what business these two unprepossessing men could have with his urbane editor, to a bench in the back of the reception hall. It would be a story, he assumed, and having vast experience with how journalists pursued news, shrugged his shoulders as if taking no responsibility for the affair.

Out of the earshot of Hughes, Marcus lost no time in acquainting Jonathan with the identity of their callers.

"These are the two fellows who abducted me, Jon, but not too bad. They let me go," he insisted obviously holding no anger toward the Hookers. Jonathan scowled but only nodded, unwilling to commit himself.

"Well, men, what have you to tell me?" Marcus urged.

"Want to see the color of your money first, cap'n. We ain't squealing for nothin', you know," Bert said with a boldness he was far from feeling.

"Quite right. How about ten guineas," Marcus suggested, not at all shocked.

"Really, Marcus. You shouldn't encourage them. They are probably lying thieves," Jonathan protested.

"Not at all, Jon. Just looking out for their interests, and you can't blame them for that. I suspect Poole never paid them a penny for the job."

"Right you are, sir. And t'was all his fault it got buggered up," Bert replied.

Heartened by the sight of the coins, Bert launched into his tale. They had been hired by Poole, he explained, on the orders of the "foreign gentleman" whose identity they neither knew nor cared, to abduct Marcus and Leslie, but more important was the next big job, the assassination.

"Wanted us to kill him as he rode through the streets."

"Another attempt at Wellington, no doubt," Jonathan guessed.

"No sir," Bert growled. "Wouldn't touch the Iron Duke. Served under him."

"Well, who was it then?"

"That old Prinny," Bert said, satisfied that he had shocked the two who stared at him in wonder.

"You mean that the 'foreign gentleman' hired you and Poole to kill the Prince Regent?" Marcus asked in disbelief.

"That's right. Don't hold no brief for that one for all he's a royal, spending money like water on his fancy women, palaces and pictures, while good men are hungry," Bert justified.

"I see. And when was this nasty deed to take place?" Marcus asked.

"When Parliament opened this fall, but I think Poole had decided to do it before then. The foreign gentleman was being a bit dodgy," Bert explained.

"Yes, he would," Marcus agreed, passing over the coins.

"You won't be having us in charge for the snatch, then," said Bob who had remained mostly silent during this discussion.

"Not at all. You are free to go," Marcus agreed.

Looking about to make sure that he had no stalwart guards ready to seize them, Bert grabbed Bob by the arm and without any more talk scuttled out of the building, leaving Marcus staring abstractly at the wall, and Jonathan fuming at his friend for allowing the Hookers to escape.

"Really, Marcus, you are a fool to let them go. We don't even know their direction and where to find them," Jonathan groaned.

"They wouldn't have told us. They are terrified of Poole. Really it took courage to tell us anything at all," Marcus said with cheerful acceptance. "Anyway they would have probably lied. And if we had hauled them before the constables they would have denied the whole business."

"Well, what are you going to do now? You have no proof of this outrageous story?"

"I want to talk to Weems, that Bow Street Runner. He is keeping on eye on Poole for me. And then I think I have enough credit with Castlereagh and Liverpool to get them to listen."

"Will they deport the count?"

"I hope so, but not before the duel."

Jonathan, in the face of this new development had almost forgotten the duel, but now he spoke up against it. "You are surely not going on with that?"

"Certainly, although I wonder why we have not heard from the man's seconds. It has been a few days since Leigh went around with the challenge. The man's a coward as well as a poltroon of the vilest sort."

"He probably is waiting for Metternich to leave London. It would not sit well with that noble minister to have one of his countrymen engaged in a duel." Jonathan suggested with a certain astuteness.

"You might be right, but that does not excuse him. Look, Jonathan, I have to get hold of Weems. He left me his direction and I am going around there right now. Do you want to come?"

"Of course. Who knows what jape you are up to now. You need a wiser head," Jonathan said with a jocularity he did not feel.

Happily they were able to catch Harry Weems before he left for his evening rendezvous with Joe Winters at the Fighting Cock. Harry greeted them with his usual insouciance. "Glad you stopped by, Mr. Kingsley. I think I have some valuable information for you. Tonight will confirm it."

"And I have some for you," Marcus replied. "Where can we talk?"

"There's quite a decent pub at the end of this street. Far better than where I am meeting my friend who is keeping an eye on Poole," Harry insisted. The three men hurried into The Three Dogs, a respectable neighborhood tavern, mostly unfrequented at this hour when decent folk were enjoying their evening meal. Jonathan paid for the drinks and took them to a secluded table in the corner. The only other occupant of the pub was an old man smoking a pipe and nursing a tankard of ale.

Without more ado, Marcus launched into the tale that the Hookers had told him. Harry listened attentively, not showing either shock or disgust, but a lively interest. When Marcus had finished, Harry nodded in agreement.

"I knew that rubbishy count was up to some villainy. He has been meeting with Poole at a low dive near the Fighting Cock. The interesting fact is that I am not the only one watching him. Prince Esterhazy, the Austrian ambassador, has bid a servant to keep an eye on the count, and we have joined forces, so to speak. Poole himself never emerges from the seedy rooms he has taken, and sends a maid to fetch him beer."

"Do you think the count intends to pursue the matter of the Prince Regent's assassination?" Marcus asked impatiently.

"I wouldn't be surprised. He certainly has some fell purpose in remaining in London beside the conquest of Miss Dansforth."

Marcus frowned. He did not want to think about Leslie now. The memory was too painful. Jonathan, too, was disturbed because he sensed Marcus' unhappiness over Leslie and felt powerless to help either one of them.

"Metternich is in London. I wonder if he is behind this plot," Marcus offered.

"Oh, surely not. However much you dislike his politics, Marcus, you must admit that he would never inspire such an attack. If it were discovered he had masterminded it, his credit would be ruined," Jonathan objected.

"You can be sure it would not be Metternich that would take the blame. I think the count has agreed to this plan to reinstate himself with royal circles in Vienna. And if he is successful there would be Metternich's gratitude to ease his way," Marcus said, convinced.

Jonathan, who was well up on European politics, and knew that Metternich had never forgiven England for not endorsing the Tsar's Holy Alliance, still could not accept this drastic plan to throw England into turmoil.

"You see, Jon, it is to Metternich's advantage to raise the fears of the government about a revolution. There is a great deal of unrest in the north and Liverpool is no liberal. He would abolish all rights, habeas corpus, open trials, the lot, if anything happened to the Prince Regent. Whatever his faults, Prinny is the heir and must be protected."

Harry, impressed by Marcus' astute analysis of the situation, remained silent. His job was to find evidence that would convict Poole, and although he believed that the Hookers' story was true he did not see how they could prove it.

"You know that Poole is still in contact with the count, Harry. That means he has not abandoned the plan. And the Hookers think he will move soon. Originally the attempt was to be made as the Prince Regent rode to the opening of Parliament, but now, under pressure from Metternich, he will act much sooner. I wish we had some idea of the

Prince Regent's movements for the next week or so," Marcus said.

"Do you want me to apprehend Poole and hail him back before the magistrate? I think Mr. Ransom would like to see Poole put away. He hated letting him go, and was quite convinced he was a wrong one," Harry replied.

"We have no proof. What I think I must do is appraise Liverpool and the Cabinet of this threat to the Prince Regent's life. Castlereagh can ask that the count be recalled. Then Poole will have no bankroll and I doubt if he would go ahead without an assurance he would be paid enough to escape the consequences of his horrible deed."

All three men brooded, appalled at the situation they felt powerless to avert. But they must take some action. Both Jonathan and Harry looked to Marcus, depending on him for a solution.

"Weems, you must keep up your surveillance on Poole and your contact with the man Esterhazy has deputized to watch the count. Poole will have to emerge to put his plan in train. He can no longer rely on the Hookers, and he will never manage it alone. In the meantime I will speak to Castlereagh about the count." Marcus at last had decided on a course to be followed, not a decisive one but the best that could be managed in the circumstances.

"Right, Mr. Kingsley. I had best be on my way then to meet Joe Winter." Even Harry's natural sang froid was quenched by this dreadful news. He had never been involved in such high level chicanery and only hoped he would emerge from it all with his life and career unscathed.

Marcus, as if sensing his uneasiness, turned to him and said, "I know we are asking a lot of you Harry. You will not lose by your efforts. And here is some money for expenses and your fee. Keep in touch. Come, Jonathan," he ordered and the three men left to continue their attempts to balk the count of his heinous crime.

As they watched Harry hurry away to his meeting, Jonathan could not repress another worry.

"You can't go on with your duel now, Marcus. You are needed to direct this business of bringing home to the count the retribution he deserves, and not by shooting him."

"We'll see. I wonder if it's too late to see Castlereagh tonight."

"He's probably at dinner. Certainly he would not be angered at such an interruption," Jonathan said.

"If he's at home. He dines out a great deal, one of the most popular men in London, sought by every hostess of the ton. Still skulking here will achieve nothing. I'll give it a try."

"You won't want me to come with you," Jonathan asked.

"No, but there is a chore you could take on for me. Like a fool I told Leslie about my liaison with Dinah and she will have nothing more to do with me. She even talks of giving up the column. Could you intercede. Just plead with her to do nothing for the moment. Make her understand how valuable she is to the paper."

"I don't think appealing to Leslie's vanity is of much use, and you probably should never have told her about Dinah."

"I wanted to be honest with her, have no secrets, and I admit Dinah is heavily on my conscience," Marcus admitted, rather shame-faced. Then feeling he owed Jonathan an explanation, he continued, "I proposed marriage to Leslie, you know, and she turned me down, with some puritanical objections that I should be proposing to Dinah, and that I was a veritable cad."

"I am sure Leslie truly cares for you, Marcus," Jonathan said, a brave admission since he knew his own chances were doomed by Marcus' determination to claim Leslie.

"She's been taken up by the Earl of Rothfield, and he will see to it that she meets all sorts of respectable fellows who can offer her far more than I can," Marcus explained, thoroughly depressed.

"I don't think worldly possessions mean much to Leslie," Jonathan comforted his friend. He was surprised at Marcus' gloomy assessment of his chances, accustomed as he was to his usual self-confidence, and success with women.

"Right now she despises me. I thought at first I would try to forget her, but I know now, I can't. Please help me, Jonathan."

Touched by Marcus's appeal, Jonathan had no recourse but to agree to his unwelcomed task, he thought. His ideals of friendship and loyalty were engrained and despite his own disappointment, realized that Leslie probably was regretting her summary dismissal of Marcus.

"I'll do my best for you, Marcus," he promised.

"You are a Trojan, Jon. I will never forget this." Then shaking off his personal troubles, he told Jonathan that he must try to reach Castlereagh this evening, and hailed a hackney to take him on his troubling errand. Jonathan refused his offer of a lift, wanting to marshall his thoughts as he, too, made his way toward an uncomfortable interview.

Chapter Twenty-Three

Leslie, as always, was pleased to see Jonathan, and urged him to remain for supper. His presence was just the tonic she needed, as she had been brooding about Marcus.

Jonathan agreed to join her for the meal. Meantime he was trying to arrange his thoughts to manage the difficult task Marcus had assigned to him. He wondered if Leslie would confide in him about Marcus' proposal and her refusal. After a good meal of roasted chicken, boiled potatoes and peas, which he did not really enjoy knowing what faced him, Leslie regarded him in a considering fashion.

"I suppose Marcus told you that he has proposed to me, and that I have refused him," she said, surprising Jonathan with her frankness.

"And that you have resigned your position on the paper," Jonathan agreed. "Are you going to live with the Earl of Rothfield?"

"Of course not. He's a dear old man, and I am very happy to have reconciled with him, but I will not give up my independence and become the cosseted relative," she insisted with some determination.

"If you married Marcus do you think you could keep

your independence," Jonathan asked with a certain shrewdness.

"Not entirely, but it doesn't matter, because I am not going to marry him. What do you know about Dinah Darcy, Jonathan?"

Oh, dear, thought Jonathan. Now I am for it, a catechism about poor Dinah. Plunging into these deep waters, he explained, "Marcus has had her in keeping for about two years. She's really a nice simple girl, affectionate and loyal, but I don't think deeply attached to Marcus. Lazy, I fear, and took the easiest way out of securing her livelihood. But he has broken off the connection."

"And broken her heart," Leslie said with a firmness that Jonathan found quite quelling.

"Not at all. She misses the money more than Marcus, but he made a very generous settlement on her. She's somewhat of a ninny, and took up with the count. Before you feel too sorry for her I should tell you she was responsible in part for Marcus' abduction by that villain, Jack Poole."

"What do you mean?" Leslie was shocked by this revelation.

Jonathan set to with all his persuasive powers to explain how Marcus had been taken by Poole and the Hooker brothers on his leaving New Albany Street after breaking off with Dinah. He had been quite honest with her, telling her he had fallen in love with Leslie, but he knew nothing about her arrangement with the count.

"That horrid man. He's at the bottom of a great deal of trouble," Leslie insisted.

"More than you know." Jonathan hesitated. Should he tell her of Marcus' challenge to the count and the information the Hooker brothers had given them? Eager to engage Leslie's sympathies on behalf of Marcus, he decided that she should be told the whole business. He could not let Marcus fight that duel and he thought Leslie was the only person who could stop him. So he plunged into the whole sorry tale. Leslie listened quietly, without interruption, although he noticed she paled and her hands clenched.

"That's a dreadful story, Jonathan. Assassinate the Prince Regent. How could even a man as callous and brutal as the count contemplate such a deed?" she asked.

"Politics are behind it. We think Metternich urged him to it and the count agreed in order to strengthen his position in the Austrian court. It's a nasty coil, and we are trying to get the count deported," Jonathan informed her. "Actually Marcus is seeing Castlereagh right now or he would have come to you to plead his cause again I am sure."

Poor Jonathan, his own chances with Leslie receding with every word he spoke, had to be honest. Ruefully he admitted his chances with her had long gone anyway and as a friend to both Leslie and Marcus, he wanted to secure their happiness, even if at the cost of his own.

"He must not fight a duel over me. That would be insane. The count will kill him," moaned Leslie.

"You do care for him, don't you Leslie?" Jonathan asked, although he had no doubt of the answer.

Unable to resist the pleading in Jonathan's eyes, Leslie admitted that she did. "But I think he has behaved very cavalierly toward Miss Darcy. I find that difficult to forgive."

"But you must, Leslie. Why ruin your future over a matter that really has little importance. Marcus never loved Dinah, nor did she love him. It was an arrangement that satisfied them both for a time, but of little moment, believe me. Most men have a mistress if they can afford it. I might have done myself if I had the income. That does not mean they do not eventually settle down and become good and faithful husbands," he insisted.

"Perhaps. I would like to see Miss Darcy and hear her views on the subject. Not that I distrust you, Jonathan, but I know you are a good friend to Marcus and would protect him."

"And I am even a better friend to you and want to protect you," Jonathan urged. "I don't think it is a good idea for you to see Dinah, but if that will reconcile you with Marcus, and persuade you to talk to him about this stupid duel, I will take you to see her," Jonathan agreed with more ease than he felt.

"Let's go now. The sooner I talk with her the more relieved I will be. I must admit I had no idea she was involved with the count. I don't know whether I can forgive her for being the instrument of Marcus' abduction. And you tell me Poole is still at large. How can we be sure he does not intend some harm to Marcus again?"

"Marcus is on his guard, and he has enlisted the help of Harry Weems, that Bow Street Runner, quite a formidable chap in his own right," Jonathan reassured her.

"Yes, I was quite impressed with Mr. Weems," Leslie agreed.

"And Mr. Weems is quite impressed with Dinah. I think he has designs on her, of the most honorable nature," Jonathan said, lightening the atmosphere with a whimsical smile.

"Let us go see Miss Darcy now."

Although he had some concern about this course of action, Jonathan agreed, hoping it would help Marcus' cause. At the back of his mind was the duel. He would do all in his power to prevent Marcus meeting the count and losing his career, and perhaps, even his life.

* * *

Whether Marcus would have endorsed this plan of action was problematical, but he had a task of his own which would engage all his skills. After changing his clothes, into de rigeur evening dress, he paid his call on Castlereagh, determined to track him down if he was not at home. But to his relief Castlereagh was at home, hosting a male dinner party, that included the Prime Minister. Fortunately his wife was in the country as that lady could be both troublesome and outrageous. The footman, who asked Marcus to wait in the morning room of the mansion in St. James Square, seemed reluctant to interrupt the diners, but a large tip persuaded him.

"The gentleman are just beginning the port, sir, so milord should be able to spare you a few minutes," the footman observed.

Marcus paced up and down the room, impatient and restless. This was a delicate maneuver. Castlereagh, like most of the Cabinet, did not look kindly on journalists and *The Times* had not always treated the government with courtesy. Would he believe Marcus' story?

At last the great man entered the room, but his countenance was forbidding.

"What is the excuse for this intrusion, Kingsley?" he asked after the curtest of greetings.

"Danger to the realm, sir," Marcus said with as much force as he could muster. He noticed the thin patrician features of Lord Castlereagh wore their usual austere cast. He was a handsome man with a great deal of outward calm which masked a volatile temperament he had managed on maturity to mask with an aloof air. Marcus' dramatic words did not appear to impress him.

"Really, well you had better tell me about it," he sighed as he sat down and indicated that Marcus should take a seat, but Marcus was too disturbed to settle. He loomed over Castlereagh and launched into his tale, omitting any reference to Leslie or his own abduction, but prepared to go further if necessary.

For once Castlereagh responded with more passion than was his wont. "Good God," he exclaimed when Marcus had finished, then rapidly regained his composure. "You realize Kingsley, if this is true, it is a powder keg."

"Just so, sir. But what will you do?"

"I cannot request that Count von Ronberg be deported without proof. Have you any?'

"Not at the moment but I have men watching him and his nasty conspirator."

"But can you believe these two rogues who laid the information. They might just be gulling you for the money?" Castlereagh objected.

Marcus sighed. He would have to tell him about his kidnapping.

"I happen to know these two fellows. They abducted me on the count's orders."

"This tale becomes more complicated every minute. What had you done to incur the count's wrath?" Castlereagh asked, now intrigued.

"Well sir, it's a rather tawdry affair and does not reflect well upon me. The count and I were interested in the same lady, although my intentions are honorable and his are not. He appeared to believe that my attentions to her were preventing him from gaining success." Marcus had chosen his words carefully, knowing that the story did not reflect well on his own character.

Rather amused by Marcus' embarrassment, Castlereagh was inclined to believe him. He knew the count's reputation with women and did not doubt that any respectable woman would find his approaches abhorrent. And Marcus appeared so shamefaced he had to think he would not have revealed the business if it were not true.

"Well, the obvious course was to bring the kidnapper before a magistrate. Did you not think of that? The lady's name need not be mentioned."

"Mr. Ransom, the magistrate in question, did not think the evidence warranted holding him. And I should mention that the kidnapper, one Jack Poole by name, a Peninsular veteran, did not know the name of his employer. The count was certain to protect his identity from further blackmail."

"What a coil. But how can I go to Esterhazy with these vague suspicions and ask him to send the count home?" Castlereagh asked, reason on his side.

"Well, Esterhazy already suspects the count of wrong doing. He has had a man following him to the dive where he meets with Poole." Marcus did not intend to tell Castlereagh of the pending duel. That would only rebound on his shoulders.

"Interesting. Unfortunately the count is close to Metternich, not that I trust that wily devil. He is quite capable of wanting to get rid of Prinny and cause havoc in the country," Castlereagh mused. "Is there no one you can produce to verify this shocking story? We cannot move against the count without a witness."

"There is a Bow Street Runner who I have employed to keep an eye on Poole and the count. He knows quite a bit, and then . . ." Marcus hesitated not wanting to involve either Leslie or Dinah in this sordid business.

"Yes, cough it up man. This is no time to have scruples. I take it from your reluctance the witness might be a woman." Castlereagh was a man of astute perception and Marcus's hesitation was not lost upon him.

"Well, yes. But poor Dinah did not know exactly what she had taken on with the count."

"Find the woman and bring her here, tonight, if possible. We cannot delay a moment. Prinny has returned from Brighton and rides about the street daily, exposed to any assassin or rogue who wants to harm him. There has already been one attempt on his life. Good God, if he is killed I shudder to think what would happen to the government, with radicals like Brougham and Hunt on the rampage."

Naturally Castlereagh would want to protect the government and the Tory party, from which his own power came. Marcus could not fault him for that. But before he could demur Castlereagh continued.

"I hope you have no intention of printing anything in your paper about this plot. Think of what turmoil any suggestion, even a veiled one, could mean?"

Although Marcus took issue with the government on many matters, on this he completely agreed with Castlereagh.

"This must be kept secret. What about the Prime Minister. Should he be informed?"

"Liverpool is an old maid, but on this matter I think I can promise he will act. If all else fails he will ask the Austrians to remove both Esterhazy and the count as a signal of our displeasure," Castlereagh spoke tersely, knowing his own influence. He had hopes of winning the office himself and Liverpool depended upon him to manage the House of Commons as well as foreign affairs.

"Go interview this woman and persuade her to see me," Castlereagh urged. "And not a word to anyone else."

"My confederate on the paper and a close friend know the whole tale as does the Runner, but beyond that there is nothing known of the threat to the Prince Regent," Marcus assured him.

"I have to trust your sense of responsibility on this, Kingsley, and hope that the lure of a good story will not tempt you."

"Not until the whole matter has been resolved," Marcus said, unwilling to go further, "If that is all, I will call on Miss Darcy and try to persuade her to tell you her part in all this. But I feel she knows little aside from the fact that the count hates me and seeks some sort of revenge."

"Well, do your best. I rely on you, Kingsley," Castlereagh said, leaving no doubt that if anything happened to the Prince Regent he would hold Marcus responsible. They parted abruptly, Castlereagh to inform Liverpool, and Marcus to face an uncomfortable talk with Dinah.

If he had realized that Jonathan and Leslie were on their way to quiz Dinah on a matter that would affect his future relationship with Leslie he would have been even more unhappy. But he must postpone all thoughts of Leslie while this complicated and dangerous business was afoot.

Leaving Castlereagh to deal with Liverpool, he wished he could have been more decisive with the minister. As he looked about for a hackney in the deepening twilight of a fine summer evening he could not help yearning to know what Leslie was thinking and if Jonathan had already intervened to soothe her anger. And even more to the point, had Harry Weems secured any evidence against Poole and the count. Why did England have these laws about a citizens rights? Then he reprimanded himself. Did he want to live in a country where a man could be imprisoned for years without trial just on suspicion? The innocent must be protected. Finally he found a cab and directed the coachman to New Albany Street, refusing to think of the awkward meeting with Dinah that lay ahead.

Chapter Twenty-Four

Jonathan and Leslie had preceded Marcus to New Albany Street, both of them apprehensive, if for different reasons. Jonathan was convinced that Marcus would be furious that he had escorted Leslie to meet with his former mistress and Leslie was having second thoughts about seeing the woman. Dinah would hate her and treat her with contempt, she was sure, and she deserved the poor girl's odium. Why should she receive her with any kindness. She paused for a minute outside Dinah's lodgings, reluctant to enter and hear about Marcus' long liaison with Dinah. Well, she had made the decision to come. She must not be faint-hearted now. Her future was at stake even if Marcus should forgive her intemperate words and still wanted to marry her. Oh, why was she such a ninny, trusting a man, that on his own admission was a libertine?

Dinah, bored and lonely, was disappointed when she saw that Jonathan was her caller, and with a strange woman in tow. She had rather hoped that Harry Weems would drop by this evening. He had explained to her after that enjoyable outing to Ranlegh Gardens that he would be very occupied with an important case during the next few days, but would try to visit her whenever possible.

"Do come in, Jonathan," Dinah welcomed him, raising her eyebrows at his companion.

"Dinah, this is Miss Dansforth, who wished to meet you," Jonathan said as the pair entered Dinah's sitting room. "And Leslie, this is Miss Darcy of whom I told you."

"How do you do, Miss Darcy. I hope we are not calling at an inconvenient time," Leslie said a bit stiffly. She looked over Dinah carefully, finding her plumply attractive with kind eyes.

"Not at all. I'm bored to tears. Do sit down," Dinah invited cheerfully. She wondered what this very respectable lady wanted with her, why Jonathan had brought her. It must have something to do Marcus, she decided shrewdly.

"This is rather awkward, Dinah," Jonathan began.

"Perhaps it might be best if I explained, Jonathan. After all it is on my behalf we are here," Leslie intervened. And before he could protest she launched into the difficult explanation with all the forthrightness Jonathan had come to expect from Leslie.

"You see, Miss Darcy, Marcus Kingsley has proposed marriage to me, and very rightly first told me of his prior arrangement with you. I understand he has broken it off, but I feel he owes you his loyalty, and should have asked you to be his wife in view of your past relationship." Leslie blushed.

"Why, bless me, Miss Dansforth, don't worry your head about me. I never expected Marcus to marry me. It was just a convenient arrangement for us both. You see, I was in the chorus of Covent Garden when Marcus discovered me, and not doing too well, I must admit. Am afraid my career on the stage was not much, and I like my comforts, so I agreed to become Marcus' mistress, because I am a lazy chit. But I always knew that someday he would find a smart, beautiful lady of virtue like yourself, and then he would leave me," Dinah explained with cheerful abandon.

"But what will happen to you?" Leslie asked, taken aback by such frankness. "Do you not care for Marcus?"

"He's a nice cove, a real gentleman, but I am not sorrowing for him, if that's what you mean. He made a generous settlement, you know, and now I have another bloke who interests me. Marcus was so serious, so smart, all that book-learning, it depressed me at times. Now Harry, my new gentleman, likes a laugh, and a romp. Much more to my taste."

"Does she mean Harry Weems?" Leslie turned to Jonathan with the question, a bit puzzled. "How did they meet?"

Jonathan had been dreading that very question but he was saved from answering by a knock on the door. Dinah excused herself and with a pleased smile went to admit her caller, convinced it was the very Harry Weems she had mentioned. Her expression sobered when she found Marcus outside, but she welcomed him with her cheerful demeanor.

"This is a surprise, Marcus. We were just talking about you," she told him.

Jonathan groaned. Now there would be trouble.

Marcus was cross, tired, frustrated and hungry. He had missed dinner in order to see Castlereagh. Looking at Leslie, Jonathan and Dinah his irritation increased. They looked like a trio of conspirators whose victim had suddenly surprised them. He had asked Jonathan to intercede with Leslie but he had not meant for Jonathan to drag her around to meet his former mistress the moment his back was turned.

"I imagine you were," he said, his tone acerbic, leaving them in no doubt about what he thought of their conversation. Leslie blushed and gave a weak smile. Dinah wisely kept silent and only Jonathan made any attempt to explain as Marcus threw himself wearily into a chair.

"Do let me explain, Marcus. You asked me to speak to Leslie about the column. She was most concerned about Dinah's feelings and I thought it best they should meet so Dinah could reassure her she felt no animosity toward you. They seem to have got on quite well together," he concluded eyeing Marcus sheepishly.

"How nice for them. I suppose they enjoyed raking my character over the coals," Marcus said sarcastically.

Both Dinah and Jonathan looked miserable, but Leslie, made of sterner stuff, joined the battle. "Don't be irascible, Marcus. Jonathan is a good friend to you, only tried to help, and Miss Darcy has been most kind and generous. Stop acting like a bear with a sore head. And for that matter, why are you here? Has something happened that demanded an interview with Miss Darcy." Leslie's tone was tart, although she really wanted to throw herself into Marcus's arms and have a good cry, so miserable was she about all these misunderstandings.

Marcus took her rebuke quite well. What a worthy opponent she was, he conceded. "Yes, as a matter of fact something had occurred that requires Dinah's cooperation. Lord Castlereagh wants to see her, to hear her story about the count. I have told him almost everything about this conspiracy, Poole's role, and the shocking story we heard from the Hooker brothers. I assume Jonathan has told you all about that," he concluded now somewhat mollified.

Leslie's presence here must mean she had not completely finished with him.

Dinah, mystified by all these allusions, and not quite understanding what was required her, determined to be as helpful as possible. Marcus seemed to be in some sort of trouble and she was only too willing to assist him. She only hoped that Miss Dansforth would not take exception to any association between herself and Marcus. That horrid count was at the bottom of the business she thought and she would like to get her own back on him. But the idea of confronting a hoity-toity lord who would quiz her held a certain amount of apprehension.

"I'll do what I can, Marcus. But I really don't know much about the count," she pleaded.

"Possibly, we'll see. What I really would like is to find Harry Weems. He is *au courant* and might have some suggestions."

Dinah brightened at the mention of Harry's name. "Actually, Marcus, I thought you were Harry. He promised to come by when he could, although I know he is busy with some case. I have been seeing quite a bit of him," Dinah offered, hoping that would calm any suspicions either Miss Dansforth or Marcus would have about any lingering feeling she might still have for her former protector.

"Well, we can't keep the great man waiting. He wants to see you tonight," Marcus urged.

"Will he press for the count's deportation?" Leslie asked, realizing the significance of Castlereagh's interest.

"If we can come up with some evidence that he is really behind this plot," Marcus said. "Come on, Dinah, get your bonnet and shawl and let's be going. I can drop you and Jonathan on the way," Marcus suggested, giving Leslie a look that boded for a future private conversation which cheered her somewhat.

Dinah, all acquiescence left the room, and Marcus turned to Jonathan. "You have not told her exactly what the plot is have you, Jon?"

"Of course not. She is puzzled but obliging. No need to strain her limited capacities."

"I think you are very harsh, Jonathan. Miss Darcy seems a compassionate and sensible woman. I quite like her," Leslie insisted.

Marcus groaned inwardly. He could see Leslie adopting Dinah as one of her causes. She would be a valiant supporter and see to it that Dinah rejected her former life and became a model of propriety.

In that he wronged Leslie, who genuinely liked Dinah and wanted her friendship. She had been surprised by Dinah's calm explanation of her relationship with Marcus, her acceptance of Leslie with no signs of jealousy or anger. A practical, rather pathetic victim of men's lust, Leslie decided unwillingly to a pass judgment. She wondered if she would have been virtuous if she had found herself in Dinah's position. Admitting her feeling for Marcus she doubted it.

In a moment the ill-assorted quartet were on the street climbing into the hackney, that Marcus had kept waiting. A good sign, thought Leslie. He had evidently not wanted to pay a long call on Dinah, and had only come on pressing business.

At Leslie's lodgings Marcus handed her out, pressed her hand and said, "You seem to have forgiven me. We will sort this all out as soon as this miserable plot is uncovered and Poole and the count brought to justice. But take care.

I don't trust either of those gentlemen. I regret our own affairs must wait upon that."

As he waited on the doorstep to see Leslie safely inside, she looked at him with a quaint considering air. "Then you have not taken me in disgust entirely."

"You little fool. I love you, more's the pity." And as Mrs. Gorey opened the door, ignoring her, he took Leslie in his hard arms and gave her a hard kiss.

"Really," sniffed the landlady, staring at Marcus's back as he ran down the steps and reentered the hackney. "On the public street. What is the world coming to?" she asked no one in particular, seeing Miss Dansforth's bemused state.

"It's a wicked place out there, Mrs. Gorey, but not quite as horrid as it was some hours ago." With these enigmatic words Leslie mounted the stairs to her room, much comforted, if still worried about Marcus' safety.

Marcus invited Jonathan to accompany Dinah and him to St. James Street, and he was only too eager to comply. He not only wanted to meet the minister but he wondered what Dinah could tell Castlereagh that would help in pinning this crime on the count.

Castlereagh had obviously been in a fever of impatience for their visit, although he managed to conceal it partially with his habitual air of gravity.

Dinah, in awe of her surroundings, the butler who had announced them, the footman who took her bonnet and shawl, and the great marble hall of the mansion, was even more overwhelmed by Lord Castlereagh. Marcus introduced her and Jonathan to the minister, who received them both with courtesy. Turning to Dinah, and sensing her nervousness in an environment completely foreign to her, he did his best to put her at ease.

"It is very kind of you to spare me the time, Miss Darcy, at this inconvenient hour."

Dinah, wide-eyed at this respect from a toff, only murmured.

"Please sit down. May I offer you some refreshment," Castlereagh asked realizing she was completely out of her depth.

"No, thank you, sir," she gasped, looking about the library where they had been received. She had never seen a room like it, heavily paneled in mahogany, with its serried rows of leather bound books reaching to the ceiling, the dark patterned Oriental carpet, and the stiff leather chairs.

Feeling he had done all he could to calm her fears, Castlereagh launched into his questions.

"I understand you have had some dealings with Count von Ronberg," he began as tactfully as he knew how.

"Yes sir. He became my protector, in a way, as I was at a loose end at the time." She resolutely did not mention Marcus's part in that condition.

"I applaud your frankness, Miss Darcy. Was this just a business arrangement or did he have an ulterior motive, beside your charms, of course," Castlereagh, ever gallant, asked.

Much heartened by the respect with which this high and mighty lord was treating her Dinah responded happily, "If you mean did he want something besides sleeping with me, yes he did. He wanted to know all about Marcus and his movements. He got quite nasty when I said Marcus was tired of me and ending our affair."

Jonathan bit back a gasp. What would Castlereagh think of such boldness. But he underestimated a man famed for his diplomacy. "And did you supply him with that information?" Castlereagh asked suavely.

"Yes, sir, and if I had suspected what he meant to do I would never have uttered. He had an ugly side for all he was a high-toned nob and he turned out to be nothing more than a scurvy rogue, not any better than the meanest cutthroat in Thrawl Street," Dinah explained with some indignation.

"She means Spitalfields," Marcus explained realizing that Lord Castlereagh would not have an intimate knowledge of that insalubrious section of London.

"And what did you tell him, Miss Darcy." Castlereagh pressed on calmly.

"Why, that Marcus was coming to see me that very evening, to break it off with me, I thought. He seemed really pleased, not that he cared a farthing for me, but just wanted to get some kind of revenge on Marcus here. And so he did, having his heavies to snatch him just as he was leaving my house."

"Why do you suppose he wanted Mr. Kingsley . . . er, snatched, as you say," Castlereagh urged.

"I don't know nothing about that, except he had it in for him." Dinah was not prepared to explain that Marcus and the count both admired Leslie, even to this lord, who didn't seem a bad sort for all his starchiness.

"Do you know his confederates, Poole and the Hooker brothers?" Castlereagh asked, surprising Marcus with his grasp of the essentials.

"Never heard of them, but if they was the villains that took Marcus I wouldn't touch them."

"It seems, Mr. Kingsley, that the count's vendetta against you is a personal not a political one," Castlereagh sighed in disappointment. "A little of both, my lord," Marcus protested. "I suspected that the count had another purpose in coming to London aside from a woman. And the

Hookers were the men who took me, and the same ones who revealed the count's nefarious plot to me."

"And these Hookers have disappeared."

"Hiding for their own safety. We know where Poole is and if he intends to go forward with his plan he must enlist some other varlets to help him," Marcus said.

"Yes, and we can't wait for that. Thank you, Miss Darcy for your time. If you and Mr. Stirling will wait a moment outside, I want to have a few private words with Mr. Kingsley, if you will not think me rude."

Jonathan rose and escorted Dinah to the door. She took one last look about the appointments and made a ducking curtsey to Castlereagh before leaving the room.

Marcus, meantime, had been brooding about his next move. Before Castlereagh could speak his mind he forestalled him.

"I think we must apprehend Poole, threaten him with dire punishment if he does not cooperate with us, and then face him with the count, hoping he will identify him. We must hint that the count has betrayed Poole and knowing the man, he will want his own revenge," Marcus suggested.

"That, of course, is illegal, but in the circumstances I think we could be excused for bending the law somewhat," Castlereagh agreed. "Yes, that appears to be the only feasible plan, but not without its dangers." He paused a moment then smiled a bit grimly. "You know, Esterhazy will be appalled by all this. I wonder how much I should tell him."

Not one bit interested or sympathetic to the Austrian ambassador's embarrassment, Marcus ignored the remark.

Castlereagh recollected himself and turned to more urgent matters. "And how will you capture this Poole?"

"The Bow Street Runners will do that. And if Poole is

threatened with hanging for committing treason I don't think he will hesitate to involve the count. He's a slippery devil and might deny the whole business but we will have to be persuasive," Marcus insisted.

"My duty is to protect the Prince Regent not inquire into the rights and wrongs of how you achieve that. I will not be ungrateful, Mr. Kingsley, if you bring this off," Castlereagh promised, knowing cynically that he would owe Marcus several favors if the editor demanded them.

"I want the count out of the country, and will do whatever is necessary to rid us of him. You need not know the particulars," Marcus said understanding what Castlereagh inferred.

On that note the interview concluded and Marcus joined Dinah and Jonathan in the hall where upon they took their leave without more ado. Dinah, not understanding what the talk with Lord Castlereagh had implied, was more concerned about the luxury of the surroundings she had seen. She chattered happily all the way back to New Albany Street about the great man's manners and his mansion. Neither Marcus nor Jonathan paid much attention, their thoughts occupied by the difficult business of bringing the count to brook. After dropping Dinah off they continued to Marcus's rooms.

"Come in, Jon, and let's try to forget this miserable affair for a few hours," Marcus invited.

"Not so easy," Jonathan insisted but he was content to sit and drink a glass of claret while Marcus ate a belated meal cooked by his man. Neither one of them said much, for their thoughts were entirely occupied with the problem of Poole and the count.

"I fear that Poole will deny the whole business, refuse to identify the count and we will be back where we started."

Marcus complained, but he was feeling a bit more cheerful after his dinner.

"Pressure will have to be brought," Jonathan advised. "If only we knew when the attack would be made."

"I am hoping that Harry Weems will give us some indication of that," Marcus said toying with his own wine and staring into space.

As if on cue there was knock on the door, and Marcus' man admitted Harry.

"I saw your light and hoped you might be at home," Harry explained. "Matters are moving. Tonight Esterhazy's man, Joe Winters followed the count to Poole's lodgings and then saw the two of them go off to the tavern where they met with two ugly looking ruffians." Harry grinned as if this news was welcome.

"And you think that they are now preparing to dispatch the Prince Regent," Marcus said.

"They are certainly planning some skullduggery. Why else would the count consort with such types?" Harry insisted.

"Listen, Harry, I have an idea. Tomorrow take two Runners, strong men if possible, and apprehend Poole. Bring him here and I will put the pressure on him. Tell him he is about to be tried for treason and the only way he can save his life is by identifying the count." Marcus frowned as if he thought it problematical that Poole could be persuaded. But what other options did they have?

"He's a tough character. He might not be easily persuaded," Harry countered. "And I will have to give the magistrate some reason for hiring these extra men."

"Tell him that Poole is a danger to the realm. That's all he needs to know. And that *The Times* is paying for the men. We can use the influence of the paper. Your employer would not want the publicity an exposé of the Runners might bring. Don't threaten him but imply that could be a factor," Marcus said with a ruthless glare that promised trouble for any official that impeded him.

"That's blackmail, Marcus," Jonathan insisted, shocked by his friends methods.

"In a good cause, Jon. And we can't tell the whole story yet."

Harry grinned. He did not share Jonathan's scruples. He had tangled with too many villains to have much faith in the nobility of man. "Sounds like a good idea. Poole would sell his mother if it insured his own safety."

"Perhaps it might be best to bring him to the paper. Then I can have a few men from the loading room standing by in case he gives trouble, but I don't think he will. He knows Ransome, the magistrate, suspects him of wrong doing and he is in a very dicey position. Our real problem is insuring that we can bring Poole face to face with the count. I don't think we can accost him at the embassy."

"Why not? If we wait about outside, hoping to catch the count when he emerges that could take days, and I fear time is running out," Harry protested, eager to get the business finished.

"Yes, and Esterhazy could not object. He suspects the count of some villainy or why have his man Winters checking on him," Jonathan offered.

"And the environs of the paper will soften Poole up. I think Poole is like most villains. When his own neck is on the block he will have few notions of loyalty to his co-conspirator," Harry said from his vast experience.

"All right, Harry. Nab Poole tomorrow afternoon late and bring him to the paper. By that time the edition will be finished and not too many people on the premises. I'll gather some recruits. We can only hope we are in time and that the count won't try something early in the day. Of course the Prince Regent is not an early riser and he is fairly well protected at Carleton House."

"If that's all arranged then, I will be on my way. I need a good night's sleep before this jape," Harry said rising to his feet. It was all in a day's work to him, but he realized his own career was on the line. If this affair concluded successfully he would be able to put his own plans into effect, and say farewell to the Runners.

After his departure Marcus and Jonathan were silent, sunk in gloom. So much depended on Harry and they each had doubts about his ability to bring off the capture of a desperate and brutal man like Poole. But they had to depend upon him. Jonathan concerned mainly for his friend had not quite so much at stake. But Marcus, like Harry, could lose a great deal if this imbroglio turned out badly. To give him credit, Jonathan thought, he was not so much worried about his personal stake in the affair as the real danger to the realm, and for that Jonathan could only applaud him.

Chapter Twenty-Five

Marcus arrived at the newspaper the next morning early, determined to concentrate on an arrears of work but as the clock slowly ticked away he found himself distracted. Would Harry be able to apprehend Poole? Had Leslie forgiven him? How would they be sure the count would be deported? There was every possibility that the devil would deny his role in the conspiracy, claim diplomatic privilege and repudiate Poole. Any magistrate would be apt to look at Poole's implication of the count dubiously, suspecting the word of an obvious villain. A great deal depended on how he and Harry handled Poole when Harry brought him to the newspaper. Marcus might have been more sanguine if he had known of Prince Esterhazy's interview with Joe Winter, the footman he had ordered to follow the count.

That morning Esterhazy, increasingly concerned that the count was up to some devious plot, called Winter into his presence. He wasted no time.

"What do you have to report, my man, on the chore I assigned you?"

Joe Winter, not overly impressed with his aristocratic

employer, came smartly to attention, and launched into his tale with an economy of words.

"The count has been meeting some very nasty men in a low dive in Spitalfields, sir. Whatever his reasons I don't think they are honorable ones."

"And how can you be sure of that?" the Prince asked looking unhappy but amenable to any proof.

"Well, sir, I have struck up an acquaintance with a Bow Street Runner, who told me that the count hired Poole to abduct the man who runs *The Times*. Then he paid Poole to try and take a lady he was interested in, a respectable one, not one of the morts you might expect. But the Runner was able to thwart that plan and Mr. Kingsley, *The Times* editor, escaped his captors. Unfortunately Poole denied the whole business and his cohorts decamped so there was no evidence to lay before the magistrate," Winter concluded.

"And does the Runner believe the count still has some interest in Mr. Kingsley?" Esterhazy asked, extremely worried. He had a healthy respect for *The Times*, London's leading newspaper. Its editor could take his revenge for this shocking act on the embassy.

"I'm not sure, sir, but obviously the count has some plot or why would he be meeting with a rogue such as Poole in The Fighting Cock," Winter explained.

"Yes, I see. Of course. Well, you have done a good job, my man. I just hope you were wise to trust this Runner."

"He's a good cove, sir, not like some of those Runners, only in it for the money." Joe would have liked to ask his master what he intended to do with this information but he had not the courage.

"That will be all, Winter. You may return to your regular duties. But here is a little tip to insure you keep your tongue about this affair." Esterhazy dismissed the man and thought about Winter's report. It was as he thought, just a sordid intrigue by the count concerning some woman and probably Kingsley had interfered so he had to be punished. Still, it might rebound on the embassy.

But was this information enough to persuade Metternich that his agent must be dismissed? Esterhazy doubted it, and the whole business worried him for it did not explain what Metternich required of the count, the reason he had sent the man here in the first place. Esterhazy's wife had told him of the count's attempt to have a woman insinuated into the embassy, and he wondered if she were the respectable lady the count had tried to kidnap. Surely the woman was the key to the affair. Perhaps he would call on her, try to wrest some more information from her. Deeply worried he sought out his wife and asked for Leslie's direction.

So Leslie was quite surprised some time later that morning when Mrs. Gorey, round eyed, announced that a distinguished foreign gentleman, a Prince, no less, had called to see her.

"Never seen him before, miss. He's not that count that used to call," Mrs. Gorey assured her.

"It must be the Austrian ambassador. You had best let him come up, Mrs. Gorey," Leslie decided.

"All right, miss. He's a real nob, this one," Mrs. Gorey concluded.

"Good morning, Miss Dansforth. You are most kind to receive me," Prince Esterhazy said after bowing over Leslie's hand.

"Not at all, Prince. What can I do for you?" Leslie retained her composure but she was certain this interview had something to do with the count. She invited the prince to sit down and followed suit.

"Are you acquainted with Count von Ronberg, Miss Dansforth?" the prince asked.

Leslie realized he was hesitant despite his worldly manner. And she wondered why this august nobleman had sought her out. Had the count appealed to him to press his unsavory cause? Surely not.

"I met him in Carlsbad and since he arrived here he tried to renew the acquaintance," she explained, unwilling to go further.

"And that was not to your taste," the prince said somewhat uneasily.

"Not at all. I rebuffed him strongly."

"The count is a dangerous man to cross."

"So I understand. He is also a libertine and unacceptable to any decent woman."

"He tried to abduct you, I have learned."

Leslie was taken aback. How had the prince learned about that distressing event? "Yes, he did, but I was rescued before he could do any damage. Thank goodness."

"I deeply regret that my countryman caused you such unhappiness. You need not worry that he will bother you again," the prince assured her, much impressed by Leslie's poise and dignity. What could the count have been thinking. There was an obviously respectable young woman who wanted no part of his lascivious suggestions. The prince was a sophisticate, well schooled in dalliance, and with his own amorous interests outside his marriage. But he also had a firm grasp of protocol. Seducing young women of virtue was not acceptable in his London circles.

"Did he happen to mention to you what his purpose in coming to London was?" the prince asked. "Aside, of course, from pursuing you."

Leslie had anticipated this question, but had decided

that she must tell the prince nothing. It might endanger whatever idea Marcus had of dealing with the count. She was tempted to tell the prince of the duel but on second thoughts decided that might be unwise and earn her a severe rebuke from Marcus. He was annoyed at her as it was and if she hoped for a reapproachment she must guard her tongue.

"No, Prince Esterhazy. The count would not confide in a woman, I think."

The prince had to accept her words, but he was not convinced. There was some mystery there. Before he could urge her to further reports, he was interrupted by a knock on the door. Leslie hurried to open it, relieved at any interruption. "Oh, good morning, Marcus," she said, pleased.

"Mrs. Gorey told me you had a visitor," he said, eyeing Prince Esterhazy with suspicion. Although he had never met the ambassador he knew who he was and wondered at his appearance here.

Was it possible this Austrian, too, had designs on Leslie? He was a jealous fool, suspecting every man who looked at her. Leslie had a very good idea of what was passing through Marcus's mind and hastened to reassure him.

"The prince has been asking me about the count," she said, after introducing the two men.

Esterhazy was quite uncomfortable. He did not want Kingsley to know that he had his suspicions about von Ronberg. But he was somewhat mollified. Obviously these two had a close relationship that the count had tried to disrupt. No wonder Kingsley disliked him, and that the count saw him as a rival.

Marcus, wary, looked at the prince with an admonitory

eye. "I have come to take Miss Dansforth to luncheon, sir. I'm sure you will excuse us."

"Certainly. So sorry to have intruded." The prince bowed over Leslie's hand again and almost scurried to the door, eager to be gone. Once the door closed behind him Marcus grinned at Leslie, much to her relief.

"You are a siren, Leslie, attracting counts, earls and princes, much less a lowly newspaper man. And why should you put up with me when you could be swanning about, covered in diamonds, the pet of the nobility of two continents," he teased.

"Don't be ridiculous, Marcus. The prince must suspect the count of some evil or why would he have called. I told him nothing." Although her tone was severe she was bubbling with happiness. Marcus had come to make peace with her, forgive her for her intemperate words. And she had forgiven him after meeting Dinah.

"I will take you out, but first I think we should settle our affairs," Marcus insisted. Putting aside any misgivings he took her in his arms.

"Have you decided I am a better value than the count. I know I am no great catch, but really, Leslie, I do love you and want you for my wife." Not giving her any time to answer he wisely took her in his arms and proved his avowal in the most dramatic way possible. And he was comforted by her response for she returned his kisses with all the passion he could have desired.

After several moments of this satisfactory solution to their difficulties, she emerged smiling from his embrace.

"That's all very well, Marcus, but what about the count. Is he to pay for his plan to assassinate the Prince Regent?"

"We have that well in train. I must return to the paper before too long to face that varlet Poole, but I could not settle to any work while I was still in doubt of your feelings." Marcus explained.

"And now you are not," Leslie agreed.

"We were both wrong. I suppose you will chivy me all our life about Dinah and I will tell you what a shrew you are. Should make for an exciting marriage. Because there is always one way to soothe your doubts." And he proceeded to show her just what that method entailed.

"We will be married as soon as this business with Poole and the count is settled. Can't be too soon for me. Now get your bonnet," he urged, putting a gentle hand over her mouth to stifle any spirited retort. But Leslie, too happy to quarrel, obeyed her future husband.

Whatever Harry Weem's struggle to subdue Jack Poole and deliver him to Marcus at the newspaper, he appeared his usual carefree self when he arrived with his prisoner. Poole, glowering and defiant, his arms securely tied behind him and in the custody of two burly Runners showed some evidence of his resistance to arrest.

And he had determined to brazen out whatever charges Marcus was prepared to lay on him. Marcus made no move to relieve his anger, looking at him for a few minutes, his face revealing nothing. He did not invite him to sit down and the two Runners hovered at Poole's elbow, prepared to exert more pressure if necessary.

Poole could not endure the intimidating silence. "You have no call to nab me. I was cleared by the magistrate," he protested.

"From abducting me, that's true," Marcus agreed. He waited a moment before continuing, and the pause obviously caused Poole some uneasiness.

"The Times has learned that you are planning an evil deed," Marcus said in magisterial tones.

"Don't know what you mean," Poole muttered but could not entirely hide his surprise.

"We have learned that you are in the pay of an Austrian nobleman who has hired you to assassinate the Prince Regent, a treasonable crime for which you could pay with your life," Marcus informed him.

"Don't know what you're talkin' about," Poole growled, but his eyes flickered away from Marcus and he lowered his head.

"I think you do. You have been watched for some days now, since you were released by the magistrate and our agents have discovered that you met with this Austrian." Marcus recited in a matter-of-fact tone as if such a heinous crime was accepted from such as Poole.

"You have no proof I meant to do nothing," Poole muttered, but visibly disturbed.

"We have enough to keep you rotting in the hulks until you tell us about your co-conspirator."

Poole looked wildly at the door, as if assessing the possibilities of making a break for it, but the Runners moved closer to him, and one of them raised his truncheon.

"Don't try it my lad or I'll be tempted to give you a clout on the noggin," the younger one said, eager to exhibit his skill with the instrument.

"You know the punishment for treason. It's death without hope of mercy," Marcus intoned.

"I ain't done nothing," Poole repeated.

"Not yet, but you intend to kill the Prince Regent. We have reliable informers, who have laid the information. I believe you know them well, the Hooker brothers."

Poole looked as shaken as his stolid stance allowed, but did not reply.

"Since you have not yet attempted what you have been paid for there is some hope I can use my influence and have you deported rather than hung," Marcus promised.

"I've got rights. You can't treat me so scurvy," Poole insisted.

"In a case of suspected treason you will find your rights have been abrogated," Marcus said, suspecting Poole had little idea of the law and no idea what "abrogated" meant. He was treading very carefully.

"What's the deal, then," Poole asked, realizing that he might yet escape his deserts if he played his hand cannily.

"We want you to identify your employer, the Austrian," Marcus said.

"Don't know his name, just he's some foreign gent with deep pockets."

"Well, we know his name, but we need confirming evidence. We will confront you with this enemy of the country and if you recognize him as the man who hired you to kill the heir to the throne, you will not die. That seems a fair bargain to me and more than you deserve."

Poole muttered to himself and threw his head from side to side as if looking vainly for a bolt hole. But none appeared. He tried another ploy. "I'm a veteran of the Iron Duke, served all through the wars. My old chief will testify for me."

"Not when it's a question of treason. Believe me, Poole, your only recourse is to do what I ask. Identify this Austrian and you will save your life. No doubt you will find some niche in the Antipodes that will suit your criminal tactics but that is not my concern. Do you agree to identify this man?"

"Don't know where to find him, or what his name is, like I said," Poole objected.

"Ah, but we do, and plan to take you there directly. And I must warn you. If you deny knowledge of your conspirator, you will end up on the end of a rope."

"Don't have much choice, do I? You want your own back 'cause I snatched you, so you are feeding me to the hangman."

"Not at all," Marcus protested cheerfully. "I am giving you a chance which is more than you gave me or intend to give the Prince Regent. Are you ready?"

"All right," Poole growled and made a few token struggles against his bonds, but stopped when one of the Runners raised his truncheon again.

"Let's be going then," Marcus said and the ill-assorted group made their way from his office and through the mostly deserted news room, where a few clerks looked up curiously but asked no questions. They had learned their editor made his own rules and any man who interfered with his actions would pay a stiff price. In the hall of the newspaper John Hughes, preparing to take a break for his evening meal, watched the parade led by his employer walk across the marble floor, but made no move to intercept them. He knew his place and that was not to quiz Mr. Kingsley, whatever his business.

Outside in Printing House Square two hefty men stood by a closed carriage, ready for trouble, having been warned by Marcus. Poole looked at the reinforcements and realized he could not escape. Hustled into the carriage he sat in sullen fury, realizing that his dreams of avarice had disappeared. Greed and violence had brought him to this pass, but he would never accept it was but bad luck that had trapped him. He glowered at Weems and Marcus sitting across from him, but he was securely pinned by the two Runners and knew that any attempt to struggle against his fate was useless.

The carriage made rapid progress through the streets and drove up before the embassy.

"Will you take him inside and demand to see the count?" Harry Weems asked Marcus, the first words he had uttered since spearing with Poole.

"Why not? We can't wait about here on the off-chance the count will appear."

The footman who admitted them took one look at the group and was about to order them away when Marcus intervened.

"Don't give us any trouble, my man. We are determined to see one of your guests, Count Felix von Ronberg," Marcus said. His demeanor was calm and his voice soft but the footman sensed that would not be denied.

"I'm not sure the count is in residence, sir," he recognized that Marcus was no common fellow but a gentleman with a commanding manner.

"Find out."

"Yes sir," the footman agreed.

Marcus, Poole and his captors waited for what seemed a long time in the ornate reception hall. Finally the count appeared flanked by the ambassador and the footman.

Esterhazy, recognizing Marcus, and fearing the worst, ordered the footman to leave and faced Marcus with more arrogance than he felt. The count made as if to retreat but then thought better of it. "What is the meaning of this unwarranted intrusion, Kingsley? You are breaching diplomatic courtesy," Esterhazy said in haughty tones.

"A citizen of your country has more than breached England's hospitality, sir," Marcus said, and then ignoring Esterhazy's attempt to protest turned to Poole.

"Well, Poole, I am waiting."

"Yes, he's the toff who hired me. Never knew his name, since he was too clever for that."

The count gasped and drew himself up. "How dare you bring this rogue here and behave in this shocking way?" he protested to Marcus, but fearing that his denials would avail him little.

"That's all we want to know." Then Marcus turned to Esterhazy. "You might not have known, I certainly hope not, that this man, Count von Ronberg, is plotting to kill the heir to the throne. We have no jurisdiction over him, it's true, but you would be advised to bundle him off to Dover as soon as possible. Castlereagh and the King will not allow you as much license as I am prepared to do."

"This is outrageous, Kingsley. Count von Ronberg is a respected member of the Austrian nobility. He would not be capable of such a dreadful act," Esterhazy sputtered, but his denial was weak. He realized this was the task that Metternich has asked the count to perform, and from the protection of the embassy. He worried for his own status and had no inclination to endorse the count. Thank God, Metternich had returned home.

"I'm not interested in the count's bona fides. He's little better than a common killer. Castlereagh and Liverpool will not tolerate you protecting him." Marcus was abrupt, not impressed with Esterhazy's denials. The count, realizing that whatever protests of innocence he made would be believed by neither Esterhazy nor this wretched scribbler. He stood on his dignity, inferring that such canards were ridiculous, but impressing no one.

"That's all our business here, Prince Esterhazy. I will

leave you to deal with your criminal countryman as you see fit, but I warn you if he is not off English soil by tomorrow, you will answer to the King and the government." Marcus turned his back on the two Austrians, and signaling to his minions that the interview was concluded marched out of the embassy, trailed by a sullen Poole in the firm grasp of the Runners. Once outside he breathed a sigh of relief. He had feared the count would mention the duel. And although he would gladly have attempted to shoot the varlet it was just as well that would be no longer necessary. His first reaction was to inform Leslie of what had just transpired. He paused on the pavement and spoke to Harry.

"Take Poole to Mr. Ransom. He will cooperate, I am sure. The man must be confined until he can be transported, which is much too good for him. But we cannot risk a scandal."

"Yes, I understand that. He won't get away this time. We have these two men to testify to his identification of the count and he will admit his own role when the alternative is put to him." Harry confirmed.

Marcus watched them ride away a great load falling from him. Until the actual confrontation he had feared a hitch, some loophole that the count might find to escape his sentence. But it had all gone off well and now he was free to seek his happiness with Leslie.

She welcomed him eagerly, all agog to know his news. He told her briefly how he had thwarted the count, apprehended Poole, and ordered Esterhazy to get rid of him.

"Can you trust that he will send him off immediately?" she asked with her usual perception.

"Oh yes, I think so. Esterhazy is not fond of his guest."

"And you will not be forced into the duel," Leslie sighed with relief.

"I suppose Jonathan told you about that." Marcus looked a bit shamefaced.

Leslie smiled but did not confirm his suspicions. And content at the outcome melted into Marcus's arms with rewarding docility.

Epilogue

Some months later Mr. and Mrs. Kingsley were breakfasting in their snug house in Wimpole Street. It was early January and outside the long windows a bleak wind was stirring the leafless trees in the small garden. But inside all was warmth and amiability. Marcus was reading his newspaper, casting a critical eye on the news he had endorsed the previous day.

"Here is an item, my love, that will interest you. Prince Esterhazy has been recalled to Vienna."

"That does not surprise me, only that it has taken so long. I quite liked the prince when he called on me, but I think he is a weakling, more interested in society than in ambassadorial duties."

"Probably. And you need to have no further fear of the count," Marcus announced. "We received this news yesterday. He has suffered a fatal accident at his shooting lodge in Bohemia."

"I wonder who was responsible for that," Leslie responded, thinking that the count was a marked man once he returned to Austria.

"Not our concern. But this is. Harry Weems came

around yesterday to tell me that he and Dinah will be married next month and inviting us to the wedding."

"How nice. They are very well suited and now that Harry has opened his own investigative agency I hope they will be happy and found a family."

Marcus grinned. He knew that Leslie had similar hopes for them, but he did not tease her.

"And how is the novel coming?" he asked.

"Quite well. I am about half way through it."

"I know it will be a success, but I still mourn the passing of Pythius. I have never been able to replace her."

"Well, you would offer her more attractive employment so you will just have to suffer the consequences."

"Just as I expected, a woman who always knew where her best interests lay," Marcus riposted smugly.

"It's time you left for the paper," Leslie reproved him but could not repress a fugitive smile. "Don't forget that tonight is the Lord Chancellor's dinner. Quite an honor to be asked."

"Not at all. You will be the chief attraction. And next week we go to Wiltshire to visit the earl," Marcus reminded her in turn.

"Yes, the dear man is so anxious to keep in touch. And he likes you, too, Marcus."

"Quite forbearing of him, since I wrested away his ewe lamb." He rose and threw down his napkin. "Who would have thought when I interrupted your rendezvous with the count at the waters in Carlsbad that just a year later we would be married."

Leslie gave a secretive smile. "Perhaps, I did."

Content to let her have the last word, Marcus gave her a warm kiss and left her idly dreaming about her happiness.

Author's Note

The hero of this tale, Marcus Kingsley, is based on a real character, Thomas Barnes, editor of *The Times* from 1817 until his death in 1841. It was Barnes, young for his post at 32, who led *The Times* to its position as the leading newspaper in the country, that it holds to this day. And it was Barnes who coined the sobriquet Thunderer, for his newspaper. He matured from a Radical Whig politically to a supporter of the Tory party. Robert Peel, when he retired as Prime Minister, thanked Barnes publicly for his support. Even Wellington listened to Barnes when the editor laid down the terms on which he would support the government. What is more remarkable his terms were accepted. Lord Lyndhurst, the Lord Chancellor, wrote to the diarist, Greville, "Barnes is the most powerful man in the country."

Unlike Marcus Kingsley, Barnes never married but lived in some splendor in Soho Square on his munificent salary of £2000 a year. Much of the material about *The Times* is based on a publication celebrating the bicentenary of the newspaper in 1984.